The
Flint Lord

THE
FLINT
LORD

RICHARD
HERLEY

William Morrow and Company, Inc.
New York

Library of Congress Cataloging-in-Publications Data

Herley, Richard, 1950–
    The flint lord.

    I. Title.
PR6058.E65F57   1985   823'.914   85-13743
ISBN 0-688-04852-8

Printed in the United States of America

First U.S. Edition

1 2 3 4 5 6 7 8 9 10

BOOK DESIGN BY JAYE ZIMET

The
Flint Lord

PART ONE

1

Fodich felt his fingers move. He touched the hard spikes of gorse. He closed his hand and made it bleed.

He was alive.

He was cold.

Needles of rain hurt his back where the flesh was open, rain in the wind like the soldier spikes in his palm.

Fodich was hallucinating. They had nearly killed him, tied him to a ladder and rendered him useless, and thrown him away to die. Night had come, yet in his brain it was still morning and he was at the ladder. That first moment had not ended. All day it had been with him, receding, coming back, filling his mind. In his mind he was still hanging by his forearms, and it was as if he had lived no other life but this, known no sensation but pain; seen nothing but the wooden rung before his eyes. The whole of his existence had become this silent, dreaming agony after the lash. He luxuriated, spread his wings, drifted in the mist, and heard his screams as at a distance.

Far above him, Brennis Gehan Fifth came to the window. He pushed aside the shutter, opening it into the wind, and looked down into the outer enclosure of the fort, beyond the spiked top of the inner palisade which surrounded his own residence.

He tapped his fingernails on the rough wooden sill. At the new year, a month away, he would be thirty, but he looked much older: a man of middle height, strongly made, his blond hair left uncut since the summer. Where his beard ended, flecked dark and light, the form of his cheekbone angled into a plane which changed shape as he opened his mouth and revealed his teeth. But it was not a smile. As he stood watching, dressed in sealskin and lynx, the soft leather of his tunic flapping at his neck, only his eyes showed that thoughts were passing. His eyes were luminous, clear, and gray; and they saw everything that was happening below.

A man was being flogged. That was the source of the screaming that had brought Gehan to the window. The man, stocky, in his early thirties, had been tied to a ladder against one of the workshops. Two overseers were beating him, watched by an ordered crowd of two or three hundred people: men, women, children, dressed in animal skins and tatters, none properly clad against the blusters of rain-bearing wind driving in from the marshes and the sea. They were slaves, and they had been brought to watch. Many of the men were still grimed with the chalky soil of the mines.

The slave receiving punishment had been stripped to the knees. His back was being flayed. With each new blow he writhed as if he would break the ladder, only to sag in the moment before the next stripe was made.

Brennis Gehan, the fifth Lord of Valdoe, studied the progress of the punishment with a detached interest. He observed particularly the reactions of the other slaves: those who watched, mulishly or in sympathy; those who turned away; the faces of the children.

A girl's voice came from the chamber behind him. "What is it?"

"A slave. Nothing to worry about."

She came and joined her brother. She was eight years younger, with waist-length blond hair tied at the neck. In texture her hair was like his, but it was paler, and in the regularity of her features could be discerned a resemblance, of attitude rather than shape: her eyes were bluer, her mouth softer, her brow more sensitive; but, unlike her brother, she had allowed her face to remain expressive and alive. He was intellect; she was emotion. She drew her furs to her chin and watched without speaking.

A heavy man in sheepskins was supervising the punishment, arms folded. From time to time some of his words reached the window.

". . . see Fodich now. He did not even reach the trees . . . away from the hill . . . and the hounds . . . let this serve you all. . . ."

The girl seemed to shiver.

Gehan turned. "Do you like to watch it, Ika?"

"Who is the man?"

"Just a slave."

"Why is he being beaten?"

"The overseers say he tried to escape."

"And did he?"

"They say he will not work. In the mines he causes only trouble. It is salutary to the others to provide an escaper now and then."

A less pensive light entered Ika's eyes as the man's screams ended and he hung limply at his bonds, unconscious and bleeding. Ika took her brother's arm. Her fingers felt the strength beneath his sleeve and moved among the sensual warmth of the lynx fur there. Something flickered about her lips, almost pleasure, perverse and incomprehensible: the overseers were not stopping. Each by turn, the two men with whips continued to step forward. The sound of it was the only noise above the wind.

"Horrible," she said. "They are beating him to death."

"It is cold here, Ika. Let us go back inside."

The Trundleman noticed the shutter closing. Under his breath he began to count the blows, almost as if its closing had been a cue, a sign of the all-seeing approval of Lord Brennis, as if the remaining supervision could be delegated now that the chief effect had been secured. The Trundleman understood. The beating needed to be severe to have any purpose. Fodich, the slave, had turned out lazy and, worse, dangerously uncooperative. The overseers had tried to make his life easier. They had given him warnings, repeated warnings which no sane man would have disregarded. Yet still he had refused to work. And then, one afternoon a week previously, he had threatened to be violent.

. . . Nine, ten . . .

"That's enough," the Trundleman said.

They cut him down and threw a bucket of water over his back. It made him cry out. Whimpering, he tried to crawl away.

The Trundleman bent at the waist and with hands on knees examined the slave's wounds. Fodich's hair was gripped and he tried to see the face looking into his own. He tightened his grasp on the soldier spikes. His mouth was open against the ground. In his hallucination a whole day had passed, a morning and afternoon, reduced to nothing. In his crawling downhill he had forced his head sideways: there was no Trundleman's face to see.

"Take him on to the hill."

They carried him from the fort. He was not worth keeping—it would take too long to make him better, and even then he would not be able to work as they wanted—and it was unlucky for him to die inside the fort. He was a savage, a wild man: better that his spirit should be released in the open. Two soldiers in

leather tunics took his wrists and ankles, and with his head hanging back and his jaw open, carried him across the wasteland that
once had been fields. Halfway down the hill, on a rough scarp of
broken soil and brown winter grass, they stopped. This was far
enough. They let him fall and turned back up the hill toward the
fort.

It was midday. Under a gray sky Fodich opened his eyes and
saw the black branches of a thornbush straining in the wind. He
rolled on to his stomach and fainted with pain: a hundred grass
stems had torn open congealed blood.

Some time later he was conscious again, in the afternoon. He
knew he had to get out of the wind. Shelter first, always shelter.
The soldiers had given him his freedom: he would not waste it.
He would not die alone, an empty soul without ancestors or tribe,
without a place among his people. He thought of his children
and his woman. They did not even know he was still alive; they
did not know he had been captured and taken to Valdoe. By now
they would be at the winter camp. He knew the way there, the
old routes followed by the nomads since the world began. He
would be with them again soon. Was he not Fodich, a hunter,
resourceful, provider of plenty?

He raised his face and saw the gorse bushes a long way down
the hill, dark green, almost black, pinstuck with yellow flowers
in defiance of winter, offering shelter, making dense shambling
screens of warmth. He estimated the distance he would have to
crawl and did not think it could be done. If he kept still the pain
reduced slowly to a constant level; otherwise it became unbear-
able, worse than it had been at the ladder. And to cover the rough
ground of the hillside would cost him too much in movement.
Each tussock would be an agony to get round. But he knew he
had to do it, to find a calm place out of the wind. If he stayed in
the open much longer he knew he would go to sleep and not wake
up.

He shut his eyes, just for a moment, very close to peace. At
once it drew nearer, blissful and warm, enticing him down.

No. He would not rest. He willed himself to think of the
morning, the ladder, the ragged crowd of onlookers, the overseers. They had cut him down and thrown icy water on his back.
It had hurt. It had made him crawl, like an animal at first, and

then like a broken man, down the hill, among the thorns and tussocks, knowing he had to want the pain to come back.

He opened his eyes and the grass-blades were different. They had changed. He must have been moving. He must have been moving and he did not even know it. He crawled like a broken man. The Trundleman gripped his hair and looked into his face; he tried to stare back, his head forced sideways in his progress down the hill. The whole day a dream, a cry of pain, darkening to dusk as the afternoon waned.

It was dark. There was something sticky in his palms. Blood. His own blood. He squeezed the vicious spikes again. Fresh blood.

Lie in this darkness and the pain will go away. A route passes a few miles from the hill. Tomorrow, or the next day, or the next, you will be strong enough to find it.

With bleeding hands he dragged himself out of the wind. He listened to the noises above him, fluted spikes on shaggy branches in the wild stream of night, pelted with rain, gusting harder; he smelled dryness and an odd scent of woody green stems, and just faintly an aromatic sweetness of the small yellow flowers he had seen so long ago.

Fodich realized he had reached the gorse bushes.

2 Brennis Gehan Fifth was alone with his wife.

He had left all the lamps burning in the chamber. The servants and body slaves were elsewhere; the dishes and trays of the night meal had long been removed, but the odors of the food lingered in the room. Outside, the wind pleaded with the walls and sent rattles of rain to add to the undersong of creaking timber. At night it could be heard most plainly, even in the wind: the structure of the fort was never silent. Gehan had learned every subtle component of its groans: the weight of logs settling, expanding and contracting in damp air or dry; the movements of joists and floorboards and rough-hewn woodwork; the cracks and stutters of suddenly released tensions. Gehan's ancestor, the first Lord Brennis, had built the Trundle over a hundred years before, and it was still alive—the oak piles and beams were still a part of the climate and the land, and in their movements it seemed as if they yearned to go back to the forest in which they had seeded and grown.

Gehan could not sleep. He lay with his eyes open, listening to the gale. There had been four Flint Lords before him, all with the same name—Gehan, the name of the family in the homelands that had grown to power through trading and ruthless elimination of its enemies. The first Flint Lord had opened Brennis, the island country, to profit and exploitation; but lesser men had succeeded him, fed on the proceeds of his vision and energy, and almost squandered his work. He had dreamed of autonomy: freedom from the taxes and imposts of the mainland Gehans, the chance to expand and take, eventually, the whole country for himself. The dream had not been realized. In the years of the second and third Flint Lords the Valdoe domain had remained subservient to the mainland, its lands restricted to an eighty-mile strip along the south coast.

Only with the advent of the fourth Flint Lord, Gehan's father, had matters changed. After twenty years of work and planning he had seized independence, facing its dangers in return for its advantages: and the advantages were enormous. At the end of his life he had begun to plan for expansion of the domain. And now, Gehan knew, it was his duty to continue and fulfill what his father and Gehan First had started. It was his duty and his destiny to make the vision real.

The first Gehan had found Brennis a wilderness of trees with isolated farming villages near the shore. The farmers, like Gehan himself, had come by sea from the German homelands. The villages he encountered were poor and badly organized, at the mercy of raiders and brigands who came either in ships and rafts from Normandy and Cornwall, or from inland strongholds to the north and west.

One such stronghold was Valdoe Hill, thrusting nearly seven hundred feet above the marshes and the coast, thickly wooded, its crown cleared by the brigands to make a fortress. On the southern slopes they had discovered rich seams of flint. Prisoners from raids were made to dig, in shallow pits at first, and deeper, until the pits branched underground and became mines. The true wealth of Brennis was its fertile land, from which grew villages of farmers who could be subjugated and exploited; but flint was wealth too, for it supplied the means to exploit: weapons, tools, ready fire. Without flints, man could be little more than an animal. With them, he could cut down trees and clear a forest, harvest his crops, kill beasts and dress their skins to wear. He could kill other men more easily and take what they had made for himself. He could win freedom from hunger, freedom from toil, by making others feed him and build his shelters.

The best flints were to be found along the chalk hills of the South Downs, and of these the flints at Valdoe were the finest.

Under the direction of Brennis Gehan First, the brigand fortress was razed and its site leveled to fourteen acres, an oval plateau circumscribed by a ditch nine feet deep. Just inside the ditch, forming a palisade twenty feet high and three-fifths of a mile in length, were erected oak trunks preserved by scorching, each the thickness of a man's chest: the product of two thousand trees, cut from the forest and dragged to the summit with ropes. Protected by this palisade, construction of the Trundle began.

In the following years the fort was completed and then improved, and smaller, secondary forts were built in a chain along the downs—at Butser, Harting, Bow Hill, Eartham, Cissbury, Thundersbarrow, Whitehawk. More of the country was taken under control, more villages and their produce secured for the use and profit of Valdoe and the Gehan family. In return the farmers received a measure of protection from attack, and a village was established at the foot of Valdoe Hill.

In the hands of their new masters, the farmers began to thrive. New villages, new communities, sprang up along the coast, peopled by settlers from the homelands. To feed them, new fields were required. Mile after mile of oak and beech forest fell before the ax, more every year. The life of any one field was short. Without proper management, of which the farmers knew little, the ground soon became exhausted. Once exhausted it was abandoned and left to become scrub, and more forest was cut to take its place. Villages shifted their sites, leaving destruction behind. Deeper and deeper incursions were made into the forest. The smoke of the clearance fires, the smell of newly hacked woodchips, the belching pyres of mangled trees moved farther and farther from the coast. Always the domain of Valdoe was on the increase, powered by the personality of one man, the representative of the Gehan family in the island country: the Lord of Brennis. His flint seams provided the axes; his artisans fashioned the tools that could be exchanged for food and skins and lumber; and his forts and soldiers watched over everything and allowed it to proceed.

With increasing prosperity, increasing boundaries, there was more to protect. The barracks at the Trundle were enlarged, and the slaves' quarters too: more labor was needed, to build roads, to dig, for every menial task. Soldiers were sent across the sea, to prey on the very communities which in other days had sailed against the farmers. The slavers came back with dark-haired, brown-eyed people, in complexion and temperament like the brigands, the original masters of the coast, whose immediate threat had now been broken and whose clans had been disrupted and enslaved.

Besides the brigands there were other natives, more elusive, with far older traditions. These were the savages, who lived by hunting and gathering, traveling the forests by routes which had not changed for hundreds or even thousands of years. The coming of agriculture, of the foreign farmers, had eroded their hunting grounds and forced them to restrict their wanderings. It was from a few such tribes that the brigands had arisen, in response to the presence of the farmers on the coast.

The savages made slaves of indifferent quality. And each time a new inroad was made into the forest there was trouble: sabotage, ambush, open attack. Every tribe was a source of delay and expense. Once deprived of its territories, if events were allowed to develop, a tribe of savages would become a horde of brigands.

During the summer the savages were scattered throughout the country, in the hills, along the river valleys, from the flat eastern coast to the mountains in the north and west; but when cold weather came they congregated at winter camps, traditional gathering-places. The tribes in the south, those which caused the trouble, used a camp some eighty miles north of Valdoe, in a valley near a waterfall.

With the aid of surprise, the soldiers of the first Lord Brennis marched on this valley and purged it. The problem was solved.

The first Lord Brennis grew old and tired; other men took his place. His policies were no longer so rigidly observed. And, as one symptom of the decline, the savages began to come back.

For many years there was no real clash between them and Valdoe. Forest clearance had slowed down anyway; old fields had reverted to woodland. What small friction there was between native and farmer was of little concern to the Flint Lord: Valdoe's interests were rarely threatened. Gradually the savages ceased to be important. Even as slaves they were negligible, of no value. They were just denizens of the forest like the other creatures there, nothing more; and like the other creatures they could sometimes be a nuisance, occasionally stealing livestock or damaging crops.

Gehan's father, the fourth Flint Lord, had restored the ideals of Gehan First. In his lifetime he had remade much that Valdoe had lost; and he had won independence from the mainland as a first step in the establishment of an empire in Brennis, but he had died before the work was finished, leaving his son to take over.

At his father's death Gehan had been twenty-three. Now he was nearly thirty. In those years he had upheld the old spirit, the spirit of the old Valdoe, of his father and of Gehan First. The consolidation was complete: expansion had once again begun. In three years, seventy thousand acres of land had been reclaimed or freshly burned. Next summer there would be more, much more. There would, in ten years, be fields and villages beyond

the Weald, thirty, forty, fifty miles from the coast. The land would be stripped of timber, the marshes drained.

There was only one obstacle. Last summer there had been a resurgence of trouble from the savages. In the northwest of the domain, they had repeatedly harried the forest clearance teams. Farmers had been captured, tortured, put to death. Stores had been stolen and befouled at a dozen sites. A unit of soldiers, twenty-five men, had been routed. And in the east, one of the most prosperous villages had been sacked and burned to the ground.

The records of Gehan First had been preserved in stories and paintings. The young Gehan had known them from his earliest days, taught by his father to revere the daring of Gehan First, the ancestor who had come to a fierce land and stolen it from the brigands. Recently the stories had been coming again to his thoughts, and with them an uneasy feeling, a foreboding, vaguely recriminating. Yet he knew there could be no guilt in his mind. What he was planning was no more than a military prerequisite of expansion. The savages were an obstacle to the smooth extension of the domain: it was his duty to remove that obstacle. He was going to march on their winter camp and destroy them.

At the latest estimate of his scouts, there were something like three hundred savages either on their way to the camp or already present. The number of soldiers that could be safely mustered, leaving enough to defend the coast, was numerically only equal to the enemy, and heavy losses could be expected in even the best-planned onslaught. There was also the difficulty of the season. The camp would not be full, and an attack would be less than completely effective, before the end of autumn. The solstice, Goele, marked the first day of winter and of the new year. Goele was the prime festival of the calendar. For religious reasons there could be no departure in the week of the festival. By then, however, it was almost certain that the snows would have started. In mild years the snow would not be too deep; sometimes there was even a thaw for a week or two, but normally the ground was frozen till spring, when the camp would quickly disperse, too quickly to risk leaving the attack until then. It would have to be made in the snow. Gehan had consulted his Divine: she had forecast a bitterly cold winter, with heavy drifts. Marching in such conditions would require many men.

The forces of Gehan First, it was said, had outnumbered the savages by three to one. They too had marched in deep snow. The extra soldiers had been brought from the mainland: the same would have to be done again. But such reinforcements took time and great expense to arrange, and the problems of transporting, feeding, and sheltering them were not easily dealt with. In winter especially, the channel between Brennis and the mainland was rough and dangerous. Weeks might pass before a calm day allowed a crossing. The number of craft available was limited; and they were small and slow, capable of carrying only a few men at a time.

However, it would be done. Even now there were ships across the channel, waiting for the swell to ease.

The alternative to an all-out assault on the savages' camp—piecemeal extermination, tribe by tribe, using soldiers already available—was tempting to consider. Not only would it be cheaper and require fewer men, but it could be carried out in favorable weather. The previous summer it had already been tried; but only when there had been no chance of a survivor carrying word to other tribes. Nonetheless, there had been several escapes, and Gehan's advisers had warned him to stop. The capacity of the various tribes for working together was unknown. Given warning by a consistent series of massacres, a force of savages might form and descend on the coast, a force perhaps of daunting size. Such an enemy would be impossible to defeat without help from the homelands, for although the Trundle itself was impregnable, and the contingency of a mass attack had been well foreseen by its designer, supplies of water inside the fort were finite and a protracted siege could not be defended.

Given all this, a sudden advance on the winter camp was the only way. Using surprise and vast numerical superiority, the savages would be dealt with once and for all, and the peaceful work of expansion would again be allowed to proceed safely and profitably. Villages beyond the Weald: that was the dream. To attain it Gehan would need all his ingenuity and courage. The details of the campaign had been crystallizing in his mind; he examined them endlessly. They brought him alive, excited him, kept him from sleep, and as the season turned and the weather worsened the anticipation had begun to consume and torment him.

He could share none of this with Altheme, his wife. Only Ika, his sister, his own flesh and blood, could truly understand. Only she knew what their heritage was.

Tonight a storm was blowing. But tomorrow it might be clear. It might be calm. Ships might be launching.

Under the bedding he put his hand on Altheme's smooth skin. She stirred drowsily and half woke, still asleep as he pulled her toward him.

Her eyes opened fully and she tensed. She seemed to draw back from him, bewildered, afraid.

"What do you want?"

Gehan said nothing. He moved on top of her, not looking at her eyes, the dark eyes that were nothing like his own. And her hair was the darkest brown before black; every night she sat combing and brushing and brushing it, no longer speaking to him; and when she undressed, she turned her back and quickly took the wrapper held up by her body slave, before her husband could see. She had given him no children, no son. Gehan ran his hands under her thighs and pulled them apart. She resisted, in silence. Always in silence now, for months, even long before Ika had come. At one time, in the middle of the day, he had found her weeping, sobbing, her face in her hands, wet with tears. She would not tell him why. Moving inside her, she would not tell him why. He tried to kiss her, to find her tongue with his own, forcing her against the pillows, his hands gripping her wrists. She went limp and the tenseness had gone. Not melted, but gone. She looked past him. Outside the gale was streaming the shutters with rain. Gehan saw her dark hair on the pillow, moving more quickly now, loveless and violent. In the channel the seas were mountains. They were keeping the ships on the beach, pounding the shingle, scouring spray along the shore, a wet night, utterly black in the sandhills where men were waiting. Breakers smashed on the line of coast, hurling weed and wood. Solid water fell on the beach and drowned the marshes beyond, reaching toward the homelands, toward Valdoe, reaching toward the hill. And despite the storm the ships were launching. He wanted to shout a warning to the men with ropes. But they couldn't hear. The ships were breaking up, the boards splintering, the sails ripped away downwind. Men were in the sea, heads and hands visible, shouting, swimming, trying to cling to wreckage. On the sloping walls of waves he saw them. They were drowning, all of them. And as

3 Tagart listened again, his head averted and his eyes unfocused on the ground, using all his concentration to filter the sounds of the forest at nightfall. The branches overhead, bare or with a few sere leaves remaining, gave no hindrance to the rain which was falling steadily from a windy sky. And as the light slowly failed, the tree trunks lost their colors: shades of green or gray migrated to dark and pale, and the shapes of unsuspected patterns emerged.

Crows were roosting somewhere far away to the south. Their raucous chorus suddenly went quiet, and started again with a few isolated cries. Tagart frowned. He was beginning to doubt what he thought he might have heard.

He was in his twenty-seventh year, dark like all the nomads, with high cheekbones and a strong, spare frame. He carried a bundle at his side; over his tunic he wore a fur stormcoat, and below it leather leggings fixed with tasseled straps. His woman Segle had made these things and her own; he had caught the animals which provided skins. His feet were bare. When winter came he would wear boots, the leather worked with tallow to make it waterproof. Later he would need a leather mask too, to protect his face from the wind, and mittens, and a fur cap to pull down over his ears. The stormcoat was fitted with a hood: this he had pushed back, the better to listen.

"Did you hear it?" Segle asked him. She was seventeen, the niece of a dead chief, all her tribe murdered by the Flint Lord's soldiers. Tagart's tribe, the tribe into which he had married, was also no more. Segle had been with him since the end of the summer. Together they had traveled the country looking for Tagart's blood-tribe, his father's people. They had gone as far as the mountains in the north, and turned back down the east coast, through the fens and inland to the southwest, but of the Waterfall people they had found no trace. Tagart knew that he would be sure to find them at the winter camp: as the autumn had begun to fade he and Segle had started eastward, along the south coast and toward the routes leading to the camp.

they went down their hair was no longer dark. It was golden; it was fair, forming whirlpools, going under, going down.

Gehan did not know whose name he had spoken, but as he slumped across her Altheme heard it and she felt her heart flood with coldness and fear. It was true, what she had guessed, what she had known. It was true. It was true and now there could be nothing more.

"Damn you," he said. "Bitch. Damn you."

She shut her dark eyes and listened to the wind.

"Did you hear it?" she said.

He had not. "What about you?"

"I might have heard voices again, just faintly."

"Which way?"

"I couldn't tell."

It was late. They had to find somewhere dry for the night; they had to build a fire.

But—if there really were a fire nearby, if they really had heard voices, then shelter, food, and company too, all would be freely given. And what if by some chance the tribe proved to be at last the Waterfall people—what if its leader were Shode, the man who with Tagart's father had taught him almost everything he knew? What if it were Shode up ahead?

"We'll go and look."

They pushed forward, between the branches of leafless bushes on each side of the path. It was hard to see detail now. More than once a branch slashed back into Segle's face. She said nothing to him; if it were not for Tagart she would be a slave still, at Valdoe, where she had been taken by the soldiers who had killed her family and friends. She would be a slave still, or dead.

The path began to climb. After a hundred paces they breasted a ridge. The faint course of the path crossed the ridge and followed the slope down. Below the tangle of undergrowth the rusty leaves of hornbeam trees lay in shallow drifts.

A hint of cooking came on the wind.

"Down there," Tagart said, and through the moving branches Segle saw a twinkle of firelight. A moment later the smell of roasting meat came more strongly, borne on a gust of wind that blew rain from the trees, and with the wind they heard voices and the sound of wood being cut.

Tagart squeezed Segle's hand and drew her on.

Near the bottom of the slope the path opened into a small clearing, and here, beside a stream, surrounding a pile of glowing logs, were eleven hump-shaped tents made of leather and fur. People were making ready for a meal; four women and a boy were splitting wood with flint hatchets.

A man stepped onto the path, holding a spear. It was nearly dark and nothing could be seen of his face, but he was dressed like Tagart, in a stormcoat, and when he spoke his voice was harsh.

"What people are you?"

Tagart told him. "We heard you from the other side of the hill," he added. "We're on our way to the waterfall camp. My father was in the Shoden."

"The Shoden." The man with the spear seemed satisfied. He looked over his shoulder at the fire. "We also are going to the waterfall camp. We are the Ospreys. Come. You're welcome to eat with us."

Tagart found the man first, half dead, in the mud of the path, his eyes open to the rain.

He and Segle had been walking with the Osprey tribe since the previous day. Their route had curved away from the coast and passed through hilly forest, on the outskirts of the cultivated land controlled by Valdoe. Early in the morning they had crossed a system of fields and then the Flint Lord's road between Valdoe and Bow Hill, following the course of an old trackway which turned north to find a gap in the downs: this was one of the established routes to the waterfall camp.

The rain had not stopped. Everything seemed to be soggy; everyone was miserable and bad-tempered. For much of the time two families had been arguing. Tagart had been glad when Visar, the leader, had told him to take his turn and go on ahead, to make sure of the way.

For a moment Tagart thought the thing obstructing the path was a rotten log, or a curious lump of earth or stone with pink showing. He did not associate it with human form. It was utterly motionless. Then he saw that it had arms and legs and a head.

The man's beard and nostrils were the color of mud; his hair was matted and knotted with it. From the abrasions on his skin it could be seen how far he must have crawled and how many times he must have stumbled and fallen. Tagart closed his fingers on the man's wrist and bent to listen to his heart. He was barely alive.

"What have you found?" Visar said, pushing a way forward.

Tagart looked up at him mutely and turned back to the man on the path.

Only when they tried to lift him did they see the furrows on Fodich's back. Blood and mud had commingled and congealed. Rain dripping from the trees made watery streaks which revealed the rough edges of the wounds, from neck to buttocks and to the backs of his knees.

The fortress at Valdoe was less than three miles away. Tagart himself had once been a prisoner there; he had once labored in the mines. He had been given firsthand experience of the brutality of the guards; he had been forced to breathe the atmosphere of corruption and despair in the slaves' quarters. The place itself was evil, the very ground infected by the man who remained unseen and for whose personal benefit so much suffering was endured. Evil: there was no other way to think of the raw force, almost tangible, which the Trundle and its master seemed to generate. It had crushed and defiled Segle, and she would never fully recover from her experience there. The Flint Lord had killed her brother and parents and every member of her tribe. And, when she had been the only one left, a Trundleman had raped her, deflowered her on the night she was due to be put into the soldiers' brothel.

A sudden constriction grasped Tagart's chest, rage and sadness, too intense for tears or words. He found it impossible to breathe. He wiped the gray mud from the man's face and cradled the back of his head as other hands lifted him from the path. Tagart stared at the inanimate features. From many small clues he already knew that the man was a hunter like himself. At some time their lives would have been almost identical—even to the point of enslavement. But there things had changed. Tagart had been able to escape intact, unmutilated. This man had not.

"It's Valdoe," Tagart said. "The Flint Lord has done this."

The women carried Fodich to the bracken and washed him. They smeared his back with herbal salves; clean, soft leather was applied to his wounds and bandaged in place. The men cut poles from the woods to make a stretcher. Shortly before noon, the Ospreys were on their way again.

Tagart offered to help carry the stretcher. Fodich lay on his front, without speaking, occasionally turning his head and grimacing when the roughness of the ground made the stretcher jolt. His eyes were open: he watched the passing leaves and mud. Toward dusk he slept.

He was strong, otherwise he could not have survived. Tagart thought he knew his face from some past winter camp. The features were square and resolute, the eyes gentle, filmed with pain. His limbs were powerful and his body well muscled. In age he was between thirty and thirty-five.

During the night Tagart and Segle sat with him, in one of the leather shelters. They gave him a little broth, in sips from a wooden bowl. He tried to clasp the bowl with clumsy fingers and spilled it on his chest. Segle eased his head back. He fell asleep again, woke, drank water, fell asleep. In the early hours he awoke sweating and retched; afterward he seemed to feel better.

He was lying face down, his head on one side.

"Can you understand me?" Tagart said. "What tribe are you? What is your name?"

He tried to speak. Segle brought the lamp closer and took his hand.

"What tribe are you?" Tagart said.

Fodich's mouth opened, wet with dribble. Slowly he turned his eyes and took in Tagart's face.

"I'll tell you," he said weakly. "But first I'd like some more of that broth."

By dawn, Fodich had finished his story.

Tagart rose. He was deeply troubled, not so much by the account of Fodich's punishment, but by everything else he had said. "This is too important to be kept," Tagart said. "I must go and tell Visar."

Three days later the rain had gone. The wind had veered to the north, bringing clear sunshine and the first real chill of the winter. At sea the waves were muddy and discolored, crested with foam. White gannets rolled with the swell and followed the coastline westward, appearing and disappearing in deep troughs, occasionally flapping higher, gliding above a horizon of rough water.

Inland the trees had been stripped of their leaves. The hues of autumn had become drab; the forest canopy was now a skein of empty branches. The rivers ran cold and dark, full of rain. A keen wind blew through the hawthorns on scrubland where old fires had destroyed the trees. Straggling flocks of winter thrushes descended on the bushes to eat the berries: redwings and fieldfares, still traveling southward in the face of the coming season.

The path into the Shode Valley, after crossing the scrubland, slowly descended between the trunks of beeches and oaks. Along this path had come most of the three hundred people, in nine tribes, who had been arriving steadily over the past weeks.

The camp lay in undulating countryside eighty miles from the coast. This was a region of dense woodland and marshes with open pools full of game. Three rivers turned southward among the hills and discharged into the marshes where the three valleys merged. In the western valley, two miles above the confluence, the river was swift and at a hardening of the rock became a noisy waterfall, from which one of the tribes had taken its name.

The Shoden, the Waterfall tribe, held first place among the people who used the camp each year. The camp had been in use for many generations: nobody knew how many. It was situated on sloping ground a mile above the waterfall, in a clearing beside the river. A few trees had been left standing, and these served to define the invisible boundaries which divided the camp into areas for each tribe. Yet at first glance no such segregation could be seen: the children ran about as they wished, the huge heaps of firewood and the cooking areas were communal, and the shelters seemed to be sited at random.

The soil in the clearing was relatively soft and easily excavated to make pit dwellings. Bundles of reeds were thatched on a hazel framework to make a thick and largely impervious roof, completely waterproofed with layers of holly and yew. An opening at one corner allowed access to the interior, which was insulated with bracken and lined with skins and furs. The opening served to ventilate the pit. It remained open in all but the worst weather; with people inside, a pit rapidly became warm.

There were about eighty such dwellings in the waterfall camp, some cleaned out and used year after year, others abandoned and used as middens, others dug afresh. No cooking was permitted inside. All food brought to the camp was to be shared at the fire, which burned continuously through the winter and was flanked by awnings to keep off the rain and snow.

Klay, the chief's son, was sitting in the sunshine by the fire, with a bone needle making repairs to a boar net. He was wearing a disagreeable look: he disliked such tasks. He was the son of Shode, leader of the Waterfall tribe. Eventually, when Shode died or decided to step down, Klay would take his name and become chief in turn. Not everyone welcomed the prospect. Something in Klay's character made him unpopular. He was twenty-four, at the peak of his strength and resilience, and just entering that state in which the older men could tell him no more about the forest and hunting. His eyes were burning and intense, his jawline hard and bunched. He liked action, sudden decisions, violence in the chase and, although he knew well enough that net mending was important, it irked him to sit still and listen to the gabble of the old women. To make things worse his two small daughters and his wife were at his side.

There was to be no hunting today. Other men and their families were cutting shafts for new arrows, holding them up to judge them true, selecting goose, quail or swan quills for the flights and flint chips for the heads, or making bindings with twine and fish glue. Others were trimming stakes for use in fences to drive game, or with the women were helping to twist rope from untidy bundles of lime-bark fiber. Shode said that it was essential to keep ahead with such work. Later on, depending on the severity of the weather, food would become scarce and poorly kept equipment might cost hardship or worse.

Shode was seated near his son, working too, discussing with Klay the change in the weather and the effect it would have in the coming days. As chief of the leading tribe of the camp, Shode controlled all hunting, allotting to each tribe its share of opportunity. Often two or more tribes hunted together, but everything had to be agreed by Shode. He was quietly spoken and introspective, his hair turning gray. In his movements could be seen the control and coordination that thirty years of the hunting life had brought. Even among the others, Shode was still a strong man. Although in his middle forties and not quite as fast as the younger men, he could run as far, work as hard, and go without sleep for as long as any. He rarely insisted on taking every privilege that was his due, but when he made a ruling his word was final. He had become chief not by inheritance, but by challenge, twenty years before. Since then there had been scarcely any threat to his leadership, and none at all in recent years. He was acknowledged to be the best man in the tribe; the best man to lead the Shoden and to give unity to all the tribes of the winter camp.

Behind him the breeze hissed in the trees and poured clean air through the valley. The sky was perfectly blue; the late morning sun still held a trace of warmth.

Shode was joined by a bulky, bearlike man, the leader of the Bubeck or Beaver tribe.

"We'll try Yote Wood again tomorrow," Shode said to Klay. "The pigs will have taken themselves in there by now." He turned to Bubeck. "Are you with us again tomorrow?"

Bubeck grinned his assent, exposing gums and broken teeth. He was almost a giant, a head taller than Klay, and supremely ugly. In his boyhood he had been caught by a brush fire and horribly burned: his face was a scarred mask, his left eye pulled outward and down. His left ear had gone, and what remained of his hair and beard grew in feeble tufts.

The Bubecks and the Shoden often hunted together. Like most of the tribes that used the camp, they were of the same lineage, tracing their descent from that part of the Sun's creation ruled by the spirit Water. Even in summer the two tribes had sometimes traveled together. They were closer to each other than the others of the spirit—the Ospreys, Dragonflies, Otters and the rest. Bubeck was also related to Shode by marriage. Despite his appearance he had taken the most desirable woman in the tribe as his wife. The chief and the chief alone had this right, taking if he wished the wife of another man; for Bubeck was leader because no one dared to challenge him. In the winter camp he was second only to Shode. He had been a part of Klay's earliest life. From Bubeck, his "uncle," Klay had learned how to shoot, how to make a trap, how to wait in silence, how to read a trail, how to follow like a shadow for mile upon mile. With Shode and Bubeck and the boys of his own age Klay had killed his first roebuck and skinned it, and been shown how to use every part of the animal, to waste nothing. From those early years Klay had spent his time with another child, a boy two years older, the son of the man who had then been chief of the Waterfall tribe. Tagart—the other child—remembered little of his father's death. A broken leg, gangrene, his mother weeping. The outcome was what Tagart's father might have wished: his friend defeated the others and took the name Shode to become the new leader of the tribe.

Tagart continued to learn in company with Klay, to be taught by the elders, and by Shode in particular. Yet even as a child of six, Tagart sensed that everything had changed. It was now Klay who was to inherit the name of Shode; Klay who received the best instruction; Klay for whom the leading beast was reserved; Klay who was expected to excel in all things. Eventually Tagart left the Shoden and married into the Owls, a tribe of the Air spirit. From then on he saw Shode and Bubeck and Klay only occasionally: the Air tribes wintered at another camp, in the east, and the Owls rarely spent any time in the south.

Klay looked up from his work, squinting. On the far side of the river his father's name had been called. He saw that a column of people was arriving, preceded by Edrin and Wone, two men from the Shoden who had been posted to watch the bank path and the bridge of logs, fixed in place like stepping-stones, which joined it to the camp.

Edrin raised his voice again. "Shode! Shode! A new tribe!"

Shode stood up and shielded his eyes against the sun. "Who are they?"

"The Visars!"

When Klay reached the river he was among a jostling crowd welcoming the newcomers, taking loads, helping to carry the heavy packs and frames, the bundles of furs and skins and shelter-poles. In a line the Visars came over the bridge, stepping one by one onto firm ground to be greeted and divested of their loads.

It took a while for them all to cross—the Visars were a large tribe, of more than forty people. Toward the back of the line a stretcher was brought across, on which Fodich of the Dragonflies had eased himself up so that he could see. Word was sent to his woman, and almost at once he was reunited with his family.

Over the heads of the crowd Klay looked at the remaining people on the far bank, where Edrin was waiting to be the last on the bridge. Beside Edrin, in easy conversation, he saw a face he knew.

Tagart was carrying a heavily laden frame, his thumbs tucked in the straps. Somewhere on his walk with the Visars he had found, or someone had found for him, purple knapweed flowers to tie in his hair. *His walk with the Visars.* The Visars. Not the Owls. Klay was suddenly apprehensive. His eyes searched for the necklet of bones which he knew all members of the Owl tribe wore. Tagart no longer had one. Then he was no longer in the Owl tribe; nor was he wearing any emblem of the Visars.

A girl preceded Tagart onto the logs, a girl with purple flowers in her hair, and all else fled from Klay's thoughts.

★ ★ ★

Her name was Segle. She was seventeen and very beautiful. Later
Klay learned that she was one of the Terns, a tribe now dead.
She had been imprisoned at Valdoe and made to work in the
slaves' quarters. Tagart had helped her to escape. Now she was
his wife.

After dark they were sitting together by the fire as Tagart again
told the story of their escape, their subsequent wanderings; he
described the things he had seen and heard at Valdoe, and the
way they had found Fodich.

Fodich was still very weak, but he had been brought to the
fire to repeat what he had told Tagart and Visar. It was something
to do with the Flint Lord and rumors at the fort. The talk reg-
istered only slightly with Klay; he did not bother to follow what
was being said. He was watching Segle. Once she looked his way,
once only, and again he told himself that she had sensed it too.
He knew what she wanted. He knew what they both wanted. He
had never spoken to her directly, never seen her before today,
but were it not for Tagart, not for his own woman and his family,
he would get up and go to her now and take her down to his
dwelling.

Klay remembered that he was the chief's son. The talk seemed
to be important. It would be as well to pay more attention.

"The snows are a month away," Shode said. "We have time
to send scouts to confirm what you say. Much as I trust you,
Visar, and Tagart and Fodich too, it goes against all our interests
to act rashly."

"Mild words," said Bubeck. "I think they're mistaken. The
Flint Lord has never dared move his men in winter before. Why
should he do so now? Has he gone mad?"

"It is possible," Fodich said. "Some say he has been visited
by demons. Others say the farmers' gods have deserted them.
Their fields are failing and the villages are going hungry."

"We've seen no sign of it," Bubeck said angrily. "Do you want
us to risk the winter just because of a few rumors in the slave
pens?"

"I repeat only what I have heard," Fodich said.

"The drought was bad this year," Shode said. "We saw ruined
crops."

"And my wife will testify that the Flint Lord has already begun killing us," Tagart said. He was becoming heated. "Didn't he murder her whole tribe? What more do you want? I suppose you won't be happy till the soldiers are here."

Shode held up his hands. Tagart, who had been newly welcomed into the tribe, was losing his sense of respect for Bubeck, a chief. "This is what we will do," Shode said calmly. "Before committing ourselves we must know how many soldiers the Flint Lord has assembled." He turned to Chenk, leader of the Kingfisher tribe. "I want you to lead the scouting party. Each tribe will give the man with the best eyes and the fastest legs. Leave in the morning; go to the Flint Lord's landing place, to Valdoe and all his other works. If you see the truth of what Visar and Fodich have said, the elders will convene and we shall decide what to do."

Tagart pleaded to be allowed to go with the scouts. Shode refused. "From this tribe I give Wone."

The other chiefs began to nominate their scouts.

Klay sat studying every detail of Segle's face. She was sitting in profile, her eyes downcast. She seemed to turn too frequently and attentively to Tagart. Klay watched her tiny movements and her self-conscious gestures, missing nothing; her shins were bare to the firelight.

"I beg you, Shode," Tagart said. "Let me go. I've been inside the Trundle. I know the other forts too, and the mines, and the landing place."

Bubeck said, "Slavery must have rotted your brains."

It was then that Segle stole her glance at Klay.

He knew at once that she had been expecting him to be looking elsewhere, at Bubeck or Tagart. She was momentarily caught out: her feelings lay revealed. She wanted what Klay wanted. Her glance faltered and she looked away.

Tagart was standing with fists clenched. Bubeck had insulted him in front of the whole camp.

But Bubeck was a chief, and this was the day Tagart had been allowed back into the Waterfall tribe; and Bubeck was Shode's close friend. Tagart sat down.

Bubeck, sprawling on his couch of skins, held Tagart's eye for a derisive moment before he turned to Klay and grinned.

But Klay did not see. He saw only Segle, at her place by the fire.

4 Bugling and whooping, nine swans flew southward along the valley, their plumage white against the gray sky above the water. Yellowed reeds stood swaying in the ripples; and in the center of the mere, flocks of waterfowl showed as dark patches.

The morning was intensely cold. It was three days before the winter solstice—over three weeks since Tagart had returned to the Shoden: in that time there had already been snow flurries and twinkling nights of hard frost. Now a sleeting north wind was blowing, numbing the face and fingers and finding a way through every layer of clothing.

Tagart and Klay heard the swans go over. They could not see them—they were crouching inside a makeshift hide of bundled reeds, watching the flooded land where since dawn the clapnets had stood open and ready to be sprung. All morning the mallard and teal had been flighting above the osiers and islands. Some had joined the coots and widgeon on the floods, grazing by the water or sleeping, heads on backs, white eyelids closed, shedding occasional feathers that the wind snared among grass-stems and dead thistles. The wildfowl slept lightly. Once a falcon appeared in the sky, drifting west, showing no interest, yet the ducks left the ground in a storm of wings and circled for a long time before returning. As they came back in pairs and parties they redistributed themselves and some chanced to come nearer the nets.

The work of waiting was made more tedious by the cold. The catch today would be consumed as part of the solstice feast, a celebration to mark the start of the new year. Most of the hunters had gone ten miles down the valley to try for a specially large boar, but Tagart had opted to work the duck traps, and he had asked Klay to join him.

The trigger cords from the nets entered the hide and lay across a branch, ready for use. In the cramped space the reeds smelled musty. Tagart put his face to the slit and peeped out. More widgeon had ventured out of the water. The grazing birds were now all round the nets; three or four were even inside.

"Not much longer," he said to Klay.

Klay grunted. Tagart regarded him for a moment before turning back to the slit.

The change in Klay's manner had not escaped Tagart's notice. The reason for it was not hard to guess. In Tagart, Klay plainly perceived a rival. Until Tagart's arrival, it seemed, Klay had seen no threat to his future. There had been no other likely successor to the name of Shode, from within the tribe at least. But Tagart was certainly Klay's equal in strength and skill, and if there were a challenge these qualities would be put to the test.

Chenk and the scouts had still not returned from Valdoe. They should have been back within a fortnight at the most, and yet Shode seemed content to wait. "We'll give them two more days," he had said that morning. Tagart thought they might have been captured; he could not understand Shode's attitude. In time, the matter might cause trouble with Visar and the other chiefs, many of whom shared the strong views of Tagart and Fodich. Bubeck, though, did not share these views. He openly ridiculed them. Shode was noncommittal; Klay had been influenced by Bubeck.

Discord over such an important issue might precipitate a challenge for leadership of the camp, and perforce of the Shoden too. But, whatever happened about Valdoe, Klay would know that when the day came, perhaps years from now, when Shode died or became too old, he could no longer be so sure of succeeding his father.

Tagart felt he understood this. It explained many things. In the past, with Tagart in another tribe, Klay had always been friendly. Now he was resentful; and his manner toward Segle too was peculiar.

And Bubeck had been hostile from the moment of Tagart's arrival. He had no son himself: Klay was his favorite. Possibly he nurtured a hope that, after Shode's death, the two tribes would merge and that he would become the chief, working through Klay.

Tagart sat looking out across the bleak marshes of the valley. The bad weather had started. Soon the meres would be solid. In some years even the rivers froze. Such times were rare, every ten or twenty winters, often following a hot summer; and last summer had been the hottest anyone could remember. The old men were already saying that a cold winter was on its way.

He opened his mouth to speak, but closed it again, not sure how best to frame his words. Out on the floods the duck were still feeding. The cloudy day made the colors of their plumage dull, blending with the grass and the thistles. Beyond them the water of the mere was blown into tiny waves; the wind flicked droplets from their peaks and drove them on the shore. The nets had almost filled with birds.

"Get ready to pull," Klay said.

"You know why I asked you to join me here," Tagart said. "I want to talk. I want to make things plain."

Klay did not look at him. He watched the nets instead. "Go on."

"I have no wish to be chief."

"If you had no wish to be chief, you would not be able to say such a thing."

"I want only to live in peace."

"You mean you are not at peace already."

"How can I be? You and Bubeck will not let me."

Klay's hands tightened on the cords. "You seek to make trouble here. Why did you come back?"

"The Shoden are my tribe."

"No longer. You left us and went to the Owls. They are dead. You are tribeless; you have no ancestors. They died with the Owls. It would have been better if you'd died with them."

"My ancestors are here."

"You do not deserve to be welcomed back."

"That is for Shode to say. What would you have us do? Spend the winter with the wolves? Die without ancestors?"

"There are other camps," Klay said.

"Where I have no friends."

"You have no friends here."

"My father was once 'Shode.' "

It was useless. Tagart had achieved nothing; less than nothing.

Klay put his face closer to the slit, cutting the conversation off. The nets were waiting and open, the cords stretched tight. Ducks had filled the fatal space: widgeon, pintail, mallard, teal.

"Pull!" Klay shouted, and they yanked the cords back.

Like folding wings the nets closed in. A teal escaped; the rest were pinned to the ground by the meshes. The other birds on the floods went up in a roar of alarm. Klay was the first out of the hide, splashing through the sleet and floodwater, a cudgel in his hand, ready to dispatch the birds they had caught.

In the late afternoon Altheme came down to the quay to watch the soldiers landing. She stood alone, almost unnoticed in the shelter of the worksheds, her hair drawn back with a carved brooch of jade and ivory. She wore a small jade earring, and a necklace of worked scales of nacre and lapis lazuli. She pushed her hands farther into the pockets of her sealskin coat, which was made of the pelts of unborn pups. Like nearly everything she owned, it was the gift of her husband, the Lord of Valdoe.

She gazed at the landing stages and the wooden vessels bumping there. Her thoughts were confused. It was three weeks and six days since the night of the storm. She tried to argue with herself: in all the years with Gehan she had conceived not once. Why then should she do so now? She was worrying without reason. It made no sense. A child would not fit the pattern, the destruction of their happiness and their life together. It could not fit: it was too grotesque.

But the night of the storm would not leave her thoughts. That was the last time they had been together. She could not forget the rain and wind on the shutters and the groaning timbers of the fort. She kept seeing Gehan above her; she kept hearing the name he had breathed. *Ika, Ika.*

The afternoon was turning to dusk. Drops of rain began to fall.

The soldiers had arrived two hours ago. The men were ashore, already finding their quarters in the Trundle four miles away. Now slaves were unloading the rest of the weapons and equipment, packing sleds to be drawn along the road that led from the quayside and the creek.

The landing stages stood near the head of the creek, accessible at all but the lowest tides. Across the water were salt marshes, and here and there on higher ground were clumps of scrub. That was where the savages, the spies, had been captured, a week or so before.

Altheme left her place by the corner of the worksheds and slowly walked toward the water. The ships, like all that was most costly, drew their design from the mainland, and ultimately from the east. The prows reared up, the heads of monsters carved and inlaid, from flat plank decking smoothed by the adzes and sand-stones of craftsmen in the homelands. From stem to stern the largest ship was twenty-nine feet. The larger vessels had two deckhouses, the smaller only one. Low masts carried leather or fabric sails, now furled with white ropes. Shipped oars stood pointing skyward, like the rays of fish fins. Hatchways lay open as the slaves passed up bags and bundles to those above.

This was the eighth or ninth such landing in the past three weeks. The number of extra soldiers was steadily growing.

"What are you doing here?"

At the sound of Gehan's voice Altheme took her hands from her pockets and turned. "I wanted a change of air, my lord."

He was not pleased to see her. He had been speaking to the harbor Trundleman, arranging for another landing stage to be built. "How did you get down from the fort?"

"An empty sled." She bit her lip. "I meant no harm. They were bringing it down anyway."

"And how do you propose to get back?"

"I didn't think."

"You never do." Gehan beckoned to a man nearby: the overseer of a team of slaves. The overseer hurried across the quay and inclined his head. "Unload that sled and take Lady Brennis back to the Trundle," Gehan said. "Make haste before it gets dark."

The road up to the fort had become a quagmire. The slaves hauled at their harnesses and struggled to keep the sled moving. Soon they were under the trees; reaching branches made a tunnel of the road. The sled turned a corner and the flickering lamps of the worksheds were left behind.

Gehan that evening arrived late for the meal. Altheme had bathed and changed, and for a long time sat alone in her chamber. She had dismissed her body slave: she wanted to examine her thoughts.

She heard the voice of the man to whom she had given herself for so many years, the man who had changed so much. He was outside, in the vestibule, taking off mud-spattered clothes.

Her thoughts returned to their first encounter, all those years ago. She had been eighteen and Gehan twenty-two. Her father, a merchant, had brought her to Brennis on a visit to see his friend, the fourth Lord of Valdoe. She remembered her first sight of the crude, wild coast of the island country; the sinister ramparts of the Trundle on the top of Valdoe Hill; the docking of her father's ship; and the sharp premonitory pang she had felt with her first step on the strange soil. She remembered a formal young man with sun-bleached hair and solemn gray eyes who had walked with her by the willows, trout dimpling the river. In him she had recognized the complement of herself. His strength of will had overawed her; but more striking had been his gentleness and his capacity for understanding. He knew her perfectly—in his company she needed no pretense.

Seven years ago. A month after their wedding his father died and Gehan became the fifth Flint Lord. At once their happiness began imperceptibly to dissolve. Gradually, over five years and more, she realized that in her inexperience she had made a mistake. His power in this country was frightening. It had invaded his sanity: it was driving him mad. His idealism had become something else.

She knew she should go, escape to her father, anywhere. That was her urge, but there was nowhere safe. She could not go home. The trade with Brennis had become too important. Even if she did try to escape, she would be sent back. Outside Valdoe she had no acquaintances, no one to whom she could turn.

Altheme rose from her couch and entered Gehan's chamber, the room where they ate and slept. His sister was seated on the bed, cross-legged, her blond hair hanging loose.

Ika looked up. "Did you hear? The other savage died this afternoon."

"I suppose you went to watch."

"For a little while." In Ika's lap was an oval box. It contained the dried female flowers of hemp, a plant brought to the homelands by traders from the south and east. Ika took some and packed it into a narrow-bowled pipe with a long, curving stem. "Pass me a taper, Altheme."

She held the taper to the nearest lamp and lit the pipe, inhaling deeply, holding the smoke in her lungs till it had lost its blueness and become brownish gray; and exhaled. She had been using the drug throughout the day. "For you?"

Altheme shook her head.

"Perhaps you should."

"No."

There was a draft as the door opened and Gehan came into the room. He went to a table by the window and poured a beaker of milfoil essence.

"Did you see the savage die?" Ika said.

"I was there, yes."

"Did he say anything?"

"Not a word." Two savages had been caught near the landing place. They had been lying in the bushes, watching the quay. According to Gehan's advisers, it was rare to find such men away from their tribes at this time of year. The clear implication was that the landings had already attracted attention and that the two were spies. When interrogated, though, neither had so much as admitted that he could understand the questions. One had been pressed to death in front of his companion. The sight had produced no effect. He had given nothing away. The guards had then exercised their skills on him, to no profit.

The incident was puzzling, even worrying. If the two men were nomads, as their appearance suggested, their presence at Valdoe might or might not indicate that news of the campaign had reached the winter camp. But if, as was possible, they were merely a couple of outcasts, or peddlers, or wanderers from some place beyond the domain, then the matter was not worth further consideration. Gehan tried to put it out of his mind.

"No guests tonight," he said. "We're eating alone."

He turned to the door and called for the night meal.

5 Tagart shouldered two more bundles of stakes and balanced them. His fingers felt cold under his mittens; his breath fumed as he stood waiting for Edrin to finish sorting through the heaps of gear. Since first light they had been working with the others, carrying bundles down the valley and into the marshes. The previous day the hunters had been unsuccessful in their attempt to catch a suitable boar for the solstice celebrations; it had been decided to try again, in a place called Yote Wood.

The Yote Oak, a hollow tree from which the wood was named, stood in the middle of an island of high ground among the marshes, an isle which the river had not yet worn away. The island was long and narrow, clothed at its edges with dense tangle. Farther in there were beeches and oaks, and it was these that brought the wild pigs to feed.

Bristly and squat, burly and dark, the pigs dug with tusks and pushed with snouts, and made small contented sounds of feeding. Their hoofs printed cleft tracks in the mud. At one end of the marshes they had made a wallow and rubbed the bark from a nearby tree. The boars were solitary, nocturnal, lurking by day; the sows traveled at night too, with their piglets, continually chiding them. In the easy soil of the marshes they uprooted tubers and insects, found and ate toadstools of many colors and kinds. Their hours were spent in continuous eating, wandering the lakesides and woodlands. Autumn was the time of feasting. And when the frosts came and the mud froze, the pigs turned to a diet of acorns and beech mast.

To catch them the hunters used various techniques. Most efficient, where the terrain permitted, was a line of beaters moving toward a funnel of wattle fencing. At the end of the funnel, catchers would be waiting with netting and spears. The placing of the wattle panels, their precise configuration, was a matter of extreme skill—a boar could weigh as much as three hundred and eighty pounds. Armed with powerful tusks, spurred by fear, such a beast could not be stopped by a fence of flimsy wattle. The fences did not prevent the animal's progress: they directed it, subtly, from clump to clump and copse to copse. Only toward the mouth of the funnel did the fences become more substantial and uncompromising. Then the posts were driven in with heavy hammers, the panels reinforced to withstand demented barging and butting. The final corridor toward the netting was made of solid stakes.

These stakes were made of the strongest oak, and were six and a half feet long, trimmed at one end to a point. They lay at the camp in bundles of six, beside the pile of wattle panels, the netting and hole borers and the rest of the equipment.

"Which are the new nets?" Edrin said irritably. He was thirty-six, small and slight, with keen brown eyes and a sparse beard. He rarely smiled or spoke idly. He was humorless and ambitious, but he had no presence and commanded little respect. Nonetheless, he held a special place in the tribe, which he had earned by his closeness to Shode, by his advice and experience in matters of the chase: his gifts in tracking and deduction were uncanny. From a blade of grass and a broken twig Edrin could compile a story, detail after detail, rejecting the irrelevant, picking out clues that anyone else would have missed. What he lacked in physique he made up for in resource and cunning. He was a man of subtle motives. A member of the Waterfall tribe all his life, he had at one time wanted to be its chief. But now all that seemed to be forgotten. Now he appeared content merely to advise Shode, to be one of the elders. He had sided with Bubeck and Klay on the question of the Flint Lord, and privately regarded Tagart and Fodich as scaremongers.

"Are these the new nets?" he said, turning the heaps over. "Klay said something about repaired nets and new ones."

"We should make sure," Tagart said. The weight of the stakes was beginning to hurt his shoulders.

"It's that pile there," said Berge, a man of twenty with wild beard and hair.

"Are you certain?" Edrin said.

Tagart said that he recalled having seen Klay with the nets earlier. Berge was right.

This was to be the final trip down to the marshes and Yote

Wood. The rest of the gear had already been deposited there. During the afternoon it was to be assembled in preparation for the drive the following day.

Tagart, Edrin and Berge set off, downhill, leaving behind the untidy expanse of the camp, the fires and shelters, the dwellings with their roofs of piled branches. The river flowed quietly among the bridging logs. Tagart felt a melting on his nose and looked up.

"Snow," he said to Edrin. "It's already starting. But where are the scouts? What has happened to Chenk?"

"He'll be here soon enough."

Tagart noticed Segle across the river, working at rope-making with the other women. He called her name, but she did not acknowledge: perhaps she hadn't heard.

Edrin, observing, said, "There are troubles nearer home than Valdoe."

"What do you mean?"

"It is not my place to say."

"Say what?"

"What you are the last to know. But gossip means nothing. The women have too much imagination."

At once Tagart understood and was angry. True, since coming to the camp it had been different between him and Segle; alone with her in the forest he had been sure of her, but here, surrounded by new influences, everything had changed. Yet she was his woman and Edrin had no right to make such remarks. Tagart's first impulse was to strike him down.

Suppressing his rage, Tagart said, "What do the women imagine?"

"I cannot say," Edrin said. "Just remember the penalties."

Tagart checked his reply. Among the nomads the marriage bond was held sacred. It was the foundation of the family, the tribe, the spirit group, and hence the foundation of Creation itself. Only a chief, whose actions were divine, could choose his woman as he pleased. For the rest, the laws were harsh. Those aggrieved by adultery could insist on severe punishment: for the man, castration and banishment; for the woman, death by burning. After only three weeks in the tribe, Tagart did not feel confident enough to challenge an elder, nor did he know exactly why Edrin had spoken as he had.

Edrin glanced sideways at Tagart and saw that he had achieved the desired effect.

They continued in silence. Berge, walking behind and whistling, had heard nothing of the conversation.

The snow shower did not persist. By the time they reached the marshes it was over.

In Yote Wood, near the big oak tree, they found Klay and Bubeck. This was to be another joint venture of the Waterfall and Beaver tribes. In consultation with Edrin and the other expert trackers it had already been established where the ending of the funnel was to be sited, here by the oak tree. They were hammering in the posts as the three men arrived.

The ground was hard with frost, but despite the cold Klay had taken off his stormcoat. He was sweating as his hands took a firmer grip on the haft of the long stone-headed hammer and he swung again, smacking the top of the post held upright for him by another man.

The corridor of posts was almost complete. It curved slightly to the right, terminating in a gap just wide enough to admit the flanks of an adult boar. Behind the gap was a framework of poles. Over this the netting would be laid, loosely, so that the animal's progress would not be halted too quickly, but quickly enough to ensure that it would be entangled in the meshes quite safely before a spear stroke brought about its end.

Tagart set down his burden.

"Take the hammer," Bubeck said.

"Yes," Klay said. "I'm sick of this." He stood back, wiping his nose on his wrist, and let the handle of the hammer fall. It hit the ground at Tagart's feet.

Frequently in the past weeks Bubeck and Klay had singled out Tagart for the unpleasant or arduous tasks. But Tagart did not belong to the Bubecks: their chief had no power to give him a direct order.

Tagart turned to Edrin, an elder of his own tribe. Edrin gave a nod: assent to Bubeck's order, turning it into a mere proposal.

Bubeck sneered.

"Let me take the hammer," said Berge, picking it up, and the moment passed.

They finished the corridor of stakes and arranged the netting on the framework. By early afternoon, work on the entire funnel was complete. Everything was ready for the drive next day; the men withdrew.

At the meal that night the Shoden, twenty-one people in all, ate as a group. They sat close to the flames, warming their hands, sheltering from an east wind. The leather awnings flapped and whipped as the wind blew the fire to life and threw sparks beyond the guy ropes and into the night. Tagart watched Edrin, who was eating assiduously, occasionally speaking to his woman and to Shode. He watched the other men in the tribe: Orick, Berge, Grisden, Phale, each with his family. He watched Klay sitting with Yulin, his wife, dumpy and dark, made drab by childbearing, her brown eyes withdrawn and resigned. More than once she glanced at Tagart and Segle. She gave food to her daughters, two small girls who clung to Klay. Klay was speaking, boasting of all the pork they would be bringing tomorrow from Yote Wood.

He noticed Tagart watching him and seemed to avoid his eye.

"This way!" Bubeck shouted. "This way! Keep him this way!"

The boar, disturbed from sleep at the very feet of the beaters, was one of the biggest they had ever seen. It had burst from a brake of rotten brushwood as the men moved forward, shouting and screaming and banging with sticks.

The men were running now, leaping through the undergrowth, trying to keep up with the boar as it crashed first one way then another, guided by the wattle panels on its headlong passage through the woods, gaining speed, its snout held low; they glimpsed its yellow tusks, the hackles of coarse bristle on its back; and abruptly it had vanished in a holly thicket, the glossy foliage slapping back to hide the place of its entry.

It was the first drive of the day, under a sky that looked full of snow. Tagart was near the middle of the line. They had managed to keep the boar well inside the funnel. The holly thicket was one of a number of such sanctuaries along the course where a quarry might go to ground—unavoidable hazards which the siting of the fences had kept to a minimum.

"Careful now! He might break anywhere! If he comes too fast let him go!"

The animal was too big for them to take chances. They had not seen it properly yet, not in the open, but it stood easily three feet high at the shoulder. If it chose to come out of the thicket

where it had gone in, if it chose to run back down the funnel—
as some old and wily boars might—it would be far too heavy to
stop.

"There he is!"

"He's coming this way!" Tagart cried.

For an instant the boar, head down, was tearing through the
brambles directly toward him. It had emerged from the holly at
a gallop, close to the place where it had entered, almost as if it
had sensed a weak link in the line of men, a slight gap between
Orick and Tagart on his left. But Tagart was moving sideways,
closing the gap. The boar came nearer: twenty paces, ten, and,
with two sudden steps, jolted to a halt. It took breath, eyeing
Tagart. He met its eyes: they were very dark, nearly black, with
rims of white showing at the bottom, bloodshot and rheumy. The
pig was looking at him. And then it turned its head and was
running again, away from Tagart and the others, more desperately
than before.

It skirted the thicket and plunged along its ordained path
toward the corridor of stakes.

"Keep him straight! Keep him straight!"

The final screen was behind; the funnel walls were narrowing.
The boar, terror-stricken, was running much too fast to take the
curve of stakes and its flank barged into the left wall, robbing it
of speed, but it kept on, goaded by the yelling and screaming
and suddenly the stakes opened and there was freedom and it
was fooled, meshed in a tangle of netting that brought it in a
slithering crash to the ground.

Men were ready with spears. Klay thrust first. The blade snapped
and he shouted an oath. He drew back; Grisden stepped forward.
The boar rolled its eyes, blood dribbling from its mouth, and
with a convulsive spasm got to its feet. Grisden raised his arms
and stabbed, badly, too quickly, goring the flank, unleashing a
paroxysm of thrashing and bucking and squealing. Shode gave
an angry cry and jumped forward to finish it, to end its pain; but
then, impossibly, the netting was somehow coming apart as the
boar wrenched its head from side to side and one foreleg was
free. Then the other foreleg came free and the netting was being
dragged behind like an old skin. Teeth chattering with pain and
rage, the boar twisted sideways and ran straight into Shode. Its
right tusk jabbed upward and pierced his groin. Tagart saw the

boar give a frenzied jerk of its head and Shode was flung down and pulled along the ground.

Other spears were plunged into the boar from behind. In a moment it was dead.

Shode was shouting, shouting through all the woods with un-human cries, a beast in slaughter. The trees, the sky, the ground—everything seemed to Tagart unreal, from some other world where emergency waited to break through. And it had broken through. What had happened so swiftly and easily could not be grasped, could not be believed.

Klay fell to his knees beside his father.

Among others, Bubeck and Edrin jumped the line of stakes, screaming orders. They dragged the carcass of the boar aside and cut away Shode's clothing.

"Hold him still!" Bubeck growled.

They stared, aghast.

"Better take him back."

6 The solstice symbolized rebirth. It was the first day of the new year. On the morning of the Creation, after the Sun had vanquished the Ice God and exiled him in the far north, the four spirits were born, released from the Sun's dazzling body in an endless stream, each separate, each remaining a part of the Sun. The spirits were a family. Together they made Light, the essence of the Sun, returning to him, coming forth. The father of the family, Fire, warlike and proud, was sent north and charged by the Sun with keeping the Ice God a prisoner. The daughter, Water, peaceful and passive, was given the south. The son was Air, whose domain was the east; and their mother, Earth, dwelt in the west.

The Moon had betrayed the Ice God and ingratiated herself with the Sun, who made her his acolyte. To her were entrusted the seasons, and each winter, when the Ice God tried to win her back, her allegiance was put to the test. At the solstice she renounced him and turned back to the Sun. It was the Moon whose slender fingers had taken the Sun's needles and sewn the threads of light he had provided: from light, from the four spirits, in greater or lesser proportions, everything was made, and, having been made, assigned its place in the world. Thus the eagle was a blend of Air and Fire, and was traditionally governed by those spirits; the bison belonged to Earth, the otter to Water. The creation of man was more complicated. His body was composed of all the spirits, but his soul was imperfect, lacking one or more of the elements that would allow him to achieve perfection or Light. He spent his life trying to repair the deficiency. If he lacked Fire, he would go to live in the north, and the totem of his tribe would be chosen from one of Fire's creatures.

There were four spirit groups, each with its winter camp in a different part of the country. Sometimes these camps split up, changed sites, fell into disuse, and then there might be five, six, or even more.

Each spirit group was led by one tribe, known as the First. The Firsts, alone among all the tribes, took their names not from a creature but from the direct manifestation of each spirit: Crase, Lightning; Shode, Waterfall; Sare, Cloud; Omber, Mountain. Their totems—lizard, salmon, peregrine, ox—were secondary symbols which nonetheless possessed great power, for each was the purest totem of the spirit.

Most tribes belonged to two spirit groups. Their summer hunting grounds, although never precisely defined, were usually adhered to and each tribe had its customary territory and rights. The Dragonflies mainly wintered in the north, at the Lightning camp; but because the dragonfly was a creature of Water as well as Fire the tribe sometimes used the Waterfall camp instead. Occasionally, finding themselves in autumn in the west or east— perhaps deliberately, for most marriages outside the tribe were arranged in winter—they might stay as guests in the camp of another First, just as the Wolves, the Bisons, and the Martens were this year wintering in the Waterfall camp.

Shode died from his wounds at nightfall. The loss of blood was too great, the damage too horrible for any hope of recovery. Yet the priests chanted through the hours of waiting, and sprinkled mineral earths on the fire, causing many-colored sparks to rise into the gray afternoon. They made prayer to the Sun, to the Moon, to the four spirits. To Water they addressed a continuous and dreamlike hymn: as chief of the Water First, Shode was the embodiment of the spirit among the nomads. There would be no rest until another had been found to take his place.

Even as they had carried Shode back to camp the speculation had begun. With such injuries they knew he was already finished. It was time for a new chief to take over. Klay's time had come.

Below ground, the Waterfall priest, Phale, spoke his prayers while Shode's woman held her husband's head in her lap. He had lost consciousness.

Shortly before dark there was a cry from the river. Chenk and the scouting party had returned. Nine men had left the camp three weeks ago; only seven crossed the bridging logs to be greeted with the news about Shode.

Chenk took the remaining chiefs, eight including himself, and gathered them together under the awnings at one edge of the cooking area. He was exhausted, filthy, dispirited; the scouts had covered the distance from Valdoe in two days. Normally it took at least twice as long to traverse, on overgrown paths, eighty miles of forest and marsh. Chenk sat down and for a moment put his face in his hands before speaking.

"Fodich is right," he said.

He described how the scouts had divided in order to survey all parts of the Flint Lord's domain. "We saw ships landing, soldiers moving from fort to fort, supplies coming from the villages. You've never seen such things. Wone and Trander are missing. They must have been taken by the soldiers." He explained that Wone and Trander had been sent to Apuldram to watch the landing place. All the scouts had been due to rendezvous on the way back; when Wone and Trander had failed to appear, Chenk himself had gone to Apuldram to find them. "There's no cover. To get close to the worksheds they must have risked being seen. We waited two days for them; we even questioned a field slave on the outskirts of Valdoe Village, but he could tell us nothing. Then we came back."

Four of the chiefs—Osprey, Dragonfly, Heron, and Kingfisher, Chenk himself, agreed that there should be an immediate convocation of the elders, not only of this, but of the other winter camps. The remaining chiefs were divided. Bubeck and Marten were still skeptical; Bison and Wolf wanted to leave the decision to Shode or his successor.

Their argument was interrupted by the arrival of Phale, the priest, tall and sharp-faced, his beard and hair almost wholly white. He was leader of the elders in Shode's absence.

"Come at once," he told the chiefs.

Klay appeared at the top of the ladder from Shode's dwelling. He stood looking round the camp for a moment before stepping forward. People began rising to their feet; the compound fell silent.

"My father is dead."

Phale pushed his way forward. "A new chief must arise!" In his right hand he was holding aloft a long staff, a carved mace intricate with flowing patterns which culminated in a leaping salmon, symbol of aspiration and the Waterfall tribe.

At his elbow, Tagart felt someone stir. It was Yulin, Klay's wife. Segle had become separated from him in the crowd.

"Who is there with strength?" Phale cried. "Who is there with strength to carry the Mace?"

Klay responded. "As my father's issue I put myself forward by choice of the spirits. Render the Mace to my charge!"

Klay's woman was standing on tiptoes, speaking into Tagart's ear. "He wants your wife," she said. "They have already known each other. If he is chief he'll take her. You will be abandoned, and so will my children, and so will I."

Phale turned to the assembly. "Does any man stand against Klay?"

"You will be cast out," Yulin hissed. "You will be tribeless. It's true. I saw them in the woods."

Tagart could not absorb what she was saying. He could not think.

". . . in the woods," she whispered again.

Murmurs were rising around him. A name was being repeated over and over again. Edrin, Edrin, Edrin.

"No!" Klay shouted. He shot out an accusing arm. "It was he who killed my father! It was Edrin, Edrin and Tagart, and Berge. They brought the old netting on purpose! It was Tagart! Tagart and Edrin!"

Edrin came forward. "I challenge his fitness to lead."

"Yes! We want Edrin as chief!"

"Klay is unworthy!"

"He cannot lead us!"

Phale raised the Mace for silence. "Klay, will you defer to Edrin? Or will you accept the challenge?"

"Do I have any choice?" He wiped froth from the edge of his mouth. "It was a plot by Edrin and Tagart to kill him!"

"That's enough."

"Murderers! Murderers!"

Phale restrained him with the Mace. "Enough, I said!"

Tagart perceived that Edrin was the choice of the majority, of all who opposed Klay. But he also perceived that Edrin was too old to challenge a man like Klay. Edrin would have better field-craft, no more, and in the forest, especially in winter, that was not enough. Klay would win and become chief. And if what Yulin had said were true, he would take Segle and drive Tagart out. Tagart would have to leave his blood tribe and his ancestors and never return. He would have to leave Segle, leave her with Klay . . .

"Edrin is old and weak," Yulin said into Tagart's ear. "Only you are strong enough to challenge my husband."

Earlier Tagart had seen the arrival of the scouts and he had already heard rumors of what they had found. At the back of his mind was something larger and far more important than Klay and Segle and his own life.

Yulin was still speaking, in a low, insistent voice. Tagart sought Segle's face but couldn't find it.

A huge man was moving through the crowd, pushing people out of the way. "Let me through," Bubeck said. "Let me through." He reached the fire and addressed Phale.

"I too challenge Klay's fitness to lead."

There was uproar.

The Shoden objected, because Bubeck was outside the tribe; they said he could not compete.

"Not so," said Phale with regret. "The Beavers are of our spirit. Their chief, and the chief of any tribe of the spirit, may challenge. This is lawful."

Bubeck grunted. "The Shoden have become too few," he announced. "They need fresh blood. Our blood. Our tribes will merge. The Bubecks and the Shoden will become one, a great tribe, the first tribe of the spirit!"

Tagart observed that Klay did not seem upset by Bubeck's challenge. He realized what it meant. It meant Edrin would stand no chance at all. Not against two.

Tagart heard his voice speaking, as though it were not his own; the words he uttered were squeezed from him by the press of people, by the firelight and the night, by Klay and Edrin and Bubeck, by Yulin, by the long hours of torment waiting for Shode to die. They were uttered for Segle, anguished and desperate words, but most of all they were uttered through the memory of Fodich lying in the mud, through terror: of Valdoe, and the carnage that would surely come if the Flint Lord remained unopposed.

Tagart faced Phale and the whole assembly.

"I too challenge," he said. "I challenge Klay's fitness to lead!"

The laws of challenge had their origin in the mists beyond memory. Their object was simple: to find the best man to be chief. In the process no one was to be killed, unless by misadventure, for no face was lost by defeat and a fair surrender was held to be honorable. In this way valuable men were not wasted, and the man who was strongest and cleverest would succeed.

Phale, as leader of the tribal elders, broke the Mace into five pieces. The uppermost fragment with its salmon emblem was retained by him. The other fragments, one to each contestant, were given to Klay, Edrin, Bubeck and Tagart. Contestants were allowed their choice of clothing, a pouch, and, through some tradition whose purpose was obscure, a coil of spear-binding twine eleven paces in length. They had no food, no weapons, no fire-making kits.

The challengers were then to be banished from the camp, in accordance with the laws. The one who came back with all the pieces of the Mace, to match the emblem and make it whole, would be recognized as the new chief.

If a man sought or accepted the help of another, or if he destroyed or lost his fragment before it could be taken, or if he returned to camp before his part in the contest was resolved, then that man would be tried by the elders. If found guilty he would be executed and all his family cast out, left to wander without tribe or ancestors, without hope of the afterlife. In winter such expulsion meant virtual death, from hunger and exposure or attack by wolves.

There were no other rules. Nothing mattered except that one man should demonstrate his superiority by finding, and having found, taking—by violence, stealth, or persuasion—each and every fragment of Mace.

The four men were separated, searched by the elders, blindfolded, and sent out secretly, each in a different direction, chosen by lot. Because they were four, each had been assigned a cardinal point. Tagart had drawn North; he had then been conducted to the edge of the camp. Only then had the blindfold been removed, so that he would not know which directions the others had taken.

No stars showed: under the trees everything was dark. Tagart made his way uphill, toward the burned-out heath where he had decided to wait till daybreak. Brambles snatched at his leggings. Branches broke under the heavy soles of his boots. He was leaving a plain and easy trail, but that could not be helped. At night, the others would be doing the same.

He had already shaped the outline of a strategy which depended upon no one but himself. That was the only way to succeed—if he tried to be too subtle, to anticipate what the others might do, he knew he would become confused and failure would inescapably follow.

It would be simple to hide among the trees, to wait, to let the others fight each other first and thus reduce the odds. But he had neither food nor fire, and what if they too were planning to hide? What then?

He knew he had to start at once, and the man to start with was Edrin. Edrin was past his best, and, though he was not to be underestimated, he would be the easiest of the three.

Tagart was afraid. Klay and Bubeck were working together, and he would have to take them both at once. They would try to kill him. They could not risk his return to camp, his testimony that Klay had been helped. So they would kill him in the woods and hide his body. And afterward Klay would take Segle and become leader of the Shoden. Disaster would come to the tribe and all the tribes of the south, for, whoever won the contest, only Tagart recognized the threat from Valdoe.

He tried to push aside all such thoughts, and thoughts of Segle too, but she was with him constantly, a dull, bewildering ache. He refused to let himself believe what Klay's woman had whispered, refused to connect it with what Edrin had so maliciously said or with what he knew in his own heart.

There was no time for her now.

At first light Altheme was standing alone at her window, looking south. She kept her eyes above the tent-filled enclosure and the spiked wooden walls of the fort, above the rough steepness of Valdoe Hill falling to bleak marshland and the sea. The sky was gray. From it, even as she watched, single snowflakes began slanting down.

It was the day of Goele, the winter solstice, a feast, and not yet sunrise, but Gehan had been up and working for three hours, leaving Altheme to listen to the sounds from the adjoining chamber.

Gehan's sister Ika was in there with a girl and a youth. The youth, Gehan's food taster, had recently been a nightly visitor to the chamber. He was tall and languid, with red hair and pale skin and green eyes. The cast of his features was beginning to betray the decadence of his life in Gehan's retinue. It was a life devoted to luxury, pleasure, sensation, with women or with men, Gehan's guests, and sometimes with Gehan himself. Altheme knew this. She was aware of her husband's tastes, the changing favor with which he viewed his other women, and the way he regarded his wife. The knowledge disgusted her. And it disgusted her to listen to Ika with the food taster and the girl. The girl was innocent, a child barely eleven years old. She had been summoned from the slaves' quarters during the night. Altheme had heard her frightened pleadings silenced; and now, at dawn, the noises were beginning again: the creaking bed-frame, growing moans, stifled cries of pain.

Altheme turned quickly from the window. By the doorway she paused to take a robe from her clothes rack. The first to hand was pale brown, embroidered with flowers and ferns of yellow, pink, lavender and green. It flowed behind her as she left the chamber and crossed the gallery, from which a twisting flight of stairs led to ground level and the Flint Lord's day rooms.

Gehan was there, in the main chamber. The ceiling of this room was low, scarcely above head height. Polished oak boards, gleaming in the lamplight, covered the floor. The walls were decorated with panels of painting, some of extreme age, others quite recent: scenes of symbolism and history, depicting demons, flames, men in battle, winged creatures spewing swarms of insects. Three wide windows overlooked the inner enclosure. Each was provided with a heavy shutter closing from within, for defense, and the door, which was made of thick elm, swung on oiled oak hinges and was fitted with four stout locking bars. A yew-wood cradle held heated rocks, renewed every hour by slaves. There was little furniture in the room: a few small chests, a kind of low bench on which stood burning oil lamps, and some leather cushions scattered on the floor. On one of these Gehan was seated, cross-legged, studying a sheet of wood marked with daubs of ink. The daubs represented hands. A hand was five: five men, a team. Five teams made a unit. Other marks separated the daubs or joined them together. A square represented the Trundle; triangles the secondary forts; a wavering line the Brennis coast.

In normal times he maintained a force of nineteen units. Seven were under the command of the General of the Coast, one unit being deployed in each of the secondary forts. Six remained permanently at Valdoe—one to guard the mines, two to guard the other works outside the Trundle, two on duty inside the fort, the sixth kept in reserve. The remaining units made up deficiencies in the secondary forts, helped with road and bridge building and repair, escorted trading teams when needed, and composed the slaving parties which made regular crossings to Normandy and Brittany.

"We must draw twelve teams from the secondary forts," Gehan said.

There were two men with him, also seated on cushions. One was fat and soft, dressed in dark gray and fox fur, with curious pink eyes, white hair, lashes, and wispy beard: an albino named Bohod Zein, agent for the forces in the homelands. Through this man, Brennis Gehan Fifth had paid in flints and goods for ships and reinforcements.

The other was General of Valdoe, a former commander from the mainland called Larr. Like Bohod Zein, he was dressed in the dark gray of the Gehans; over his garments he wore a military tunic of plain hide. A white scar marked his forehead, an old ax wound. His eyes were black and penetrating, his face fleshless and hard. In the army of the Gehans the ranks were few: soldier, team master, unit leader, commander, general, lord. Larr had begun as a soldier at the age of ten. In twelve years' slaving he had advanced to team master, unit leader, and commander. Under Gehan's father he had been brought to Brennis and then, at the age of thirty, had been made general, one of two in the island country.

"My lord," said Bohod Zein, "if you take so many from the General of the Coast, will your forts there not be weakened? I can respectfully arrange for three more units to be sent, trained men, all experienced, at a price scarcely greater than that negotiated before."

Gehan considered. At this moment over three hundred men were waiting across the channel, consuming food and supplies. Two hundred more had already landed and were overcrowding the barracks. The expense of the campaign so far was giving worry. The output of the mines for the next three years had been mortgaged. If the weather worsened and the crossings were impeded, the expense would become ruinous. But he knew that the agent was right. To leave the secondary forts under strength would be dangerous.

"Arrange it."

"As to price, my lord—"

Gehan arose as Altheme entered the room. Larr stood too, lithe and controlled. Bohod Zein struggled to his feet.

"My lady," Larr said.

Bohod Zein eagerly stepped forward and took Altheme's hand. "My lady."

His familiarity far exceeded the bounds of etiquette. Gehan observed Altheme's uncertain glance, noted the lingering clasp of Bohod Zein's fingers. With a courteous smile she drew her hand away.

"I am sorry, my lord," Altheme told Gehan. "I did not mean to disturb you here. But have you seen outside?"

Already there were white ridges on the roughness of the inner palisade. Gehan strode to the nearest window and looked out and up.

The air was filled with tumbling feathers and stars, multitudes and multitudes coming from a darkening sky.

The snows had started.

7 Klay heard the camp coming awake. From his perch in the boughs of an old beech, he looked across the river toward the compound and tried to see movement, but too many winter branches were in the way.

He took off one mitten and held up a licked finger. East, the wind was coming from the east, and when he studied the sky he saw that it was sliding majestically, a dense, almost featureless mass of cloud tinged with yellow that meant snow for certain.

He replaced his mitten and started down the tree. In snow they would be able to find Tagart very quickly; and then, when the first of Shode's murderers had been dealt with, he and Bubeck would go after Edrin.

Edrin would already be in hiding, somewhere safe, somewhere impossible to find, for Edrin was the finest tracker and his wood-craft was too good for any of them, even for Klay himself. To search for him would be wasted effort. Better to let hunger bring him out. Meanwhile, they would find Tagart and kill him.

Klay wondered what Tagart was planning, and how far he had managed to think things through. He was stupid: he would not have guessed that Edrin was in hiding. But then . . . was that really what Edrin was doing? Was it safe to presume anything? Suppose Edrin weren't in hiding at all. Suppose he intended to find Bubeck or Klay and keep his distance. Suppose he saw what they did to Tagart and went back to the camp to tell Phale. Or suppose he joined forces with Tagart. Suppose . . .

The confusion in Klay's mind multiplied. He did his best to sweep it away. One thing, at least, could be depended on.

In the lottery for direction, Klay had drawn West. He had left the camp under the eyes of the elders and disappeared into the darkness. Two hundred yards from the edge of the compound he had halted and climbed into the beech tree. There was no sense in going any farther. In the morning he knew he would be meeting Bubeck. He knew Bubeck would be nearby, because this was what they had arranged in whispers. Together they would circle the camp and find Tagart's trail, leading in one of the two directions that they themselves had not drawn. There would be little doubt about whose trail it was: Tagart was taller and much heavier than Edrin, and, unless Edrin went to immense and improbable pains, that could not be disguised.

Klay reached the ground and looked about him. Bubeck had instructed him to walk sunwise, following its circle. Bubeck would walk the other way, and in this manner they would quickly meet: so close to the camp it would be unsafe to linger. The solstice feast had been canceled, and for the duration of the contest there would be no hunting excursions; even so, now in the gloom of first dawn, there was a risk of being seen by someone in the camp.

Klay set off. The ground was hard underfoot from days of frost. When he came to the gurgle of the river he waited near the bank, reluctant to go in. The water would be very cold, and he would have to cross with bare skin, for contestants were allowed no spare clothes. The river flowed southeastward; Klay had drawn West. Bubeck, not knowing—their whispering had taken place before the lottery—had told him to walk sunwise.

Klay nipped at his cheek lining. One or other of them would have to cross.

Suddenly there was movement on the far bank, among the thicket of elder and dogwood that grew right to the water's edge, the branches in the twilight overhanging the swift current. Klay drew back in alarm.

"It's me!"

Bubeck broke the branches aside. He was clad in a bearskin stormcoat, shaggy and dark, tied with a horn-buckled belt, and his leggings, also of bearskin, were tucked into high leather boots. On his head was a peaked fur cap with flaring flaps, and his hands were protected by fur mittens. He brought them together with muffled claps, then swung his arms in the cold. "Come out of there, Klay!"

Klay appeared, glad to be alone no longer. Bubeck hissed the good news across the intervening yards. "Tagart drew East. He's left a trail like an aurochs'."

"You've already found it?"

"Yes. Come on. Get across the river and we can start."

Klay hesitated. The water here was deep as well as cold.

"What did you draw?" Bubeck said.

"West."

"That means Edrin drew North. I drew South."

"You've already crossed once?"

"On the stepping-stones at the waterfall." Bubeck gestured impatiently. "It's not that cold. Get your boots off."

"It looks difficult here. I want to try farther up. At the swamp."

"Don't worry," Bubeck said. "It's shallower than it looks. You can cross all right."

"I'm not sure about it, Bubeck."

"I've done it myself here. Come on. You're wasting time. If we're not quick we'll lose him."

Reluctantly, Klay undressed. The air was so bitingly cold that his teeth began to chatter at once. The water would be worse. However, he would soon be across and back in his dry clothes. Shivering uncontrollably, he squatted naked, bundling his stormcoat and wrapping it round the pouch and the rest of his things.

"Heave them over," Bubeck told him, and Klay did so.

Klay neared the water's edge.

"Hurry up! What are you waiting for?"

When Klay's foot touched the water he gasped. Water of such intense coldness was not possible. With his right hand he was gripping a branch. He let it go and gingerly put his other foot forward, probing for the riverbed.

It was not there. The current was strong and fast and had cut deep. The water seized Klay's foot and pulled at it like a playful animal. It was scalding his calf, his knee. How much colder would it be on his thighs, on his genitals? Too late, much too late, he realized he wanted to change his mind and he scrabbled for the safety of the branch, but he was losing his balance, his left foot slithering: he knew his equilibrium had gone and he was falling. He shrieked and hit the water with a clumsy splash. At once the grabbing, caustic pain clawed at his skin: in an instant all sensation had been destroyed. He was nerveless, dead with grinding cold. He thrashed his arms, but could not stop his head from going under and the river was dragging him with it.

Numb feet found the bottom and he managed to stand up, against the flow. He had been carried some yards downstream. He opened his mouth, gaping for air. His thorax seemed to have collapsed.

Something hit the water in front of him: a bundle of clothing and a pouch. The pouch had been plundered. The fragment of Mace was missing. And when he looked toward the bank, so was Bubeck.

Tagart frowned. Someone had been in the river here, less than an hour before. He plucked a blade of meadow grass from the tangle of vegetation on the north bank where the man had pulled himself out. The grass, bright green even in winter, was freshly bruised.

Tagart stood up, with a practiced eye examining the faint impressions in the ground, the disarray of twigs and leaf litter, the clues which seemed to lead toward the camp. He turned his eyes to the far bank, trying to see where the man had entered the water. There. Upstream.

He worked his way along the water's edge. Opposite the spot he found new damage to the elder branches. From the number and thickness of split fibers which had so far resumed their shape, he deduced that everything here must have happened at about the same time. The man in the water and the man on the north bank had been here together. Tagart pictured the scene, a grim smile growing on his face. It seemed that Bubeck hadn't been planning to violate the laws of challenge after all. And how did this affect Tagart's quarry—how did it affect Edrin?

At dawn, Tagart had come down the hill to quarter the eastern side of the camp, searching for a recent trail. Those who had drawn West and South would have started from the other side of the river.

So near the camp there were many confusing signs of coming and going, but all were at least a day old. It had not taken Tagart long to find tracks that were unmistakably recent, and from the stride and weight of the man who had left them, he concluded that the trail was Bubeck's and that it was Bubeck who had drawn East. That meant Edrin must have drawn West or South and would be on the other side of the river. If Edrin had gone to earth, that would be where the contest would be resolved. Tagart would have to cross. There were not many places to cross safely, and at any one of them an enemy might be waiting. Tagart, despite his decision to start with Edrin, had to know what Bubeck was doing. He had followed Bubeck's trail to the river, where he had found what he took to be Klay's trail, leading out of the water and toward the camp: the trail of a beaten man.

Tagart resumed his pursuit of Bubeck's trail. It ran generally beside the river, heading upstream. At times it made detours, favoring the easier passage away from the thickest undergrowth. Tagart followed. All his senses were alive; but the woods seemed empty and reassuring.

The wind was keener now. The sky was dark. Soon snowflakes were falling one by one. As they touched the water they vanished and were carried onward. A mile or so above the camp, the river curved away from him and became a wandering stream in a rushy swamp. The snow was falling more quickly. Snipe, harsh-voiced, sprang from the frozen rushes as Tagart approached; they flew up in towering spirals, calling incessantly.

He found the spot where Bubeck had removed his boots and did the same, placing his bare feet in the marks that Bubeck had left, paddling through the icy black mud and into the stream. The water was painfully cold. There was gravel underfoot and between his toes. Tiny fish, black in the pellucid water, streaked away from his feet. The water came to his knees; he crossed as quickly as he dared, afraid of losing his footing, afraid of an ambush, knowing that he was vulnerable here.

On the other side of the swamp, where the ground began to climb, Tagart pulled on his boots and found Bubeck's trail again. It led south—to Edrin.

Tagart stopped on the rise above the valley and looked back. Over the landscape and down into the gray, leafless woods, the sky was shedding snow.

The flakes softly found their way through the branches and, no longer melting, began to settle on the forest floor.

Klay knew the dangers of what he was doing: if he were caught, both he and his family would be tried and punished. His wife and two daughters would be made tribeless, and he would be disemboweled, the manner of execution reserved for the lowest criminals, those who had betrayed the trust of the tribe.

But, however great the dangers, they could not compare to Klay's rage.

Yulin was still asleep when he came down the ladder and into his dwelling. He was certain he had not been seen. His dwelling was near the edge of the camp, and by crawling and rolling he had reached the ladder unobserved.

His immersion in the river had left him weak and chilled, but his furious resolve had given him new strength. Bubeck, the man he had followed and respected always, was now revealed, laid bare. His treachery was like the eruption of some obscene fungus that had finally reached its season and burst. So Klay had retrieved his clothes from the river and put them on. In his wet stormcoat he had made his way to the camp and to his ladder and had climbed down it.

Yulin awoke as he pulled off his coat and threw it into the corner. "Hide this, and the rest of it," Klay said. Above him in the camp, he could hear someone talking. Soon the first meal would begin.

He gestured at the two small girls curled up together in their bed of furs. "Keep them quiet," he said. "I want dry clothes. My second stormcoat. And food. Plenty of it."

Yulin looked at her daughters in the half-light of the pit. They were wide-eyed with fear. She enjoined them to silence with a finger on her lips, and from the traveling bags unpacked fresh clothing for Klay. She knew better than to speak.

"Get the food, woman! Hurry!"

"I'll have to go above ground."

"Then do it!"

She moved toward the ladder, urging herself to betray him, for then he would never be chief and her daughters would never be without ancestors: they would never be expelled and made tribeless.

"Let no one suspect!" he said, seeming to divine her thoughts.

"No one," she said, and climbed out.

Klay's eyes seemed to be burning in their sockets. His fingers were tingling. Impatiently he turned out Yulin's pouch—he had no other—and started to cram it with weapons and supplies. First, a fire-making kit in a wallet of tallowed skin. A leather purse with a dozen bowstrings. From pegs on the wall he took down his best longbow. This was not a toy for killing coots, not for hares or squirrels: this was for felling big animals. He unhooked his quiver and filled it with suitable arrows, each one tipped with flint. Lastly he took down his prized hunting spear.

The weapon was heavy with magic. It had impaled many beasts.

Its point was still stained with dried blood; the shaft was of flawless yew, shaped and tapered to take a perfect trajectory from Klay's arm. His rage blazed more fiercely. The spear had been made for him alone, a coming-of-age gift from Shode. It was the work of a master weaponer, now long dead, a man from the Eagle tribe whose very name meant Spearmaker. The grip was bound with colored twine, making a herringbone pattern of yellow and brown. This spear was a javelin, designed purely for flight; in its making Spearmaker had breathed his spirit into it, and now it had its own life and its own desires, seeking the heart of its prey. Bubeck's heart.

"I want you to look outside," he told Yulin, once he had packed the food she had brought down. "Go up the ladder and look. If it's safe I will leave."

Yulin had come close to giving him away. At the fire she had almost spoken to Phale's woman; but she was afraid of Klay.

"Please, Klay. You have been defeated. There is no dishonor. Tell Phale and let the others fight among themselves. Your place is here with us." She drew in her breath, frightened that she had dared to speak her mind. "Please, Klay. Please."

He studied her contemptuously. At another time he might have struck her. "Get up the ladder."

She obeyed and urgently beckoned. For a moment the way was clear. Using every inch of cover, he darted from the ladder and ran, bent almost double, to a fallen log, to the trunk of a tree, to a pile of firewood, and in moments he was out of the compound and running into the forest.

When Bubeck saw smoke rising from the hillside below him, he knew why the fire had been lit.

After taking Klay's fragment he had followed the river upstream, in order to cross safely at the swamp. It would have been quicker to circle back and cross at the waterfall, but he had already found Tagart's overnight trail and he knew that Tagart would be returning to the vicinity of the camp at dawn to look for signs of the other contestants. Bubeck did not want to come upon Tagart unexpectedly; he also wished to leave him a plain trail to follow.

But that trail had been quickly obliterated by the snowstorm. By midmorning, after two hours of heavy snowfall, the wind had freshened to a blizzard and Bubeck had been forced to shelter in the lee of some bushes. Later, looking for traces of the others, he had wandered southeastward, near the river. From there had climbed to the highest slope of the valley and into the top of a beech. His view, of undulating hillsides covered in trees, was grizzled by the continuous falling of light snow. Since noon the light had steadily got worse. It was now too drab to pick out moving figures: Bubeck had searched the valley for minutes at a time, his eyes watering in the cutting east wind. He had almost given up hope when he saw the thread of smoke.

He tried to fix the position of the fire in his mind and came down the tree.

For most of the day he had managed to keep moving, to keep warm, but even so his hands and particularly his feet were suffering. If he were hiding somewhere like Edrin, not daring to stir, he knew he would be afraid of frostbite.

But he also knew that Edrin would have anticipated this thought. And he knew that if Edrin wanted a fire, he could make it burn perfectly well without any smoke to give his position away.

That meant the fire could have only one purpose. It was a signal: an invitation, an admission that the snow had made tracking a matter of chance and not skill. Above all, in this dangerous weather, it was a ploy to hasten the end of the contest. Whether Edrin would be nearby was doubtful. He would be elsewhere, safely awaiting the outcome of whatever encounter his fire produced.

Bubeck started downhill. His feet crunched and creaked and crushed snow into the mouldering leaves and litter of the forest floor; his breathing, wet and warm, returned to him in the confines of his mask.

He stopped to listen.

The silence was not encouraging. The hairs on the nape of his neck began to prickle. He waited a very long time; snow accumulated on his hat and shoulders, on the sparse and disordered tufts of his eyebrows. He licked meltwater with a small, furtive motion of his tongue.

The fire could not be seen from here, but he knew it could not be very much farther down the slope. He looked in vain for the smoke. Sky and snow had made it invisible.

Finally, measuring each footfall, he continued downhill, stopping every few yards. The woods here were of oak and birch;

clumps of brambles were tangled and clotted with white. He sniffed. A faint tang of woodsmoke met his nostrils. Another dozen steps. He could see the fire, a mound of sticks whose center had collapsed to leave a bed of embers. The bracken round the fire had been roughly cleared.

He whirled round, but no one was lurking among the trees. Perhaps he was the first to get to Edrin's fire.

In a conversational tone he called out: "Who's there?"

No answer.

Resisting the impulse to retreat, Bubeck went forward to the fire. He looked round uneasily and squatted to make a rapid study of the half-burned sticks. Judging from the embers, the fire had been burning for two or three hours.

He stood up and yet again looked round, sensing the presence of something malignant. The wind moaned. Grains of snow flittered to the ground.

Bubeck examined the bracken round the fire. After missing it twice, he found the first of what looked like a series of footmarks, a pocket of crushed bracken shaped like a bird's wing. He took a twig and disturbed the snow in the pocket. Its surface was powdery and new, but, underneath, a thin layer of snow had been compacted by a man's weight. The thickness of the powdery layer told him that perhaps two hours had elapsed since the footmark had been made.

His eye followed the line suggested by the mark and found another mark, and another, making a trail. The gaps between them were not great: they had been left by a man of less than average height—Edrin!

He stood up. He had two choices. He could wait here in the hope of catching Tagart unawares, assuming Tagart would be drawn by the smoke: this was obviously what Edrin was hoping for. Or, he could follow the trail to Edrin and the third fragment of Mace.

The decision was easy to make. He had anyway decided earlier to leave Tagart till last.

Placing his feet in the marks—just to puzzle Tagart—Bubeck set off. He had not doused the fire: he wanted Tagart to come after him.

He followed the trail downhill and toward the river. More than once he became confused, only to find the trail again by dint of patient searching. The whole of his attention was given to the ground ahead. He was ill-prepared for the blatant message that had been strewn so carelessly across his path; it took him momentarily by surprise. Human urine had been splashed in a place where the footmarks had become vague, near the base of a sturdy durmast oak.

Bubeck had just enough time to look up, half knowing what he would see.

Falling from the height of a bough, plunging toward him, accelerating, came the boot-first weight of a man in a stormcoat, a man who had been waiting up there for two hours.

Tagart took the impact in his knees. His boots struck Bubeck in the throat and chest, and his hands, gripping each end of the piece of Mace, brought it down with a dull crack on the upturned mask. It hit the bridge of Bubeck's nose, and with an odd quiet grunt he collapsed.

Tagart was thrown to one side. His piece of Mace spun away and landed in the snow, making a slot for itself.

He lay on his back, dazed, his eyes wandering in the pattern of twigs and branches above. He remembered building the fire, and he remembered working and working his makeshift bow drill, in his palm a concave pebble to press down on the spinning stick: the first miraculous wisp when friction made smoke, renewing his efforts, blowing on the spot, until the flame caught and burned in the dry punkwood he had scooped from a rotten birch. From the fire he had left a trail with deliberately shortened strides, and climbed into the oak to wait for Bubeck.

Nonetheless it had taken him a moment to adjust to the shaggy presence of the man below who had stopped to peer at the ground.

Then he had launched himself.

Bubeck lay groaning. His groans ceased and blood oozed from one corner of his mask, staining the snow.

On unsteady legs Tagart got up and stood over him. Bubeck's breathing was labored and hoarse. He had fallen on his pouch. Tagart knelt down in order to roll him out of the way and undid his mask to help him breathe.

Tagart could scarcely believe his luck. After the blizzard he had been forced to give up hope of finding Edrin; instead he had been made to concentrate on Bubeck. And now by this simple ruse of the fire he had given himself a huge advantage. He was three quarters of the way to victory. All that remained was to find Edrin.

Bubeck was heavy, like a dead thing. The strength had gone from Tagart's arms and he feebly and repeatedly tried to push Bubeck off the pouch and roll him aside. It was no use.

He found the strap of the pouch and tugged. The pouch came free at last: Tagart delved into it and brought out the two fragments of Mace. The wood had been varnished by the handling of years, but the splintered ends were newly white. Tagart tried to fit them together. As he did so he sensed movement in the field of view beyond his hands. He looked up.

Klay was a hundred paces away, approaching at a trot, following the line of footmarks from the fire. He was fully dressed in dry clothing. A bow was slung across his back, an ax dangled from his shoulder, and held to the ready was a hunting spear. At the sight of it, Tagart began to rise.

He had not noticed Bubeck's eyes opening.

Bubeck's kick caught him in the side of the head and sent him sprawling. The two fragments of Mace were flung from his fingers. His shoulder struck the bark of the durmast oak and he tumbled into the snow, face up. Bubeck was on him at once. The weight of his body crushed Tagart against the ground. Bubeck's hat had gone; his eyes were mad gleaming points in smudges of shadow. A choking stench of sweat, foul breath, and stale fur caught at Tagart's throat as Bubeck raised his fist to deliver a single tremendous blow.

With a hiss the spear sliced under Bubeck's arm and carried something with it. A fine red spray hung sprinkled in the air: the point of the spear slammed into the tree, penetrating to the heartwood before its flight was arrested with a loud and plangent humming of the shaft.

Bubeck stared at his forearm, at the inexplicable red flow that was gleaming and welling across his sleeve, and as the humming died he turned to see where the spear had come from.

Ax in hand, Klay hesitated a moment longer. He had missed, and in his panic he saw what he must do. It meant leaving the spear behind, certain evidence of his return to the camp, but he did not consider that. He saw only that he had missed, that Bubeck and Tagart were unhurt, that they were two to his one; and he saw that three pieces of the Mace were lying in the snow, waiting for him.

He snatched them up and ran.

8 Bubeck got to his feet and chased him, shouting abuse. Fifty yards from the oak tree Bubeck tripped and fell. Tagart ran past him, carrying the spear, its flint tip broken, but Bubeck's kick had left him weak and dizzy and Klay easily outdistanced him. He saw Klay disappear into the trees.

Tagart looked back. Bubeck was on his feet again, clutching his arm, approaching with lagging steps. "He's been back to the camp!" Bubeck called out.

Tagart began to retreat.

"No! Tagart! Stay! I want to talk!"

Tagart smiled inwardly; Bubeck hurried his pace. Snow was still falling lightly.

Tagart knew Bubeck. He had already guessed what was coming, but he did not want to seem too eager to listen. However, the contest had taken a new and desperate turn. Klay now had at least three of the four fragments. If he had already taken the fourth from Edrin, or if he did so before Tagart, the contest would be over and Tagart would have lost. By the laws of the challenge, it was true, Klay had cheated, but Tagart did not know how much credence the elders would give to his accusations, especially if, as seemed possible, Bubeck were to refute them for reasons of his own. Even the spear could doubtless be explained away.

Tagart's best hope was to get to Edrin first: this would be true no matter what Bubeck was about to propose. And it was no more than a hope. Klay may well have got there already, something which would soon be confirmed if his trail were seen to lead directly back to camp. But it seemed likelier that Klay had simply been drawn by the beacon fire after a morning of aimless wandering.

A race was on to find Edrin. If Klay won the race, he would also win the contest. If Tagart won the race, the contest would be prolonged and he would have a chance of taking the rest of the Mace from Klay.

Where was Edrin? More than elementary woodcraft would be needed to sniff him out. But he would not have made his hiding place impossible to find. The cold would tell on him more severely than on the others, and he would scarcely want to prolong matters needlessly. Some process of deduction, then, should give the key to finding him.

What was more, Tagart knew that Edrin would not be simply waiting to be found. He would be busy making preparations for the arrival of his visitors. The nature of those preparations would, ideally, need to be revealed by some third person.

Bubeck, breathing hard and warily eyeing the spear, stopped a few paces short. His stormcoat was badly bloodied, the bear fur caked and white where he had been rolling on the ground. One of his leggings had worked loose and hung at the top of his boot. The flow of blood from his nose, where Tagart had hit him, had ceased and congealed in his beard; he was still nursing his wounded arm.

He nodded in the direction of Klay's tracks.

Tagart prepared to listen.

Toward midafternoon the snowfall stopped altogether. Bubeck and Tagart were following the river south toward the marshes. Beyond Yote Wood it broke into several streams; the valley floor was filled with beds of sallows, osiers and reeds. On slightly higher ground were open leas, profuse with low growths of annual plants and with close clumps of grass which could withstand months of submersion. With the rains, the ponds and puddles of the leas coalesced to form small meres.

Bubeck was leading the way, his arm bandaged with a spare boot lining. He was continuously aware of Tagart behind him with the spear, but he felt hopeful, for once Tagart had been persuaded to listen, it had been easy to dupe him into apparently joining forces to find Edrin. Tagart had agreed to Bubeck's proposal almost at once; he had even fallen for his glib reply to the question of which of them would keep Edrin's fragment. "We'll worry about that later. For now, we must reach him before Klay."

So far Bubeck had scrupulously observed the rules of the contest. He had arrived alone at an idea of where Edrin might be: he had neither consulted Tagart nor asked his opinion of the idea, though Tagart had expressed his doubts about its logic.

Bubeck did not share them. It was plain that Edrin would have picked a hiding place that could be found by inference rather than tracking. As a result of his seemingly casual questioning of Klay at the river, Bubeck had deduced that Edrin had drawn South. Thus Edrin was probably somewhere south of the camp. But where? He might be waiting by one of the established paths in that area; or he might be waiting close to the camp. Or if there were a hunting shelter, he might be waiting there. But there was no hunting shelter. The only shelters for miles were those actually inside the camp—and it was forbidden for him to hide there.

Then it had come to Bubeck. It was so obvious that he marveled he had not seen it before. There was only one man-made structure outside the camp. It lay on the south side of the river. It would offer Edrin protection from the weather, and moreover it would allow him to sleep, for no one could approach without giving warning by the crash of breaking ice. Lastly, and Bubeck saw this as the finishing touch of ornament on his theory, the structure's name proclaimed the purpose to which Edrin had put it.

The hide was near the edge of the marshes, on the western side of the valley, overlooking a sheet of water three or four acres in extent. Behind it was a channel of the river and a gloomy copse of alders. A makeshift log bridge spanned the channel, leading to a causeway of broken branches which had been strewn in the mud along the fifty paces to the hide. The hide was the height of a man's chest, large enough to seat two, made of reeds bundled on to a crude framework of poles, the joints lashed with strong cord.

Tagart and Bubeck came to the copse of alders. The channel here was eleven feet wide, bridged by the log. Stubs of broken branches projected from it: one trailed in the water, slitting the surface and sending a wake of ripples downstream. A crust of snow covered the log; it had been disturbed during its formation by the passage of feet. Edrin had been here. At the end of the causeway the shape of the hide was visible.

"He's done something to it," Bubeck said.

Many of the reed-bundles had been untied and the framework looked lopsided. Too much light was showing through. The front of the hide had been removed.

"What do you think?" Bubeck said.

"He may have wanted the lashings."

"Let's look."

Tagart glanced round uneasily. This was a good place for an ambush.

"You're armed," Bubeck said. "You check the hide."

It was too late for Tagart to argue: possession of the spear had trapped him. Bubeck was using him in just the way he had meant to use Bubeck.

He went out on the log. It was precariously balanced, and the snow made it more dangerous still. He cautiously reached the other side and started along the causeway.

Bubeck stood watching. The light was failing and he did not notice the heavy, water-logged willow bough that came drifting downstream, gaining momentum. Behind it stretched a long tail of thin twine—spear-binding twine. Ahead, the bough was overtaking yards of sodden, knotted cord which preceded it to the bridge. The bough barely broke the surface of the channel; it passed under the log without a sound and traveled onward. Ten yards from the bridge, the cord tightened in a straight line underwater. Its end had been tied to the projecting stub of the log, the one that had been partly hidden by the current. As the cord tightened the log jerked and slewed and was gently dragged into the channel, and at a distance followed the willow bough as it resumed its stately journey downstream.

The bridge had gone. Tagart heard the splash and looked round. He and Bubeck had been separated by the width of the channel, a width too great to leap unaided.

Tagart checked his shout of warning and allowed Bubeck to be taken unawares. Behind Bubeck Edrin came at a run from the copse and with a grunt brought down a length of broken branch on his head. The power of the blow struck Bubeck squarely on the back of the skull and he staggered. With the second blow he went down on his knees. Edrin hit him again. He pitched forward and lay still. Edrin dropped to his knees and tore open Bubeck's pouch.

Tagart sprinted toward the channel. Edrin rose to his feet and made for the copse. His movements were stiff and slow: he had been waiting all day for the arrival of his adversaries.

Tagart was three yards from the bank. Barely slowing, he planted the tip of Klay's spear next to the water and hoisted with all his strength. The vaulting motion carried him almost across the channel; he smashed into the ice and slime on the far side and at once felt the disastrous soaking in his boots, and, tangling with the spear, slithered on the snow as he pulled himself clear and tried to stand.

Edrin had vanished. His feet already freezing, Tagart ran after his tracks, past Bubeck's slumped form and into the alder copse.

He saw Edrin then, climbing the slope among the trees, struggling in the snow. Edrin was running as if wading. He looked over his shoulder and redoubled his efforts.

Tagart caught him fifty yards on, by a bramble patch. He seized Edrin's shoulders and dragged him down, punched him in the face, and Edrin gave in. Tagart ripped open his pouch: the piece of Mace was not there.

He turned Edrin onto his stomach and forced his arm up against his shoulder blades.

"Where is it?"

"I wasn't . . . expecting a spear . . . You've cheated . . ."

"Where is it?"

He gasped with pain. "Klay took it!"

Tagart, already tired, cold and hungry, was beginning to lose his temper. He shoved the arm further and felt something tearing. Edrin screamed.

"By the waterfall! In the poplar! In the poplar! I hid it in the poplar!"

"The hollow one?"

"You've broken my arm!" He screamed again. "Yes! The hollow one, the hollow one!"

Tagart considered this reply before easing the pressure. Although he was disinclined to believe anything Edrin might say, the words had sounded convincing enough. It made sense that Edrin would hide his fragment somewhere.

Using the strap from Edrin's pouch, Tagart bound his wrists.

"What are you doing?" Edrin said in alarm.

"I want your boots." Tagart took them off, removed his own and tossed them aside. With his spare linings he dried his feet as best he could before pulling on Edrin's own, fur-lined hunting boots.

"I'll lose my toes!"

Tagart did not bother to answer. He added his spare boot linings to those already in Edrin's pouch. "Put your feet in there."

When he had done so, Tagart tied his ankles with twine and tied the bindings at wrists and ankles together. He left Edrin lying in the snow and went back to the alder copse and the channel.

Bubeck was unconscious. Even his thick skull had been unable to withstand such an onslaught of blows. When Klay eventually found him he would be in no state to defend himself. Edrin too would be helpless.

That was a matter for Klay's conscience. Tagart trussed Bubeck and tied him to the bole of a young alder.

Taking Klay's spear, Tagart set out. By the shortest route, across the hills, the waterfall was three miles away at most; but he would lose his way under the trees. If he wanted to travel by night, under cloud, he would have to follow the riverbank and let it guide him along the trail he and Bubeck had already made. At the confluence of the first tributary—the one that came down from the camp—he would branch left and keep with it till he came to the waterfall.

But he managed to cover only half a mile. At first the remnants of dusk had enabled him to proceed, but soon all trace of daylight had gone. Everything had been reduced to black and grayish white, the snow picking up the faint and general luminescence afforded to the clouds by the stars behind. It was too dark to see the way.

This was the second night Tagart was going to spend in the open, and the prospect worried him. He had not eaten since the previous day, and he badly needed warmth, but with Klay searching for him he could not risk lighting a fire or being found asleep.

Nearby was an old willow with a big spreading fork fifteen feet above the river. Tagart climbed into it, refastened his mittens and made sure that the drawstrings at his wrists, neck, waist and legs were tight. He pushed the edges of his mask deeper into the sides of his hood, which he drew down over his brow, leaving just a slit for his eyes.

Through it he could barely discern any variation in the quality of the darkness. The cold was getting worse.

Hugging himself more tightly, Tagart prepared to wait out the night.

During the afternoon Klay had followed the trail of Bubeck and Tagart, down from the woods and along the river as far as Yote Wood, where failing light had forced him to stop. He had sheltered for the night inside the Yote Oak; at dawn he woke and emerged from the tree.

He returned to the river and was perturbed to find a new set of footprints heading toward the camp. They were indistinguishable from those Tagart had left yesterday.

"He's passed me in the night," Klay said aloud.

He took another piece of hardtack from his pouch and chewed it, trying to understand the meaning of the new tracks. Had Tagart returned to camp? Had he been beaten? It seemed likely, for if he had been seeking Klay, he would surely have followed his tracks to the Yote Oak and surprised him there—unless it had been too dark for Tagart to see tracks when he had passed. Perhaps Tagart had beaten the others. Perhaps he had the fourth fragment and had gone to Phale to accuse Klay of cheating. Or perhaps he was searching for Klay despite everything.

Klay placed his hands on the three fragments of Mace protruding so reassuringly from his pouch. He needed only one more. Then he would be chief, and not only of the Shoden, but of the whole camp. His first act would be to put Tagart and Edrin on trial, and Berge too, for the murder of his father. All would be disemboweled; he would do it personally. Bubeck would then be tried and found guilty of conspiring with Tagart in the contest—their tracks had crossed and recrossed; they had been together. Bubeck would be stripped of power and shamed, and the Beavers would become part of the Waterfall tribe. And then, once the spirits had been appeased, Klay would take Segle for his wife. He would be divine, a demigod, almost one of the spirits himself. Did he not already feel greatness? Had he not already shown himself superior? Had he not won three of the four fragments?

He wanted the fourth. He had to know whether Tagart had it.

Klay started north, his ax in his belt, his bow across his back. For part of the way along the river, as far as the place where yesterday's tracks came down from the woods, Klay's own tracks of the previous evening were plainly visible. They had been ignored—or missed. Beyond that place, Tagart's trail continued alone, through virgin snow, still keeping by the river.

Klay forced his pace. He was beginning to feel warmer. He had breakfasted well, on nuts and dried fruit and venison hardtack, and now the loneliness and discomfort of the night were receding and he was becoming eager to make an end to the contest.

At the tributary, Tagart's tracks turned with it, still heading for the camp. The footprints went on and on, keeping with the river path, through the alders and crack willows, leading Klay between the steeply rising sides of the valley.

After another mile he stopped to listen. He was getting near the waterfall. A little way off he could hear its roar, churning the gray morning air with subtle variations in pitch and volume.

He was about to continue when he thought he glimpsed movement among the trees ahead. His heart suddenly pounding, he stared at the spot; trunks and branches of hazel and alder impeded his view.

He unslung his bow, nocked an arrow, and went slowly forward.

9 The waterfall was two miles above the confluence. Green water slid over the lip and tumbled in a dense sheet to explode on the pebbles in roils and froths of white which curved in on themselves in standing waves that dragged the riverbed. A few yards on, the dazed current recovered itself and continued downstream. Spray from the fall had accrued as grotesque icicles on either bank; withered curls of hart's-tongue had been frozen solid and encased.

A line of stepping-stones crossed the river just above the waterfall. On the north bank stood a hollow poplar, old and gaunt.

All sound lost in the din of falling water, Klay drew back his arm and took aim. The dark barbs of the flight quills scraped his cheek as he readied himself for the shot, eyes focused with deadly purpose on the air slightly ahead of Tagart's moving profile, his wrist and arm smoothly traveling with Tagart's progress across the river from right to left. Tagart seemed to be knee-deep, walking in the waterfall, but that was just the angle of view. The range was about a hundred and ten paces, and still Tagart had not noticed him. Klay's vision became a lucid tunnel. His whole will and intent slowly merged with the arrow's flint tip. He wanted to strike Tagart's skull, to burst his brain in a flurry of blood and skin and hair. He waited for Tagart to gain solid ground, one heartbeat, two, three, four, and when the arrow could go nowhere but down the axis of the tunnel the string was no longer in his fingers and the shaft had been released.

But Klay, contrary to the teaching he had received, had left his bow strung overnight. Away from its protective envelope of leather, the string had become slightly dry. The constant tension of the bow had stretched it and impaired its elasticity. And, during the night, he had leaned against the quiver in his sleep, crushing some of the delicate barbs, unhooking the tiny barbules that linked to make a smooth vane for flight. These imperfections took expression in the arrow's path and it flew six inches wide.

Klay saw Tagart jerk instinctively back as the wind from the arrow raked his face. Klay reached over his shoulder for another arrow.

Tagart recovered his footing and for the first time seemed to see Klay. He ran down the rough slope beside the waterfall, coming straight for Klay; his pouch fell to the ground behind him and with his right hand he took a throwing grip on the javelin.

Klay aimed again, more rapidly. He tried to concentrate on the shot: this was just an animal running toward him, not Tagart, not Tagart, just a large animal, sixty paces away, fifty: Klay let fly.

Tagart dodged and in a single fluid sweep the spear was in the sky, flickering against the branches, curving down, plunging so rapidly that Klay had only time to turn. The broken point struck him as he was turning, a hammer blow at the base of his neck. Something heavy exploded inside his head and his mouth was full of sharp, granular snow. He was on the ground. A merciless weight was crushing his spine: he could feel Tagart's knee in his neck where the spear had struck. This was a pressure point, a death-place. Tagart was shouting. Klay could not understand the words: his ears were filled with a roaring like the center of the waterfall, the center of the world. Through a carmine fog he saw Tagart's wolfskin mittens gripping either end of a piece of Mace, forcing it upward across his throat.

The pain had become a single continuous blare louder than anything he had ever known. His neck was breaking. If he did not give the sign now he knew Tagart would pull with one more ounce and he would die.

He beat his hand on the snow.

The pressure relented. Tagart was still shouting.

"Shode's death was an accident! Say it!"

Klay croaked.

"Say it! Say it!"

"Accident."

"And what will you call me? What will you call me? What's my name?"

"T . . . T . . ."

"What's my name?"

Then Klay understood. Tagart had the whole Mace. He had all the pieces. He had got them all.

"Shode, Shode," he said.

"Again!"

"I . . ."

"Again, I said! Louder!"

"Shode! Your name is Shode! Shode!"

Klay remained for a long time with his face in the snow, listening to the waterfall, before he realized that Tagart had gone away.

PART TWO

1 "What is it, my lady?"

Altheme shook her head, too sick to speak, and though nothing more would come she leaned over the bowl again and retched. On waking she had felt nauseous, but it had not been until she had sat upright and put her feet on the cold floor that she had lost control. Rian, her body slave, had come running into the room with an empty wooden laver.

Rian had borne three children. She knew well enough what was ailing her mistress.

"Let me help you," she said, putting her arms round Altheme's shoulders and easing her backward against the pillows.

Rian summoned her under-slaves and quickly the room was fresh again. The floorboards were scrubbed, the bedclothes changed, and the heated rocks renewed. Altheme was washed and, after she had been wrapped in clean marten furs, looked gravely at Rian and spoke in a low voice. "Sit by me, Rian."

Cracks in the shutters admitted slits of gray light; the draft toyed with the flames of the rush lamps burning by the bed.

"There can be no more doubt," Altheme said. "I am going to have his child."

Over the past few days she had confided her fears to Rian.

"You should be glad. Perhaps this will change everything."

"No. It has come five years too late."

There was no bitterness in her voice, but she could no longer conceal the extent of her misery. To the older woman, Altheme looked like a child, a pale child, ill and overwrought. Rian had been serving her for two years. Her predecessor, for some reason that had never been divulged, had been dismissed by the Flint Lord himself. Rian was almost twice Altheme's age. She had been a slave all her life.

Altheme took her hand and held it closely. Shadows covered the ceiling and walls. The doorway was in gloom; beyond it, down the stairs, were men's voices. From outside, from the enclosure where many soldiers' tents had been erected, from the overcrowded barracks, came ceaseless shouts and the sound of work.

"How many soldiers are outside, Rian?"

"Too many for me to count, my lady. I hear the landings are half done. More ships are due when the snow stops."

"They say there will be six hundred foreign soldiers here soon."

"Yes."

Rian noticed sparkles of light at the corners of Altheme's eyes. Tears slowly welled and ran down her cheeks.

"You must tell him, my lady."

"I cannot."

"You must."

"And have him change toward me just because of the child?"

Rian had already had this conversation with her mistress, but there was a new firmness in Altheme's voice as she added, "The baby is my only weapon."

"But he will find out soon enough."

"Let him."

"I beg you—"

"I will dress soon," Altheme said curtly.

"You are too ill to rise."

"There is nothing the matter with me. And I have instructions for you. Tonight I want no slaves near my chamber. Not even you."

"As my lady wishes."

Altheme squeezed her hand more tightly. She studied the bed-clothes, unable to look Rian in the face. "There is a man," she said presently. "There is a man called Bohod Zein. I must . . . Your master says . . ."

Rian stared at her. She had seen the agent from the homelands, Bohod Zein, a fat, white-haired albino, and she had seen his pink eyes following her mistress, but she could not believe what was being said.

"Gehan has no more flints," Altheme went on. "He has promised them all away, and still he wants soldiers. Bohod Zein is rich. In the homelands he has twenty villages. He owns ships and many cattle. And he . . . he wants . . ."

Rian opened her arms as Altheme broke down and wept. Eyes closed, Altheme crushed her head against Rian's breast and allowed herself to be comforted. Rian gently stroked her hair. "You must tell my lord about the baby," she said. "He will never permit it then."

Altheme shook her head and began to sob. Rian felt her shoulders heaving and tried to calm her with soothing words; but then she too was overwhelmed and began to grieve, not only for her mistress, but for her own plight and the plight of every slave. Through her tears she brushed her lips against Altheme's cheek to give her a child's kiss, and, as on the vulnerable skin of a child who has been ill in the night and washed by its mother, Rian tasted but did not mind the musty, bittersweet odor she found there.

Envoys to the other winter camps were sent out as soon as Tagart had formally received the Mace and the name of Shode.

On returning from the waterfall he had given the broken pieces of Mace to the elders, as tradition required. Everyone was summoned to watch Phale as he crudely repaired the Mace and matched it to the tribal emblem. Tagart was prepared for the ceremony by the other chiefs: no women were allowed to witness his ritual washing or the slow process of dressing in robes and mask. Dyes and daubs were applied to his skin and hair, in cream, white, pale-blue and green. He sat as if numb, elated and exhausted. He was to be the chief and leader of his own blood tribe and the winter camp, first man of the spirit. Upon him had settled the divine choice of the Sun: he was to be Shode.

Dragonfly and Heron reverently unpacked the striking and beautiful salmon mask with its glossy eyes and hooked lower jaw, each scale of its skin cut from mother-of-pearl and left the native color, or stained and finished with crimson and olive green like the skin of a living salmon. In the compound, the sacred foods were nearly ready.

Meanwhile men had been sent to find the other contestants. Edrin was unhurt but, like Bubeck, badly chilled. Bubeck had been concussed, though not seriously, and he seemed to bear no grudge; indeed, he had trouble in dissembling his admiration of Tagart's victory. Klay, on Tagart's instructions, had been brought back to the camp in a hood with his hands tied.

At last Phale gave the signal and Tagart was conducted into the open.

The ritual of making a new chief was an occasion of urgency

and awe. There was rarely time to prepare elaborate costumes such as were seen at other ceremonies during the year. The chief of each tribe wore his mask and robes; the others wore the best they had. There was no feasting, nor was there music save the measured speech of the elders. This was a time when the spirits were very near. As if to acknowledge their presence, the trappings of the ritual were both simple and powerful. The holy, magic, forbidden wood of the spindle tree—from whose branches the Sun had fashioned needles to sew the threads of his Creation—was gathered and used to heat the morsels of dried man orchid that conferred divinity on the new chief. With them, because this was the Waterfall tribe, a few scraps of salted salmon, the sacred food of the water spirit, were also made ready and heated on a flat stone.

The whole camp had assembled. It was about noon when Phale began to speak. In a freezing wind, under heavy cloud, the river flowed past; the snow on its banks was packed hard. Here and there across the compound were small movements: the motion of smoke, a hanging strip of leather.

Watched by the people of nine tribes, and eight chiefs in bird, beast and insect masks, Phale held the pieces of orchid to Tagart's mouth.

"This becomes your flesh."

Another elder recited a prayer and brought Phale the platter of warm salmon.

"This becomes your spirit."

Tagart ate. It was very salty; a fine bone stuck in his cheek.

The fish mask was placed on his head.

"Your tribe calls you."

One by one, everybody in the Waterfall tribe walked past and spoke the name "Shode."

Last but one came Tagart's woman. Through the apertures in the mask, he saw on Segle's face mixed apprehension and hope; and she had passed.

Now Phale stood before him again. As he spoke the name he gave the Mace into Tagart's hand. It had been repaired with twine and leather: a new Mace would be carved soon. As Tagart's fingers closed on the knots and twists of the binding and felt the firmness of the wood beneath, he sensed for the first time the reality of what had happened.

"You are the holder of the Mace. You are our chief. You are Shode."

After the ceremony he called all the chiefs together. Chenk, the leader of the Kingfishers, the man who had been sent as a scout to Valdoe, and the other chiefs who previously had been in favor of a convocation to discuss the Flint Lord, with Tagart's new authority managed to persuade Bison, Wolf and Marten, the doubters, to join their view. Bubeck alone resisted for a while; finally he agreed that envoys should be sent to the other winter camps.

"But not for a convocation," Tagart said. "It is too late for that. We must call for help."

"Shode is right," Chenk said. "I have seen the soldiers. Talk will waste time. We must defend our lands; we must ask for warriors to join us."

Eventually even Bubeck consented. Token tributes of flint spearheads and presents for the chiefs' women were got ready, and Tagart chose three pairs of envoys, each pair led by a man who had himself seen the preparations at Valdoe. Men were picked from the Herons and Beavers, and from the Dragonflies went Fodich, who was now almost completely fit. They were accompanied by men from the Wolf, Marten, and Bison tribes—tribes which did not belong to the water spirit but to the spirits of the other camps: in the north, east, and west.

"Tell them what you have seen," Tagart said. "Tell them we must fight together or be driven out."

The envoys left in the afternoon, in the middle of Klay's trial.

The trial was over by nightfall. Testimony was heard from Tagart and Bubeck, Yulin was interrogated, and the clothes and weapons he had unlawfully used were held up and displayed to the camp.

In turn, Klay accused Tagart and Bubeck of cheating: he said they had colluded to find Edrin. But Bubeck said that Tagart had offered no help in finding Edrin; he had merely used Bubeck and his ideas, and so had exercised nothing more than the "stealth" that was permitted under the rules. Edrin confirmed that Tagart had made no attempt to help Bubeck.

Phale pronounced sentence. Klay's woman and children were to be expelled and made tribeless: when at last they died, of cold or hunger, or were eaten by wolves, their spirits would be unable to join the ancestors. It was a terrible punishment. Yulin sagged and collapsed. The penalty for Klay himself was that which was always paid by those who had betrayed the trust of the tribe.

Final authority rested with Tagart. He was sitting in the middle of the line of elders, stroking his beard, studying Klay, Yulin, and the fire. At his side was Bubeck. They briefly conferred. Tagart glanced at Segle, and looked again into the fire.

"Sentence will be deferred," he said. "At the next moon, the elders will reconsider."

Klay, who was still bound at the wrists, stared impassively forward.

Tagart arose. There was one more matter to be resolved.

He left his place by the fire, took Segle's arm, and pulled her toward their shelter.

2 Six miles northwest of the Trundle, on the highest point of a five-peaked hill, the secondary fort of Harting dominated the sweep of the downs and the fertile plain to the north. Between Harting and its companion fort to —— the west, Butser, lay some of the richest farmland in the Valdoe domain. At the base of Harting Hill was the village of Fernbed, which, in a sheltered valley, cultivated acre after acre of barley, wheat, oats and millet.

Gehan's sleigh passed a snow-whitened clump of gorse and Harting fort came into view, a black palisade on the distant hilltop. Behind it, in contrast with the snowy landscape, the sky was solid and gray. Colder than the snow, an east wind blew behind the sleigh and piled drifts against the gorse bushes and the roadside banks. It beat against the leather hood of the sleigh and left stray drafts of exhilarating air in its wake.

Ika turned to him and laughed. She was excited to be making such an adventurous journey in the snow. The business to be dealt with, Gehan had told her, would be unpleasant; the journey, and the overnight rest at Harting, would not be comfortable. But in the sleigh it was warm enough under the thick furs, and Gehan took pleasure in the proximity of her body on the padded seat. The wind had brought a high color to Ika's cheeks. Her eyes shone. In this severe winter light, her blond hair just showing beneath a fur hat, she seemed more beautiful than ever. "What is the name of this village again?" she said.

"Fernbed."

"A lovely name."

Gehan nodded and, reminded of the destination, went back to his thoughts of the difficulties in hand.

In some ways he saw himself as the expert husbandman of a complicated and volatile herd. The beasts of the herd were the farming villages in his domain; his muzzles and harnesses were the soldiers and traders who enabled him to maintain the balance that produced the heaviest yield of profit. There were over a hundred villages, stretching seventy or eighty miles along the coast and up to twenty miles inland. A few were prosperous, with palisaded compounds, wood and stone houses, granaries; most were squalid collections of huts whose inhabitants lived in constant fear of starvation. Over the centuries these people had come to the island country to escape oppression in the homelands: it was important to ensure that things did not get so bad that any were tempted to return. It was important, too, to allow them a measure of hope, for this was a most effective stimulant to hard work.

The farmers depended for their implements on flint. At one time it had been possible to gather good quality flints from anywhere along the surface of the downs. No longer. Today, they had to be mined. Most of the mine-workings were in the region of Valdoe Hill and on the hill itself; all were the exclusive property of Brennis Gehan Fifth. The flints, cut and ground by his craftsmen, were taken by trading teams to the villages, and there exchanged for food and goods.

The price exacted by the traders was carefully regulated. In years of bad crops, the price went down. To prevent retailing between villages, the price at any one time was fixed throughout the domain; but the larger and more successful villages, those which were able to acquire a surplus, were subject to a harvest impost determined by inspectors from the forts. Attempts to bribe or deceive the harvest inspectors were rigorously punished; failure to pay the imposts likewise brought soldiers. Such punishment was rare—the harvest impost normally took no more than two thirds of the surplus. Despite complaints, the village head-men felt this was not only reasonable, but, considering the power of the Flint Lord, almost generous.

In times of very great hardship, Valdoe sometimes waived all taxes and distributed free tools, even free seed-corn, to distressed villages. Conversely it occasionally made an additional levy for special purposes.

A levy in respect of the campaign against the savages had already been made. From each village an amount equivalent to half the harvest impost had been assessed by the inspectors, and from every fifth family the eldest son had been pressed into nonmilitary service. The preceding summer had given a poor harvest because of drought: fewer villages than usual had managed a surplus, but some, like Fernbed, had done well and had been assessed for the impost. The levy should have left Fernbed with enough food to last the winter, and with seed to sow crops the following spring, but with no more.

However, an informer from a neighboring village had been to Harting to tell the unit leader of a secret storehouse in the forest outside Fernbed. Here also the eldest son of the head man was in hiding, avoiding his duty to Lord Brennis.

A unit of twenty-five men was stationed at Harting. Fifteen had accompanied their unit leader to investigate these charges. They had found the storehouse, cunningly camouflaged in the woods: it had been in use for years, and it held several tons of first quality grain.

Duplicity of this kind so close to the fort had enraged the unit leader. Some of the blame would attach to himself, for it was his duty to make regular searches of the countryside for just such caches. And, in view of the orders from Valdoe, evasion of service by the head man's son could only be seen as a direct challenge to his authority. He had wanted to execute the youth and his father at once; but permission for executions had to be obtained through his superior, the commander of Harting, Bow Hill, and Butser, who in turn had to petition the Flint Lord himself.

On receiving the request, Gehan had taken advice from the General of the Coast before issuing his personal instructions in the matter of the head man and his son.

Yesterday the signalmaster at the Trundle had read a message from Harting, relayed by the intervening fort at Bow Hill. In dark and light smoke the message had slowly taken shape. *The . . . punishment . . . at . . . Fernbed . . . ordained . . . by . . . Lord . . . Brennis . . . has . . . begun . . . We . . . await . . . his . . . illustrious . . . presence.*

Gehan's sleigh, drawn by ten slaves in harness, flanked by guards, passed through the open gate of the palisade and into Fernbed. It was early afternoon: the journey from Valdoe had taken four hours.

A crowd of over two hundred people parted to let him through. The sleigh stopped by the head man's house and Gehan alighted. The commander, a heavy, gray-bearded man named Awach, came forward and saluted. It appeared that, like the crowd, Awach and the soldiers of his units had been waiting in the snow for some time. Their armor of horn and leather, overlaid with winter dress of fur capes and leggings, had been meticulously cleaned.

Gehan looked about him. The village had changed little since his last visit. The palisade enclosed a compound of twenty or thirty dwelling-houses built round a small open space. Two low barns stood behind the village pond, where a few ducks, their feathers ruffled, huddled on the bank beside the ice; another building, a bakery, occupied a slight rise near the north gate. There was no meeting house in this village. Instead the head man's house was unusually grand, with a long extension on one side into a chamber for public meetings.

The village showed unmistakable marks of prosperity. Most of the dwelling-houses were made of stone and timber, with pitched roofs clad in boards or turf and window apertures shuttered for the winter with planks. Some of the houses had integral pigsties; many had two, three, or even four rooms. The head man's house seemed to have at least five rooms besides the public chamber. A paved precinct by its entrance had been brushed free of snow. Part of the precinct was sheltered by a wooden portico supported by two great posts; as he passed between them, Gehan paused to notice the carvings, of twining barley-heads, that climbed the posts from floor to roof. A boss in the lintel depicted the Earth Mother, serenely guarding the doorway.

The entrance gave directly into the public chamber. This was twelve paces long and half as wide, floored with boards of pale beech which had been finished with beeswax. The walls were rendered with clay, smoothed and then whitened with lime. A simple and elegant system of beams held up the roof. At the far end of the room, below an open window, was a stone altar. Beyond it the window looked out on the whiteness of Harting Hill. Gehan could hear the cawing of crows. That, and the screaming from the compound, were the loudest sounds in the village.

In front of the altar, geometrically arranged on the polished wooden floor, a repast of many small delicacies had been surrounded by an oval formation of leather cushions. Gehan motioned that Ika should be seated. He sat down next to her.

During the meal, Awach nervously gave an account of the events leading to his request for execution of the head man and his son. Awach also confirmed that all instructions from Valdoe had been followed. A priest or the head man from each and every village in the domain had been commanded to present himself at Fernbed, to witness the punishment. Today was the fourth day of the Goele festival, when it was considered unclean to travel: a fact sure to impress still more deeply on the villagers the significance of the occasion.

"And what is the name of this old woman, the head man's wife?"

"Lythou, my lady."

"She is the son's mother?"

"Yes, my lady."

Ika accompanied them when they went to watch. Smoke was rising from the open ground faced by the houses. A scaffold had been erected there. Below it, a clay caldron of water was being gently heated. Lythou, the head man's wife, was naked, suspended on a noose under her armpits; the rope ran over the top of the scaffold. Since yesterday she had been repeatedly immersed in warm water and raised into the wind.

She made no sound: she was nearly dead. The screams were those of her husband and son, who had been locked in two pillories close to the fire. They had not been physically harmed.

Gehan felt Ika moving nearer. Her hand discovered his.

By her touch she had joined him in the invisible radiance that set him apart from all others. From villagers and soldiers alike Gehan sensed a surge of hostility and outrage, but it was inextricably mixed with cowardice and he knew he was safely in control. He had judged them accurately.

With a glance from Gehan the commander began his prepared remonstration with the villagers, while his men brought bundles of brushwood which had been stored nearby. Lythou was raised clear of the caldron; the soldiers started to build up the fire, heaping bundles against the pillories. Three of them fanned the flames with boards until, unable to bear the heat, they had to move back.

The head man and his son were silenced. Their charred corpses, still kneeling at the blazing pillories, began to burn alone, without aid from the brushwood, sending fierce flames above the general fire. Awach, without pause, continued to harangue the people of Fernbed and to warn the others of their fate should they seek to deceive the inspectors. He said that the Flint Lord, benefactor of all the villages, had ordered the special levy for a secret purpose

that was vital to everybody. The conscription of eldest sons was
a part of this purpose also. Those who tried to evade it were
traitors to the common good. In view of events here at Fernbed,
a second, voluntary, levy would be accepted by Valdoe until the
new moon after next. The source of any goods so received would
not be investigated; but, after the period of amnesty, deceit would
be shown no mercy.

The water in the caldron was boiling as the speech came to an
end. Gehan gave a curt nod and the rope was released. Ika tightened her grip on his hand; Lythou fell into the water. A moment
later the caldron cracked. It broke into clumsy earthenware pieces
and drenched the fire in a rush of steam and smoke. Ika's hand
relaxed. With wide eyes she watched the aftermath of the punishment, her hand lingering in Gehan's own.

That night Gehan was again unable to sleep. The hours since
Fernbed had passed with a curious, heightened awareness: the
journey up to the fort, the inspection, the meal, the entertain-
ment. Awach had provided dancers, girls from his villages, accompanied by three musicians. One had played a flute; another
had kept time on a little drum. The third had used his voice in
a song without words, droning, repetitive, weaving and looping
through the rhythms of the dance.

Gehan was lying in the chamber usually occupied by the commander. He stared into the darkness, his thoughts colored by the
musician's song. The room had been refurbished for his visit,
and he could smell some indefinable herbal redolence in the luxurious coverings on the bed. It was a scent from his childhood,
an old-fashioned perfume that evoked a pang of memory just
beyond reach.

The door opened from the next room. Before it closed again
he saw Ika's silhouette. She moved across the floor to the bed
and sat down beside him.

"Can you sleep?" she whispered.

"No."

"I keep thinking of that fire."

He tried to make out her face, but the room was too dark.
Hesitantly, timidly, she shifted her position on the edge of the
bed. It was as if she were gauging an unknown resistance, waiting
for a sounding before daring to proceed.

The silence was total. Ika's fragrance was beginning to reach him, from her skin and hair, from the folds of her robe, from her breathing. It mingled with and overwhelmed the herbal scent and entwined the musicians' song.

"It was a nightmare down there," she said.

"Are you afraid to go to sleep?"

"Yes."

Her next action seemed inevitable, like the succession of time, like the pervasive rhythm of flute and voice. She slowly bent over him.

He had abstained from drink during the evening; she had tried several essences. A rich, decayed sweetness remained on her breath. He tasted it as she hovered over him. They were separated only by the last remnant of her uncertainty, a narrow stream of darkness that was part of the larger night: secret, private, utterly quiet.

Trembling slightly, she touched his lips. The pressure of her flesh, miraculously subtle, was such that he could not tell precisely when the kiss had begun: he knew only that it was happening. As she became more confident her mouth opened a little; yet still she hesitated before crossing the last shred of darkness. Gehan hesitated too. Above all else he wanted to succumb, to acknowledge that he and Ika were of the same. She was perfect, golden, immaculate. She had, in the village today, glimpsed the frontier of the will, the vision of Gehan First, the frontier beyond which stretched the limitless sea of absolute freedom. She alone was worthy to join him on that awesome beach where he had dwelt in solitude for so many years.

He felt her hair fall across his face. In the villages, anywhere else, it would not matter that they were brother and sister. But he was the son of Gehan Fourth: he was the master of Brennis, the Flint Lord. And this was weakness.

He pushed her away. "Go back to your room."

"What is it?"

"This is wrong."

"No, this is right." She leaned forward again and whispered. "We can do anything we want to. You proved that today."

"Go."

"Let me rest beside you, if nothing else."

"You must go."

"You want me to stay."

"I want you to go."

When she had returned to her room, Gehan tried to compose himself for sleep. Again he breathed the herbal scent. And suddenly he saw an image of sun-colored flowers and smelled pungent green leaves, and he recalled that in his boyhood the house slaves had hidden sprigs of tansy among the most valuable heaps of pelts and fleeces. It was supposed to deter insects. He strove to recall more clearly the clusters of flowers like little buttons, the spreading fernlike leaves; and he saw again a bright window-ledge, a lonely playroom, and a barren view of hillside and sea. Ika had been a mere baby. At the age of six she had been sent to the homelands: Gehan's days had been shaped to some other purpose, filled with discipline, schooling, instruction; somehow, standing on tiptoe and peeping out, the empty vista beyond the playroom window had contained no explanation of it at all.

In the early hours, resigning himself to another night without sleep, he went to the shutters and opened them. The night was hard and freezing. Over a mile away to the southwest, and two hundred and fifty feet below his window, he saw a solitary twinkle of light. It disappeared and returned, disappeared and returned, sometimes disappearing for such a long period that he thought it had gone out. At this range the buildings of Fernbed could not be distinguished, but among them somewhere a fire was still burning, and he knew it was not the pyre his men had made, but a memorial flame at the altar. The priest would have lit it to mark the mourning of the village and the passage of three more souls to the gates of the Far Land.

Gehan barred the shutters and rested his head against them. He stood like that for a moment, turned, and went back to his bed.

3 The snow deepened; for fifteen days the sun was not seen. Everyone in the camp who was not hunting was put to work, mending, sewing, making boots and mittens and clothing, cutting pelts and curing skins to make water carriers, packing food, binding spears and axes and hammers and knives, shaving arrows, carving bows and spear slings. All spare leather and fur had been commandeered: those who stayed behind would be cold as well as hungry.

From nine tribes Tagart had selected a hundred men of fighting age and forty women who wanted to join the march to Valdoe. Only the very old and the very young, or those who could not be spared, had been forbidden to go.

Each day he calculated again how many people he might expect from the other camps, and when they would arrive. Sometimes he felt there would be none, that the envoys would fail; at other times he thought they would come, but too late. He counted the days needed for the envoys to reach the camps, to persuade the chiefs, for the preparations to be made, for the journey to the Shode Valley, added time to allow for the difficulty of traveling in the snow, subtracted it for the loyalty of this or that tribe which he knew to be friendly and helpful, added it again for those chiefs who were said to be uncooperative or who were likely to be indifferent to the troubles of the tribes in the south; and each day arrived at a different answer.

His strategy would depend on the amount of support he received. As his estimates varied so did he evolve and discard a dozen battle plans, retrieve some, examine them afresh, and then in a fit of doubt or depression reject them all. At such moments he wondered whether perhaps Bubeck was right. Tagart would be committing all his people to fighting something that might not be killed by spears alone. He had been to Valdoe; he had seen what sort of men were there; he had seen the villages along the coast. Thousands of farmers relied on the Flint Lord: if they came to his defense there would be no hope.

But, on the fifteenth day after the envoys had left, a hundred and nineteen people arrived from the Cloud camp in the east. The next day Fodich arrived. He had brought nearly a hundred and fifty from the Lightning camp in the north: all that remained was the arrival of those from the Mountain camp in the west.

Tagart sent for Klay. Since his trial he had been given lowly duties and kept within the boundary of the camp. As Tagart revealed to him what his part in the march was to be, Klay saw why he had been reprieved. He listened with growing dismay to Tagart's detailed instructions. This was worse than the original sentence. He was given food and appropriate clothing and allowed to make his farewells to Yulin and his children. If he carried out his mission with honor they would be pardoned. They would no longer be considered tribeless, and his own sentence would be rescinded in full.

But it was with a heavy heart that Klay crossed the bridging logs and left the camp behind.

The stone bowl, supported by three squat legs, was half filled with charcoal which sent smokeless heat up into the rafters. Lamps burned on poles set round the bowl. They projected distorted shadows of the Divine as she finished her prayer.

Gehan watched from the darkness. Thille, the Divine, had read the sky that day and from the flight of crows had discovered that portents for the campaign had changed. All six hundred soldiers had been landed; the army was ready to leave. But the omens were bad. For confirmation, the Divine had taken a dry briar branch and on it, with a magpie quill, had inscribed seven runes.

"Fire, fire, speak to Thille! Fire, fire, do thy will!"

She threw the briar branch into the bowl. It lay on the charcoal, stubbornly refusing to ignite. And then at one end spitting flame crackled and scorched some of the runes. "Aih has been burned," said the Divine. "The weather will hold." The flame cleft into prongs and spread along the branch, wavering and fluttering, while the Divine studied its progress, circling the bowl. Her feet shuffled on the stone floor. Next to Gehan came the asthmatic breathing of Bohod Zein.

Bohod Zein leaned toward him. "Your Divine would be prized in the homelands," he said. "Is she a native?"

"The daughter of a slave, born here in my grandfather's time."

"She has a gift."

"She has second sight."

"Is she ever wrong?"

Gehan shook his head.

The briar branch had been consumed, reduced to a worm of gray ash. Taking a linden spoon, the Divine scraped it up and deposited it in a small leather pouch. Her attendant came forward and covered the bowl with a heavy stone lid; the Divine arranged on the lid a precarious tripod of three bone wands, their feet in some secret pattern that only she could memorize.

The attendant lit the rest of the lamps in the divination chamber.

"My lord," said the Divine. Her robes were green; she wore yellow slippers. She was old and bent, but her eyes were direct. "My lord, the fire has spoken. The flame was slow: there will be delay, and this is propitious. It will avoid disaster. Aih was burned first: the weather will aid you. Tsoaul glowed strangely and was enwrapped by blue flame: your enemy will be strong, but you will surround him. Gauhm burned yellow and will take no part. The briar crackled, and so the fighting will be very fierce. For every crackle a man will be slain. This was foretold by the crows."

"But what will be the outcome?"

"In our question to the fire we spoke only of the savages. The answer is confused, as though you had another enemy, a more powerful one. There will be much killing and suffering. Order will be overthrown. By the shape of the ash and the burning of the four outer runes, the portent is very bad. The fire begs you to think again. No purpose will be served."

"But you say the savages will not defeat me?"

"There is neither defeat nor victory here, my lord."

"There will be no defeat?"

"Not at the savages' hands, my lord."

Bohod Zein turned to him. "If there is no defeat there must be victory."

"I agree," Gehan said, "since we are to take the offensive. There must be some slight confusion in the ash. Is this possible, Thille?"

"Perhaps, my lord."

"You speak of another enemy. Who could this be?"

"I cannot say, my lord. It is . . . forgive me, my lord."

"It is what?"

"It is as if the enemy were yourself."

Bohod Zein whispered in his ear. "Preposterous!"

"What does the fire tell us about the delay?" Gehan said. "Will it be long?"

"It urges you to wait till the moon wanes."

"The full moon is seven days hence," Bohod Zein said. "We have been delayed too long already."

"There will be certain disaster if you start in a waxing moon, my lord."

"Of what sort?"

"On the march. There will be disaster on the march."

"Does the fire say any more?"

"It speaks of the sea, my lord. I do not understand it."

"The sea? The question has nothing to do with the sea."

Bohod Zein revolved the white marble ring on his forefinger. "The prophecy seems somewhat nebulous and inconclusive," he said to Gehan. "You say she is never wrong. Could it be, Thille, that we posed our question wrongly?"

"I cannot say. I speak only of what the fire tells me, and the fire gives a bad omen. I must repeat, my lord, that order will be overthrown."

"A matter of opinion," said Bohod Zein with an incipient smile, which died the moment he saw Gehan's face.

"Leave us, Thille," Gehan said.

She bowed and, taking the leather pouch of ash, was followed by her attendant from the room.

Gehan rubbed his forehead. "Another seven days! I must speak to Larr."

"The delay is probably wise, and the General will concur," said Bohod Zein, thinking of the extra rations the soldiers would consume, and wondering how much might be charged for them. "The Divine was quite specific on that point. But as for the rest of it . . ."

Gehan stood up; Bohod Zein did likewise. "There is nothing ambiguous in Thille's words," Gehan said. "As a child she taught me how to view a prophecy. If you do not understand it at first, you must let it soak into your thoughts. Intuition will give you its meaning."

Bohod Zein hitched his robe over his shoulder. "Our divines in the homeland are much less reticent."

"And much less accurate."

The albino stepped aside and allowed Gehan to be first through the door. It was after dusk; stone cressets, set in the walls or suspended from roof-beams, gave their dismal glow to the next rooms. These were hawk mews which, together with the divining chamber, an office for the astronomer priest, and a room of maps and charts, made a single block set inside the main palisade on its northern side. There was only one exit: to reach it they had to pass through the mews.

One of the falconers was present, attending to a sea eagle, a huge bird which sat hunched on a padded perch, its head covered with a plain hood. As Gehan and Bohod Zein entered, the falconer saluted.

Gehan stopped to exchange a few words with him. "Is that Larr's eagle?"

"Yes, my lord."

"Is it ill?"

"He is hunger traced, Lord Brennis." He gently indicated the folded wing.

"Let me see," Gehan said, but even as he reached out the eagle unfurled vast wings and from the hood came an anguished cry. Its wings flapped once, twice, thrice, and the pressure of wind lifted it from the perch. Leather straps arrested its ascent; it fell forward and dangled by its legs, shrieking and twisting its head. The great wings hung awkwardly, brushing the flagstones, and three dark pinions broke away and fluttered to the floor.

Gehan and Bohod Zein departed at once, to leave the man and his charge in peace.

"It means nothing," said Bohod Zein, unnerved by the incident and by Gehan's glowering silence. They were crossing the outer enclosure toward the inner palisade and Gehan's residence. "A sick bird, my lord. An eagle in a rage."

"A sea eagle," Gehan said strangely.

On all sides they were being hailed and saluted. The enclosure was crowded with leather tents, each occupied by five men waiting their turn to go inside the barracks to be fed. Every foot of space in the Trundle was full: the two barracks, the armory; soldiers had been billeted in the dwellings of the craftsmen and in the overseers' quarters; vacant animal sheds had been taken over; even a spare cell in the prison had been appropriated. Some of the mine slaves, whose cages were always kept outside the Trundle, had been taken from the chalk face and put to work in teams, helping the soldiers to carry skins of water up the hill from the river, for the reservoirs inside the fort were inadequate to the needs of a thousand men. Other slaves stoked cooking fires, stirred caldrons, carried trays of steaming coarse bread; and others yet dragged sleds up from the sheds at Apuldram, where the rest of the stores and supplies had been unloaded.

The Trundle had been designed as two separate forts, one inside the other. The outer palisade, twenty feet high, with its guard towers and ditch, carried a parapet from which projectiles could be rained upon rebellious slaves or besieging brigands. The gallery below this parapet was used to store a variety of ingenious equipment, some of it dating from the first days of the Trundle and conceived by Gehan First himself. The two gates of the fort, at northeast and southwest, swung on armored hinges and were barred with enormous beams of oak, to which could be added sloping buttresses fitting into oak-lined pits. Constant vigil was kept from each of the sixteen guard towers: Valdoe Hill had been cleared of trees, so there would always be ample warning, in daylight at least, of approaching danger—even in the extreme and unlikely circumstances that neither of the neighboring forts at Eartham and Bow Hill was able to send signals or render support.

The inner fort was the Flint Lord's residence, enclosed by another palisade of greater strength than the first. It had one gate, and a single wooden building on two stories—three, counting a platform for the signal station. Part of the building formed the barrack for his personal guard, trusted men who received double pay and the best rations. The rest was divided into chambers for sleeping and eating and storage, on the upper floor; and much of the lower floor was taken up by one large dayroom. There were side chambers for stores of emergency rations, a small armory, and a cistern of drinking water which was renewed by rain pipes from the roof.

In theory the gate of the inner enclosure was to be kept open whenever the Flint Lord was not present, and locked when he was inside; in practice it was locked only at night.

None of the Trundlemen, the freemen who managed the various workings of Valdoe—the mines, the slaves, the harbor, the fort itself—slept in the inner enclosure. Their quarters were situated just outside its gate. Apart from his retinue, bodyguards, and members of his family, only the General of Valdoe was allowed free access to the Flint Lord's residence. Even guests were expected to sleep in the main enclosure, although in the case of important visitors such as Bohod Zein an exception was occasionally made.

He had been given the principal guest chamber, a room four yards by three, furnished with sumptuous hangings of umber and scarlet. Above the bed was a mural on whose cracked surface a family of seals, hauled out on a sandbar far from land, basked in peaceful sunshine that had been faded by age.

After a long evening in the company of Lord Brennis, Bohod Zein retired for the night. He was washed and changed by the two women who had been appointed as body slaves for the duration of his stay. The women finished tying his robe and left the dressing room; Bohod Zein fastened the catch behind them and passed into the sleeping chamber.

Altheme was already in the bed. She had entered by another door; earlier in the evening Bohod Zein had intimated to Gehan that her presence would again be welcome.

"I hoped you would come," Bohod Zein said. He put out all the lamps except one at the bedside and pulled back the covers.

She was lying supine, staring fixedly at a point on the ceiling. To Bohod Zein it seemed that her pale skin and abundant dark hair had been invested with a new and healthier beauty, as if the past nights, when she had manifested signs of revulsion and repugnance, had after all secretly pleased and agreed with her. If it was possible, she had become even more desirable: not only was she the wife of the most powerful man in the island country, but now she was beginning to respond to his expert nocturnal tutoring. Suppress it as she might through pride—and he found her feigned contempt a source of additional stimulation—the evidence was in her face. Soon she would yield openly, willingly; what passions might then be released? At bottom, like all her kind, she was a harlot. When at last the floodgates opened, he knew his teachings would be richly repaid.

With a pleasant feeling of flattery and anticipation, he snuffed the remaining flame and climbed in beside her.

4 Ika had been out on Valdoe Hill with a party of servants and villagers, among them the head man, who owned the dogs with which they had been coursing hares. At midafternoon, being near the village, the head man had invited her to his Meeting House for refreshments.

Rald, the food taster, was at Ika's side as she sat sipping a hot barley tisane. It was spiced with thyme and cicely, and their flavors rose in the steam and mixed with the smell of hemp smoke: Ika and Rald had been sharing a pipe.

The village council had gathered in Ika's honor. The Meeting House, open at one end, was warmed by a log fire. The floor gleamed with polish; the walls were paneled with rush matting to keep out the draft. Ika, inwardly amused by the deference the villagers were showing her, had shocked them all with her open and brazen intimacy with a menial, a food taster, a person of lowlier rank than anyone else in the coursing party. Insulted and outraged, the council men had done their best to hide their feelings, for she was the sister of Brennis Gehan Fifth. Nonetheless, the conversation in the Meeting House was stilted and contrived, and at the sound of a commotion in the village compound the head man seemed grateful for a chance to leave the room and investigate. Presently he returned.

"What was it?"

"Nothing of importance, my lady."

"Tell me what it was."

"Merely a runaway, my lady. Some of my people caught him on the outskirts of our village. He claims to be a wandering peddler, but we know him for a slave and, his lordship your brother permitting, we will present him to the fort."

"At a price."

"We must cover our costs, my lady." He snapped his fingers at a girl who was waiting meekly with a wooden jug. "Will you take some more tisane?"

"Let's see this runaway. Bring him in."

"He is uncouth and smells foul, my lady."

"Bring him in."

With a resigned glance at the other village elders, the head man went to obey.

The main intake of labor at Valdoe was supplied by slaving sorties to the mainland, when ships would bring back twenty or thirty or more captives to work in the mines, in the Flint Lord's fields, in road gangs, or in the forts. Rarely did a month pass, though, without at least one native addition to the slave quarters. Most often this would be a farmer luckless enough to be out alone and caught by a trading team, who would be paid a bonus for their enterprise. Anyone alone and defenseless was deemed fair prey. Occasionally savages would be taken; occasionally a wandering herdsman or peddler.

Ika put her hand on Rald's leg as the slave, hobbled with rope and with a line binding his wrists, was led into the Meeting House. His clothing was rude, grimed with mud and travel. He had apparently been subdued with plentiful blows about the head: a rivulet of blood had dried on his temple, and his cheekbone was bruised and swollen. But he was unbowed and he returned Ika's appraisal with defiance. Tall and dark, he was about twenty-five. Ika found him striking. Something in his primitive, uncompromising bearing excited her and she leaned closer to Rald, squeezing his thigh.

"Do you think he's interesting?"

Rald gave a cryptic smile.

The head man jerked the slave's chin aside. "Show respect!"

For reply the slave spat in his face. The head man struck him; unable to retain his balance, he toppled to the floor.

"How quaint!" Ika whispered. She moved her hand higher, watching as the slave was pulled to his feet. "Do you find him beautiful, Rald?"

"We will take him away now, my lady," the head man said.

"No. Not yet. I think Rald would like to know him better."

Impulsively she stood up and started toward the slave. She sensed the disapproval of the room: the air had become charged. For the first time today her boredom was forgotten.

"Be careful, my lady."

"He won't hurt me." She reached out and ran her fingertips across his lips. "See? He didn't bite."

The head man massaged his hands nervously. "It is nearly time to go back to the hounds, my lady, if we are to have any more sport today."

"We have sport enough here." She beckoned to Rald.

The slave was slightly taller than the food taster, and in every way quite different. Ika was thrilled by the contrast between the two men, in manner as well as appearance: one civilized and refined, with all the merits that culture could bestow, the other a rough bumpkin, a clod, an animal from the wildwood. And yet . . . there was some fire, some spark in this clod that Rald had lost. Rald had never looked at her like that. She stood back while Rald studied his face. Rald too reached out and touched his mouth, palpated his bruised cheek, and then, entering into the full spirit of his mistress's game, and with a conspiratorial smile for Ika alone, he began to walk round the prisoner, examining him from all angles.

Rald completed the circle and looked her way. Some subtle signal passed between them: Ika grew more animated still.

"My servant and I wish to speak to this fellow in private," she said to the head man. A flush was rising in her cheeks; her eyes seemed to have grown wider.

"The council will withdraw, my lady," the head man said.

"Are there blinds to close the doorway?"

"There are."

"Then bring them."

"Of course, my lady," said the head man in bewilderment.

"And we shall want a knife. And some fresh rope."

"What does my lady plan?" He indicated the altar. "I . . . I must remind you . . . this is a sacred place . . . my village . . . the elders cannot . . . they cannot permit . . ."

"You'll have your price for him. Do as I say! He won't be killed."

"That is not the point . . . we cannot permit . . . we cannot permit . . . sacrilege, forgive me, my lady . . ."

One of the older men stepped forward. "We give allegiance to the Flint Lord, my lady. This is Valdoe Village: what we have belongs to him. It is so with this runaway. The slave is Valdoe's now and of course you are free to dispose of him as you would of any slave. We make no claim on him at all." He paused. "But our head man is absentminded and has forgotten that a council meeting is due to be held here in a short while. Might my lady care to conduct her conversation in some other house? Perhaps in the head man's house?"—he glanced for confirmation at the head man, who nodded reluctantly—"His dwelling is nearby, warm and comfortable, screened and shuttered for privacy. Here I am sure my lady would feel more at ease."

Ika assented. At her direction, the slave was bathed. He shouted and struggled as six of the villagers tied him face-downward on a bed, spreadeagled by taut ropes from his wrists and ankles to the pillars of the room.

The head man tried to conceal his dismay. He was the last of the villagers in the house.

"One more thing," Ika said. "Post some men by the door to see that no one enters. Give them weapons. If he becomes troublesome I want help at hand."

The head man nodded. Rald blew out one of the lamps.

"Now go."

The head man backed away. The doorway was low and led into a tunnel porch: he crawled into it backward. As he lost sight of the room he heard Ika say something hoarse and unintelligible, and he saw Rald beginning to disrobe.

Nearly four hundred slaves spent their lives, by day or by night, in Brennis Gehan's mines. About thirty were stationed at the small workings at Findon, a similar number at Blackpatch nearby, and forty at Raven Hill. At Bow Hill, three miles west of the Trundle, eighty miners occupied the slaves' quarters below the fort. The rest, some two hundred men, were prisoners at Valdoe.

The mines here were the most productive and yielded the best flints. They lay on the southern slopes of the hill, just under a mile from the fort itself. The vegetation had long since been burned off, and only coarse turf and a few thornbushes remained. The area was strewn with spoil heaps of stark white chalk rubble, piles of timber, and was crisscrossed by muddy paths. Plank structures, roofed with skins, protected the mineshafts from the rain, and a small shed gave shelter on site for the mines Trundleman, a man named Blene. He was forty, with pale gray eyes and close-cropped hair. Born in the homelands and of a wealthy family, Blene held the most prestigious nonmilitary post in the island country: he was responsible for all flint production in the Valdoe domain. From the aspect of a hill, from the way the land was shaped, he could guess where the flint seams were likely to run. At his word the overseers would direct the probing gangs to their work. Ropes and flags would be used to mark out the test pits, and samples of stone and soil would be taken back to the Trundle for examination. If all was auspicious, a shaft would be started, driven up to seventy feet underground, and from the shaft a radiating system of galleries would be dug. It was here that Blene's real genius displayed itself. He was an artist in the manipulation of loads and pressures and thrusts. As if by instinct he knew when a tunnel had gone far enough, and at the moment of imminent collapse work in the gallery would cease. By inspired use of timbers he kept shafts open long after they should have fallen in; and by means of his own inventions—rope transport and movable ladders—he ensured a smooth flow of work inside the mines. Sometimes there were failures: sometimes a few slaves or even an overseer would be lost in a cave-in, but this loss was small compared with the gains from Blene's efficiency. It was Blene who had been instrumental in helping Gehan to summon his present military strength: Bohod Zein had to be paid in flint.

Blene took an acute interest in the quality of workers provided for him by the slaves Trundleman. Most were "Valdonen"—men who had been born in slavery or who had spent all their lives at Valdoe. From these the overseers were recruited, as were most of the skilled men—the carpenters, joiners, probers, and rope-men. The unskilled force, with the exception of a few who performed surface duties, worked at the chalk face, in pairs, eleven hours at a stretch. After each shift they were marched uphill to their quarters, a compound enclosed by tall incurved palings.

Shifts were changed at midmorning and in the evening. The outgoing shift would be woken and fed an hour beforehand, and locked in a holding cage just outside the compound. A flag or flame signal would then be made to the mines and the other shift brought above ground. Only when the incoming men were safely locked in the compound would the holding cage be opened and the new shift released.

The compound covered a third of an acre by the southwest gatehouse. Inside the palings were leather tents and shelters for the overseers and guards, canopied kitchens and an eating area with benches and long tables, and an inner cage for sleeping. This had a wicket gate and a wooden floor, sloping slightly downward to a shallow gutter, and a roof made of poles and skins. Above waist height the walls were open to the weather: the bars, vertical and horizontal beams of ash, allowed nowhere a gap of more than a hand's width. While the incoming shift ate a meal of beans, lentils, meat and bread, and while they used the troughs and latrines, women with brooms and buckets sluiced the cage; and then the miners were counted through the wicket and locked up.

They were thinly dressed: in winter they shivered. The floor was always damp, often icy, and there was little protection from the wind. Sometimes during the long nights one of the older slaves got so cold he did not wake up. For this reason it was considered lucky to be a night shift man: underground, below a certain depth, the temperature varied little.

"It is not my fault," Klay said to the man who was to be his partner, a thin, grumbling foreigner called Wouter. Wouter's partner had broken his leg. As a result Wouter had been moved from the night shift and teamed with Klay, who, having been examined by the slaves Trundleman, had been approved for duties underground and put in the sleeping cage some time before midnight.

"Filth. They're filth," Wouter said. He was gray, no longer young, stoop-shouldered, with tiny veins in his nose and in his watery brown eyes. His beard was lank; his joints and knuckles were red and swollen with rough work and the cold. "Anyway, go to sleep," he said wearily. In the faint lamplight, Klay watched him lean back and find a space on the floor. His eyes closed at once and his mouth sagged open. In a few moments his breathing became a snore.

The moon had risen. Above and beyond the high bars of the cage, beyond the compound, Klay could see it drifting mysteriously behind scant, luminous cloud.

With misery in his eyes he watched its passage in the sky. He could not forget what had been done to him, there in the village at the bottom of the hill. Afterward the villagers had dressed him and taken him up to the Trundle and he had not seen the green-eyed youth again, nor had he seen the blond woman who at first had merely watched, urging the youth on, and then, slipping off her clothing, had participated. At the depth of his shame Klay had shouted out in humiliation and pain. With vile clarity he now recalled each detail, the first touch and the weight of the youth on his back . . . he clapped his hands to his face and sharply breathed in: he wanted to be sick, to vomit, to expunge from his thoughts all evidence of what had taken place in that loathsome room; but he knew that even if he could scrub his mind clean, he could never rid his body of its sense of dirt and violation. Tagart had not warned him of their customs; he had told him nothing of this. One more grief to add to Tagart's score! And that score would be settled—on the way south, trudging alone through the woods, Klay had vowed it. Tagart had cheated in the contest; Tagart had treated him unjustly and cruelly. His honor had been impugned, his family and ancestors belittled before the whole camp. The threat of banishment still hung over Yulin and his children, and he, Klay, a chief's son, true heir to the name of Shode, had been given an impossible mission as an alternative to public execution. Plainly Tagart had hoped he would fail. Well, Tagart would be disappointed! He would not fail! He would redeem his honor and restore the name of his family, demand a retrial, demand another contest, and this time the laws would be properly observed by all! And at last, Klay would depose the strutting impostor who had usurped his birthright, taken over his blood-tribe, shamed the memory of his father; and he would choose with dignity the woman he wanted for his wife. Yulin and her children would be well cared for and respected as members of his family, and he and Segle would govern the Waterfall tribe and all the tribes of the winter camp. This was the future: he would not fail it.

He looked up again. Most of the miners were sleeping. Grunts, sighs and moans broke from the huddle of men. Behind him, from the corner, came the sound of someone defecating. Klay tried to ignore it. For a while he studied Wouter. In ten hours or so they would be going underground, he had said, and Klay wondered when the best time would be to break his silence. He surveyed the sleeping men. They were ignorant of his identity; they had no idea why he had come; they were completely unaware that in a matter of days the secret he had brought would change their lives forever.

He sat thinking for a long time, but he supposed later that he must have fallen asleep during the early hours, because he felt Wouter shaking him and opened his eyes to find that it was day.

"Come on," Wouter said. "Come on if you want to fill your gizzard."

The miners were being counted out of the cage and were passing into the refectory, where they seated themselves at the tables. Serving women were already ladling stew.

"Over there, to the left," Wouter hissed, pushing him from behind. "We want to get on that table. She gives you more."

They were beaten to the coveted places by the other men.

"No matter," Wouter said. "We'll be quicker after the shift."

Klay squeezed in beside a middle-aged foreigner with greasy black hair. Across the table every face was turned toward the caldrons: eyes watched and gauged the movements of the ladlers, counted heads to see where a bowl would end up. Some of the men drew shells or wooden spoons from their clothing.

Klay ate with his fingers. The stew tasted unpleasant: it was thick with strange vegetables; globules of pallid fat floated just below the surface. The meat, which Klay could not identify, was stringy and almost inedible. When he had chewed the last piece he followed Wouter's lead and drank the rest of his stew straight from the bowl.

Women circulated with osier baskets, handing out wads of loam-colored stuff. Klay had never seen its like before. He could only compare it to fungus or rotten wood. He touched it with his tongue, licked it, bit some off.

"The bread's always stale," the foreigner whispered. Talking was forbidden: he glanced warily at the nearest overseer, who stood swinging his cudgel on its strap. "Give it here if you don't want it."

"Silence!"

This man, who was called Gabot, was assigned to the same part of the mine as Klay and Wouter. After the meal, they and the rest of the shift, having been given a few minutes at the latrines, were counted out and, in their pairs, ordered into the holding cage. This was another enclosure of wooden palings, with a tall gate locked by a bar. Gabot and his partner were almost the last pair through. Wouter pointed Gabot out.

"Don't trust him," he said. "He's an informer. He sleeps in the cage and works at the face and pretends to be one of us, but he's been seen coming out of an overseer's tent."

"Do they give him extra food?"

"No one knows."

"He seemed hungry just now."

Wouter shrugged. "Perhaps they've got his woman in the Trundle. They do that sometimes. A woman, or a child."

The holding cage was secured; the chief overseer of the day shift called to a soldier on the battlements, who waved a flag. Farther down the hill the signal was relayed by another soldier. At the mine-workings a gong was sounded above each shaft and the men came to the surface. They were counted and checked, and each was given a load of stone to carry to the Trundle.

Half an hour later they were locked into the compound. To Klay, watching through the bars of the holding cage, the night shift looked more like walking cadavers than men: they were slow, haggard, whitened by smears and dust of chalk. Some were bleeding from cuts and grazes.

The sight of them gave form to Klay's dread of the coming day. The holding cage was crammed with men. Suddenly he could no longer bear to be trapped; but already the chief overseer had removed the bar at the gate and the day shift were leaving the cage.

"What's it like?" Klay said to Wouter. "What's it like in the mines?"

"You'll find out soon enough."

5 At the start of his second day underground, Klay and fifteen others, who yesterday had been working as a team, were kept waiting in the cold while the Trundleman, Blene, discussed something with the chief overseer.

The men stood in a line on the white ground, shivering and stamping their feet. Klay embraced himself and buried his chin in his shoulder. The wind was blowing at his back, flinging sleet across the face of the hill from the northeast. Far away to the south the hill ended in a belt of aspens heaped with drifted snow, beyond which, spreading three miles to the sea, were white, yellow and dun marshes, reed beds, tidal flats. The sea was the color of flint itself; sluggish waves pushed at the snow on the beach.

Gabot, the foreigner, was standing next to Wouter. The previous day he had made a point of eating his midshift meal in the same place as Klay. It was as if he had been told to make a report on the new man. During the night, Klay had awoken to the sound of faint whispering. Through his lashes he had watched Gabot conversing with an overseer through the bars of the cage.

At last Blene concluded his talk with the chief overseer and the slaves were told to collect their tools. Yesterday they had been set to deepening the shaft. Klay, Wouter, Gabot, and the rest of the unskilled men had taken turns to dig out the chalk and haul it to the surface, while three pairs of carpenters and joiners had cut and fixed new ladders and shuttering to support the walls. Today they would be doing the same.

Gabot went first, carrying an oil lamp. His partner was to have gone next, but Klay jostled him aside and grabbed his load, a bundle of antler picks. The partner said nothing and took a second bundle. It made little difference who went down first or last, as all the unskilled jobs were rotated throughout the day. The worst job was perhaps digging at the very bottom of the pit, where a persistent foot or so of water seemed to collect and form a creamy slurry with the chalk despite all their efforts at baling.

Klay ducked through the shaft-head shelter to see Gabot starting down the first ladder. Gabot's lamp dimly illuminated the shuttering, lit his face and chest; but below was unfathomable darkness overlaid by the darkness of his own shadow. The bottom of the shaft was at least forty feet down, and presumably the night shift would have taken it even deeper.

Holding the lamp in his left hand, Gabot began to descend. Klay climbed onto the ladder, the bundle slung across his shoulder.

"Not so quick," Gabot said. "You nearly trod on my hand."

Klay's face was level with the top of the ladder; he checked that Gabot's partner had not yet entered the shelter.

"I can't go so quick, fool!"

Klay rapidly moved down two rungs more and felt his foot crushing Gabot's fingers. He pushed with all his strength downward. Gabot cried out and dropped his lamp. It fell, still burning for a moment before going out. There was an appreciable interval before it splashed into the slurry below.

Gabot clawed at Klay's ankles with his free hand. Keeping his right foot firmly in place, Klay descended another rung and lashed downward with his left heel. It struck Gabot in the mouth. At that instant he released Gabot's fingers.

Gabot fell. He scrabbled for the rungs as he lost balance and tumbled backward, striking his head on the shuttering. Limply and clumsily he dropped into the shaft. There was a splintering noise near the bottom and Klay heard him hit the slurry.

"What's happening down there?"

Klay looked up to see Gabot's partner, a hand on either rail of the ladder, outlined in the twilight of the shelter. He was moving his head from side to side, trying to see.

"Gabot's fallen!" Klay answered.

Weak groans were coming from below: he was still alive. Without waiting for the overseer's interference, Klay hurriedly continued down the ladder. Gabot's partner was shouting something. Klay ignored him.

Near the bottom of the shaft, Klay reached the place where Gabot had smashed the ladder in his fall. His foot failed to find a rung, and in the blackness he crouched down and fingered the jagged edges of the broken rails.

"You down there! What's going on?"

The overseer, leaning over the ladder, looked very small. "He's hurt!" Klay called up the shaft. "I must help him!"

Gabot's groans had become quieter. It was hard to tell how far away he was. Klay looked up again to see someone climbing onto the ladder. There was no time to lose: Klay jumped.

He was surprised to find that the bottom of the shaft was only two or three feet below. He landed on Gabot's legs and stumbled against the chalk wall.

Gabot gasped with pain and feebly snatched at Klay's clothing. Klay kicked his arm aside and got one leg across his chest; his hands found Gabot's forehead and forced it down. The injured man resisted for a few seconds. With a supreme effort he arched his back, gurgling as his face came clear of the slurry. Klay pushed harder. He felt the slime closing over his wrists, rising toward his elbows. Gabot relaxed.

Presently the overseer, bringing a lamp, reached the bottom of the ladder. "He made a strange noise," Klay told him. "He made a strange noise and then he just let go. I think he had a fit. When I got to him he was already dead."

The overseer gave Klay his lamp to hold and pulled Gabot's head and shoulders toward the light. Gabot looked like an effigy of himself in wet, white stone, but his tongue was partly pink and his teeth were brown and black. The overseer scrutinized Klay.

"It's just an accident, boy. Don't worry about it." He glanced up the shaft. "Wouter! Wouter!"

"Yes, master!"

"Send down a rope!"

Klay fastened it to the dead man's ankles. Using the fixed pulley at the top of the shaft, the other slaves drew Gabot to the surface and laid him in the snow outside the shaft-head shelter.

They gathered round the body.

"His little girl is in the Trundle," one of the carpenters said. "I'll pass the message on somehow."

"All right," the overseer said. "We've wasted enough time here. Let's get to work."

Valdoe Village, where Klay had been captured, was sprawling and prosperous, with many wood and stone houses, two granaries, several barns, and a large variety of sheds and workshops. The Meeting House was the finest in the Flint Lord's domain. The aesthetic pitch of its roof, the sweep of its eaves, proclaimed from a distance the extravagance of materials and virtuosity of craftsmanship that had been expended on its construction. The proximity of the Trundle did away with the need for a palisade round the village, and it was as if all the cost and labor saved thereby had been lavished on the Meeting House: its architect had been the chief builder in the service of Gehan Third, a man who, like many of the Trundle officers and craftsmen, had kept a household in the village for his family, away from the military atmosphere of the fort.

This custom was still maintained, and of the seventy or so houses in the village fewer than fifty were inhabited by those who held no direct post under Lord Brennis. These were freemen following every conceivable trade, all of whom paid a tenth of their earnings to the fort, with an additional annual tax reckoned proportionately to the harvest impost. The village fields belonged to Valdoe and were worked by slaves who lived in a small settlement on the outskirts.

The village lay in the valley between Valdoe and Levin Down, a hill whose summit was two miles from the Trundle and a hundred feet short of it in height. The southern slopes were partly under cultivation, but the rest of the hill, especially on its north side, was covered in thick woodland or scrub. Where the soil was poor there were patches of gorse; farther up were stretches of dogwood and buckthorn. These gave way near the summit to mixed woodland and coppice of ash, oak, beech, rowan, whitebeam, with occasional stands of pure oak and here and there a yew tree. Some of these yews were very ancient: the largest had a girth of ten yards and had been standing for as many centuries, during which it had become hollow. Over the years the hunters, farmers and soldiers too had cut wood from it for bows and spears and tools; at one time or another all the hill had been visited for timber. Many of the trees had been felled a hundred years before, during construction of the Trundle, but the old hollow yew had escaped.

A raven, perching on the topmost spray, craned its neck in alarm and then took wing; in silence it slid over the treetops and across the hill, away from danger and the approaching sound of men.

From his time as a slave, Tagart had learned that the Gehans had placed their forts on the most strategic, and usually the highest, points on the downs. The forts communicated by smoke signals, were connected by roads that remained passable throughout the year, and were each occupied by a unit of twenty-five men. He had also learned that the Flint Lord lived inside the Trundle and very rarely ventured beyond Valdoe.

Due west of Valdoe, three miles away and within signaling range, was the fort at Bow Hill. There was another fort, Eartham, southeast of the Trundle, also within range; but the road between Valdoe and Eartham ran through open farmland and provided little cover. The road to Bow Hill, however, passed for much of its length through deep forest.

Tagart knew the landscape of the downs, and his plan depended on this knowledge almost as much as on the three separate forces of nomads, each more than a hundred strong, that had converged on the Shode Valley from the other winter camps. Some had never been so far south before; others Tagart knew personally. Almost every tribe was represented, every totem: the camp was overcrowded and overstretched. Old animosities were laid aside, feuds tacitly forgotten, and under Tagart's leadership the strategy for killing the Flint Lord was explained.

They had left for the coast in two forces. The first, sixty experts in trap-building led by Tagart himself, had left two days after Klay's departure. A day after that the main force, four hundred and eighty-three people, had started, led by Bubeck. He was to take them as far as the Rother, a river in the south of the Weald. Here, well away from the villages and the Flint Lord's roads, he was to await further orders.

The march from the winter camp had taken Tagart and his men six days. Bubeck's force, traveling more slowly, would take seven to reach the Rother, which gave Tagart two days in which to make the necessary preparations in the countryside near Valdoe.

Most of Tagart's men had already gone on to the woods near Bow Hill. Tagart himself, Fodich, and six others, taking cord, axes, and hatchets, had hidden their packs in the undergrowth at the base of Levin Down and clambered up through the snow-covered scrub, cutting bundles of gorse which they had dragged to the top of the hill.

With his hatchet Tagart moved aside a branch of the old yew tree for a better view of the Trundle.

Sleet was falling across the hills and into the valley. They could make out the black timbers of the fort, the pennons flapping on their staffs above each guard tower. Fodich pointed out the slaves' quarters, just visible at the right-hand shoulder of the hill. Winding past them, issuing from the southwest gatehouse and coming down the vast white flanks of the hill, a line of posts marked the descent of a trackway, four hundred and fifty feet to the village below.

"That's Valdoe Village," Fodich said.

"Let's start," said Tagart.

They arranged their bundles of gorse around the trunk of the yew. On the bundles they heaped twigs, bark, sticks, larger branches, and a layer of wet leaves that reached well above the lowest boughs of the yew. From his pouch Tagart brought out a pocket of tallowed leather and checked its contents—it was a fire-making kit, which he hid under a piece of bark.

They were three quarters of a mile from the village and hundreds of feet above it, and the wind was blowing hard: there was little risk of their hatchets being heard below. They lopped a few branches from neighboring trees and trimmed the undergrowth near the yew to improve the flow of air.

"No more," Tagart said. "We don't want anything to be seen from the village." He turned to the man whose duty it would be to light the beacon. "Can you remember this spot?"

"I think so."

"You must be sure."

"I'm sure."

Tagart was satisfied. With a last look round, he led the others back the way they had come. They collected their packs and started southwestward, toward Bow Hill and the rest of Tagart's men.

"Why did you kill him?" Wouter said to Klay.

Klay poked a piece of bread into his mouth and chewed it. There were no galleries yet in the shaft: the overseer had ordered the sixteen men to the surface to eat their midshift meal. Klay and Wouter were sitting a little apart from the rest.

"Why did you kill Gabot?"

"He fell and drowned in the slurry." Klay pulled his tunic closer to his neck. "It's cold out here."

"His partner says you kicked him down the ladder."

"He fell. He had a fit. Who cares?"

Wouter mopped up the rest of his stew. "They might put me back on the night shift," he said hopefully. "You could team with Gabot's partner."

They sat for a while in silence. Klay squinted at the sea. Keeping his profile to Wouter he said at last, "Have you heard these rumors about a rebellion?"

"What's that you say?"

"Someone in the cage told me. They said the fort was going to be attacked and we can be set free, if we play our part."

Wouter looked round for the overseer; he was out of earshot.

"There will be smoke on Levin Down," Klay said. "That's the signal. When we see it we're to open the gates from the inside and let these people in."

"How can we open the gates from here?"

"Word has to be sent to the slaves in the Trundle." Klay looked Wouter in the eye. "Do you think that could be done, Wouter?"

Breaking from the disbelief and fear in Wouter's mind came a sudden gleam of hope. "This man in the cage," he said. "Your friend. When did he say these people were coming?"

"Soon. In a few days."

"Do they know about the army? Do they know about the foreign soldiers?"

"That's what it's all about."

Wouter's insides were churning. He had been a slave since the age of eight. As a boy he had often dreamed of escape—they all had. During the passing years he had thought of it less and less often. Now he was not sure if he wanted it anymore.

But then he remembered that the meal break was nearly over. Soon they would be going back to work. There could be no question of a choice.

Wouter saw again Gabot's white corpse lying in the snow. He thought of what the carpenter had said, that Gabot's daughter was in the Trundle. It explained why Gabot had spied on his fellows; it explained what had happened to him in the shaft. Wouter felt thankful and relieved that he had chanced to mention Gabot to Klay. If he had kept silent he might have jeopardized the only hope of freedom he would ever have.

"We must keep these rumors from the guards," Klay said. "Can everyone be trusted?"

"Yes," Wouter said. "They can be trusted." He looked over his shoulder at the overseer. "I think even he could be trusted. He'd take his freedom if he thought they wouldn't chase him and bring him back."

"But you won't tell him."

"No. Of course not. Of course I won't tell him."

"This man in the cage told me we should all pass the message on."

Wouter looked levelly at Klay. After his first excitement he was beginning to have doubts. "Where did you come from?" he said. "What are you?"

"A peddler."

"We have them here sometimes. You're not what you say."

"It doesn't matter who I am."

"Then who are these friends of yours mad enough to challenge the Flint Lord?"

"Just remember the signal. Smoke on Levin Down."

Wouter was growing suspicious. He wanted to ask more questions. But he had no time: the overseer decided that the break had ended, and for the rest of the day there was no safe opportunity to talk.

Gongs sounded: the shift was over. The slaves, about a hundred in all, were brought above ground and formed into ranks.

After the first count the chief overseer, accompanied by another overseer carrying a torch whose flame was blown about by the wind, came and stood next to Klay's rank.

"Which man here was on the ladder when Gabot fell?"

"I was, master."

The torch was put near Klay's face. "What is your name?"

"Klay, master."

The chief overseer studied him with experienced, skeptical eyes. Wouter watched. Throughout the afternoon his thoughts had been consumed by wild and changing moods. He had tried to keep calm, but it had been impossible. Talk of escape on its own would have produced no effect on him—he was too wise, too much a slave. No, it had been the circumstances of Klay's arrival that had given some credence to the talk; and then, and then, the blinding realization of what Klay had done to Gabot and why!

Of course, it was probably all nonsense! For some reason Klay had been trying to impress him. Or perhaps they had found out that Gabot was known as a spy. What more convincing way for a replacement to establish himself than to kill his predecessor?

But still . . .

The chief overseer plainly suspected Klay of something. This was no act. Wouter's heart soared.

"I'll be watching you," the chief overseer said.

A second count was made. Tailed, flanked, and led by bobbing torchlight, the miners were taken uphill once more to be fed and locked in the compound for the night.

For the first time in over forty years, Wouter was looking forward to going into the cage.

6 The army was now complete. Twenty-four units of foreign soldiers had been acquired through the mediation of Bohod Zein and brought, twenty or thirty at a time, in ships from the home port. Twenty of the new units had come directly from the Gehans' barracks; of these, eighteen, the last to arrive, had been drawn from the Vuchten, the "shock-squad," an elite body that gave fanatical allegiance to the Home Lord. Others were rougher and cheaper recruits, from as far east as Greifswald on the Baltic and as far south as Giessen, soldiers of the Felsengehans; from the Frisian Islands came mercenaries who spoke a harsh dialect and who wore no armor save crude tunics of sealhide and fur. Among the more outlandish recruits was a man of indeterminate age, hairless but for a small waxed topknot, his nose cosmetically removed—the practice of his western tribe—and the two nares forming the centers of whorls of tattooing in green and blue, which descended to his throat and spread out in fans across his chest. Another, dressed wholly in black, was a deaf-mute who conversed in a fluent and eloquent sign language, refused to eat any food of vegetable origin, and insisted on sleeping in the open, even if snow were falling.

These men were arranged into teams and units and were issued with armor and shields. Over leather tunics they were to wear coats of mail made from horn cut into ovals; over this fitted thick leather plates at breast and back. They were given shinguards and armguards and helmets of plain, gleaming oxhide. The helmets of the team masters were differentiated by a ridge from front to back, those of the unit leaders by hackles of feathers, the color and shape identifying the unit. For protection from the cold, they were issued with fur-lined boots, mittens, masks, and fur or sheepskin stormcoats.

The Vuchten wore different armor and clothing, darker, giving a more unified appearance, with helmets fashioned into hideous faces designed to frighten the enemy.

They held themselves aloof from the others and trained apart, spending long and grueling hours on the hill. Their weapons practice was always attended by an audience, drawn by displays of strength, speed and accuracy in spear throwing, archery, and combat with axes and hammers.

It was by now common knowledge among the slaves that the Flint Lord's army would be leaving on the morning after the next full moon, two days hence. The craftsmen, the overseers, the traders and tradesmen who came and went, all knew in lesser or greater detail the plans for the campaign. Some had sensed a strange expectancy among the slaves. Blene, the mines Trundleman, felt that the slaves were hoping for Gehan's total defeat.

There were ten Trundlemen. Their posts varied in importance between that of Asch, in charge of brothels, and that of Blene. In status Asch was equivalent to a unit leader, Blene to a general.

Blene and the Trundlemen for roads, trade, ships, and slaves, had been summoned to a conference in the main chamber at the residence. It was late afternoon; a young girl was lighting the lamps as another slave closed the shutters.

The Trundlemen were seated on cushions facing the windows. Lord Brennis was speaking. On his right sat Bohod Zein, who tomorrow would be taking ship and returning to the homelands; on his left was Larr, General of Valdoe. Beside Larr sat Hewzane, General of the Coast, a taciturn, pale-haired man of thirty.

Lord Brennis was describing the final plan for encircling the savages' camp. The army was to be led by Larr. Under him would be eight hundred and fifty men, most of them foreign.

Larr was of low birth—it was even said there was a slave or two somewhere in his parentage—and lacked the refinement of his fellow general, Hewzane. Blene came from a family even better than Hewzane's, and of the two men he preferred Larr, whose exalted rank had been earned by hard years in the teams as well as by ruthless leadership and intelligence. Hewzane appeared to lack all humanity. Blene had heard that it had been upon his advice that Lord Brennis had specified the unnecessarily cruel form of punishment at Fernbed. There were many other stories from the outer forts, most doubtlessly embellished, and tales of an atrocity at a village in the west. In mitigation it had to be said that Hewzane's task, maintaining the cohesion of the domain, was scarcely suited to a weak or pliable man. He had held his generalship for two years, having been purchased directly from the service of the Home Lord.

Blene, who was ten years older, remembered Hewzane's predecessor and regretted his absence. Perhaps this whole campaign—which Blene and, he suspected, a number of his fellow Trundlemen secretly regarded as unjustifiable, even foolhardy—could have been averted. Lord Brennis, who had only just turned thirty, might have been deflected from this lunacy by a few timely words; yet Larr, under whom in normal times were twelve units, seemed to have less influence with him than did Hewzane, who controlled only seven.

"Only two units will remain here," Gehan warned Blene and the slaves Trundleman. "Your overseers must be specially vigilant. I suggest extra food and perhaps beer for the miners, but postponement of rest days till we are back to strength. We must give them no opportunity for revolt."

At last the conference came to an end. As Blene was leaving, he passed by Lord Brennis. "Will you be supervising the attack, my lord?"

"Of course. Larr may be the general, but I am in command." He took Blene's elbow. "Come. Let us walk together. We haven't talked for weeks."

Blene suddenly saw him not as Brennis Gehan Fifth, not as the Flint Lord, but as the boy of twenty-three newly bereaved by his father's death and burdened with crushing duties, someone in need of friendly understanding and advice. Blene felt impelled to risk a reprimand and voice his doubts about the campaign: perhaps even now Gehan could be persuaded to reconsider, or at least to refrain from exposing his person to danger. As they reached the doorway, Blene resolved to speak his mind.

But Hewzane was approaching. "My lord!"

"Tomorrow," Gehan said to Blene. "We might have time to speak then." He turned to Hewzane and together they left the room, already deep in conversation, and Blene was left to reflect how much change the last six years had brought.

Gehan woke long before dawn and spent the morning with the provisioners and the quartermaster, making sure that nothing would be lacking the next day. Before lunch in the barracks he inspected the Vuchten, and after it the rest of the men, who were paraded by their commanders on the hill. At midafternoon Bohod Zein took his leave; despite Gehan's express instructions, Altheme was nowhere to be found when it was time for the sleigh to take the agent down to Apuldram and the turning tide.

For the rest of the day Gehan conferred with Larr. The Vuchten would lead the attack; Gehan would travel with the units of his own men.

Late in the evening a final divination was performed by Thille. And last, as a formality, the astronomer was sent for. He confirmed that the moon was about to achieve its perfection: in three hours it would be on the wane.

Gehan looked up at it as he passed through the gate. The sky was clear, another good sign.

He decided to bathe. Upstairs he was received by his body slaves, who removed his cloak and leggings, his tunic and underclothes, and washed him with unguents and hot water. When he was dry they brought a clean new houserobe and helped him into a marten robe. With soft fur boots on his feet, he was ready for the night meal.

"Where is my wife? Bring her here."

"She has already eaten, my lord, if it pleases my lord, and she has told her slaves to make up a bed in her own chamber."

"Bring her to me!"

"It's all right. I'm here."

She came through the doorway. With a motion of his fingers Gehan dismissed the slaves. He waited impatiently for them to leave. Altheme stood by the doorpost. She was wearing a maroon robe. Close to her throat was a necklace of small jade beads.

Gehan hit her across the face with the back of his hand. The necklace broke, scattering beads; Altheme fell against the wall, a crimson patch rising on her cheek.

"That is for eating without me and for leaving my chamber without permission," he said. "If I wish you to sleep elsewhere I shall say so. Get up."

He had never been angrier. This was the eve of the most important day Valdoe had known since Gehan Fourth had won independence from the Home Lord. He had wanted to savor these hours. At dawn tomorrow would begin the fulfillment of his destiny in the island country, the fulfillment of all his father's dreams. He, her husband, had worked for months—years—to bring this about. Not once in all that time had she offered him the slightest support, nor had she shown the slightest interest in the campaign that was to herald the new empire. She was unworthy of him. Even this afternoon her indifference had disgraced the Brennis name and embarrassed him in front of the central figure in the negotiations with the homelands.

"I suppose you know how deeply you have offended Bohod Zein."

"My lord, I was ill."

"How dare you absent yourself against my orders?"

"I was ill, my lord, and—"

"That's enough, you whore!"

"If I am that," she said quietly, "it is what you have made of me. Don't you think he had already seen enough of me?"

"You are a whore," he said, "and good for nothing else. Where is my son? Where is the son you promised me? Where is the son to carry on the Brennis line?"

Her eyes flashed. "Here! It's here! Here in my belly!"

"You're lying, you foul slut!"

"What do you think made me ill today?"

"Get out!"

When she had gone he put his fingers to his brow. They were trembling. She had implied that Bohod Zein could sire a son and he could not. She had called him sterile. And it was true. In all his liaisons he had never once fathered a child. Sitting on the edge of the bed, he shut his eyes and buried his face in his hands.

The room waited, utterly indifferent: the bed with its soft mattress and its covering of ermine and marten, the hangings of dyed and embroidered cloth, the shuttered window overlooking the enclosure, the six oil lamps on their turned poles. A slight draft was blowing in from the door; the flames by the window fluttered like moths' wings.

When he looked up, he saw his sister standing at the doorway.

"They are waiting to bring your meal," she said.

"Have you eaten?"

"Not yet."

"Then call them."

She did so, crossed the room and seated herself on the end of the bed. Her skin seemed very delicate, translucent; the cloth of her pale gray robe was stretched by the swell of her body and revealed her ankles, forearms, and neck. Gehan noticed that her eyes, usually so blue, had been all but taken over by the large, black pupils. Briefly their intense, receding reflections contained minute images of himself; and she looked away.

The aroma of hemp smoke still clung to her clothing and to her hair, which, in the lamplight, was densely composed of tints tending toward gold; where it was drawn up at the back of her head, the lines of tension seemed to draw their direction from the rise of her shoulders. It was held in place by a single ivory pin, like a trigger ready to release its charge.

The food taster and three girls entered with trays of steaming vegetables and meats, cheese and bread, and placed them on the eating dais. The girls adjusted dishes, spread facecloths and trickled clear water into wooden bowls.

They began. Rald seated himself just behind Gehan. The girls withdrew to the floor and squatted on their heels, watching.

Once Rald had approved it, Gehan poured cups of essence for Ika and himself.

"To tomorrow," she said.

"To tomorrow."

At the end of the meal neither she nor Gehan had eaten very much. Rald appeared distant and withdrawn as he helped the girls to collect the dishes and load the trays.

"You may all retire," Gehan said.

They watched the slaves go. Rald turned to shut the door, looking back into the room. His face was expressionless.

"It is too early for me to sleep," Ika said. "Are you tired?"

"No."

"Is the moon full yet?"

"Nearly. Very shortly. Perhaps even now."

"Can you tell when it's full?"

"The astronomer takes measurements. He could tell you."

All through the meal he had felt their speech becoming stranger and less natural, and now it had become drained of any but a kind of brittle, superficial meaning.

"Shall we look at the moon?" she said.

He went to lift the locking-bar from the shutters.

"No, wait! Let's open them together." From the wall she took down the snuffer and put out the lamps one by one. "It's too bright in here," she said. "We must do this properly." As the last lamp went out the room went black. In the swirling, particulate darkness Gehan slowly made out the dimness of the doorway and, turning, he saw the vertical filaments of silver where the shutter boards did not quite meet.

Ika put her hand on the locking-bar. He did the same. Their fingers were almost touching.

"Together," she said.

He was acutely aware of her presence so close beside him. He could hear her breathing; some heavy reluctance was preventing him from lifting the bar. It was affecting her too. They seemed to be waiting for the moon to complete its orb, synchronizing their heartbeats so that, at the precise moment, they could throw wide the shutters and let perfect moonlight flood in. But the moon was outside, high over the sea, and he and Ika were here, behind the shutters, standing next to each other.

He recalled the night at Harting Fort, her fragrance as she had hovered over him. He had despised himself then, but now he knew he had been wrong. This was not weakness. This was strength. At last he would no longer be single, cold, remote. With her he would be safe.

He put his warm hand on hers and took it off the locking-bar.

7

The road from the Trundle to Bow Hill was three or four miles long, a track wide enough to take six men walking abreast. It came down the long western slopes of Valdoe Hill and turned slightly to the south, avoiding high ground, before resuming its westerly course. A mile from Valdoe it entered the forest. Some way farther along it began to climb, and it was here, on a curving two hundred yard stretch, that Tagart and his men had concentrated their attention. With relays of lookouts protecting either end of the chosen stretch of road, and more lookouts in the surrounding woods, the intricate work had begun.

They had been interrupted frequently by false alarms, and more often by small parties of soldiers or farmers using the road. The delays had been agonizing. Tagart's scouts had counted almost a thousand men exercising throughout the day on Valdoe Hill: the Flint Lord's army would soon be leaving. Perhaps too soon. Again and again Tagart had wanted to ignore his own imperative of caution, to return more recklessly to the work after each false alarm; but he had not dared. If the Flint Lord got wind of anything untoward, the whole plan would be ruined.

And so they had taken nearly three days to do what should have been accomplished in one. Four tall oaks had been selected, like two pairs of gateposts, one at each end of the stretch of road, and interfering boughs and undergrowth skillfully cut away. Two hornbeams, partly rotten, had been felled and hoisted into position fifty feet above the ground and fifty feet back from the verge. A ditch had been dug on the south side of the road and lined with angled, sharpened stakes.

By late afternoon on the third day it had all been done. The road looked as it always had: a peaceful stretch of woodland track overarched by the graceful branches of lofty trees. There were no unusual footmarks in the snow, no furrows to betray the heavy hauling that had taken place, not a splinter, not a shaving. All freshly hewn wood had been smeared with earth; the ditches had been disguised with brush, and everything given a seemingly artless sprinkling of snow.

Only at the ends of the traps might something have been noted by a suspicious eye. Between each pair of oaks, fifty feet up, a stout rope passed across the sky and on into the woods to the place where a long and bulky mass had been suspended in the treetops.

Tagart and all but two of his men withdrew to wait for morning.

The two he sent to the camp at the Rother, nine miles away, carrying orders for Bubeck.

Bow Hill was a long hump of land, rising as high as Valdoe Hill, three miles due west of the Trundle. The fort stood at the highest point on the hill. Near its gate were the miners' quarters, and, a few hundred yards away on the slopes, were the spoil heaps and shelters of the mine workings. Three shafts were in use. Bubeck could hear voices below the ground, picks and hammers and shovels, the slow creaking of ropes.

The moon had set, tired and yellow, but there were so many stars that it was easy to see the way. Bubeck came up on the guard from behind. He had no time to make a noise. He dropped his spear and fought with insane strength to tear away the constriction at his throat, a loop of rawhide, knotted in the middle, its ends bound to a pair of wooden handles.

Steadily Bubeck continued opening his arms and the knot crushed the man's windpipe. His struggles became feeble. He slid to the ground.

Bubeck looked once again toward the fort. It stood as before, silent, unroused: nothing had been heard.

The other guards were dead by now. There were five, all strangled by Bubeck and his men. Behind Bubeck, in the hawthorn scrub, were twenty-five more hunters. He motioned to them and they arose and came forward, dividing into three groups, one for each shaft.

Bubeck led his group to the nearest shaft. It was covered by a wooden shelter, a leather curtain across the entrance. Lamplight showed at its edges.

Bubeck ducked under the curtain. A man with curly hair and a thick beard, dressed in a ragged doeskin tunic, his legs bound with scraps of old fur, was pulling something up the shaft on a rope. Next to him stood an overseer in a sheepskin jerkin.

"Greetings," Bubeck said, before the overseer had time to react, and thrust a spear into his heart. With all his strength Bubeck shoved him against the wall of the shelter.

The slave stared in horror. He let go of his rope: the load fell with a rasping hiss, and from below came a cry of anger and dismay.

Bubeck's companions laid the overseer on the floor of the shelter.

"Is there another one down there?" Bubeck asked the slave.

He was unable to reply.

"Is there another overseer in this shaft?"

"No."

"Then tell your friends to come up. You're free."

A second overseer was found in another shaft and killed; in a few minutes the whole of the night shift, forty-two men, had been brought to the surface and armed with spare weapons brought for the purpose. In the first light of dawn the whole force of seventy advanced on the slaves' quarters.

Bubeck and, in his planning, Tagart too, had underestimated the effect that sudden liberation would have on the slaves. Most of them seemed maddened, intoxicated. They smashed the palings of the slaves' compound and breached the sleeping cage, freeing the day shift. One of the guards managed to escape; the rest were cut down in a frenzy of axes and hammers. Despite Bubeck's shouts and the efforts of the other nomads, the miners pulled the cage to pieces and carried one of its sides to the palisade to serve as a scaling ladder.

The fort, like all the outer forts, had been made with a single enclosure and a single gate. Its palisade resembled that of the Trundle: a high fence of oak trunks, sharpened at their tips, set firmly in the ground and surrounded by a ditch.

The attackers were repulsed at the ramparts by soldiers with battle hammers. Several were dragged over the spikes and clubbed to death. The soldiers' forked siege poles thrust aside the makeshift ladder and its burden of screaming men; marksmen started to shoot. By the time the slaves fled there were twelve bodies in the ditch.

The survivors joined Bubeck's men and the rest of the slaves, who had been positioned just out of bowshot in the thorn and tussock scrub on either side of the road, commanding the gate. None of the nomads had been hurt.

Bubeck was watching the fort. A soldier had appeared on the platform at the top of the main building. He busied himself with bundles of wood and a firebrand and shortly a wisp of smoke appeared.

Most of the slaves seemed undecided whether to run or stay. Several had been wounded in the skirmish at the palisade; one man, an arrow in his leg, was groaning as a woman, a kitchen slave, tried to help him. Those who had not been wounded were arguing and shouting about the bodies in the ditch. After a while they chose a leader, a man of about fifty who had been prominent in the assault on the ramparts. He was sallow and swarthy, a foreigner. At his approach Bubeck stood up, rising to his full height. The slave was tall, but Bubeck was taller.

"We want to get into the fort."

Bubeck returned his stare.

"We're going to kill them all."

"And end up like your friends in the ditch?"

For support the slave looked over his shoulder. The others averted their eyes.

"If you stay with us and do as you're told," Bubeck said, "you can have something better than killing a few soldiers."

"What do you mean?"

The wisp had become a stream of white smoke gushing into the sky, rising for thirty or forty feet before beginning to drift downwind. As they watched, it changed color from white to blue.

Bubeck turned and pointed to the Trundle and the east.

"My lord! My lord!"

Gehan opened his eyes, woken by his body slave pounding on the door of the bedchamber.

"My lord!"

"What is it?"

"An urgent message from the signalmaster, my lord! Bow Hill has been attacked by brigands and the slaves are loose. General Larr has already stopped the departure, but he is awaiting your consent to answer Bow Hill's request for aid."

"I'll be with him as soon as I'm dressed."

"Shall I assist you, my lord?"

"No."

To judge by the intensity of light at the shutters, it was almost sunrise. He had wanted to be up much earlier, to see off the first units, and at another time he would have been angry with his body slave for letting him oversleep. However, Gehan told himself that his presence at first light had not been essential. All the preparations had been made.

He had changed. He felt he was no longer the indecisive coward who had permitted himself doubts about the glory of the future. Ika had guided him to that summit, that vantage, from which all was visible and all attainable. She was beautiful. She had shown him, more clearly than he could have dreamed, the boundless territory that was their birthright. It was the legacy of a supreme and masterful genius, of Gehan First, a man who had transcended mortality to seize the very flower of the gods themselves.

The body slave's knock at the door had woken her too. She was regarding him calmly, triumphantly, her head on the pillow. "Lord Brennis," she whispered. He leaned over and kissed her on the mouth. She responded at once, drawing him closer, pressing her body against his; Gehan felt her leg sliding across his own and she was on top of him.

The bedcovers slipped down her back as he measured her waist in his hands. His thoughts returned to the night, marveling at the softness of her skin and the lightness of her touch. Now at dawn she wanted unmistakably to begin again that rhythmic, mystical climb.

"I must speak to Larr," he said.

"Soon."

Gently, reluctantly, he pushed her aside. "Now."

The last group of soldiers had almost crossed the line traced by Tagart's eye from tree to tree. He turned in his seat, held up his hand, and signaled to Fodich.

Fodich was twelve yards behind him and to the left, astride a low fork. A harness was strapped to his chest and shoulders, attached to a rope. The rope led upward and was lashed to a branch, fifty feet above the ground, whose end had been carved into a hook-release for the suspended weight: a ton of hornbeam trunk, connected by two thick cables—one stretched tight and the other loose—to the two oak trees on either side of the road.

A similar arrangement and a second man in harness were waiting two hundred yards farther on toward Bow Hill.

The sun was rising among the trees. Here by the road the forest was still in blue shadow. The snow, crisp after the night's frost, sounded icy under the soldiers' marching feet.

Tagart had counted a hundred men in armor, led by a young man in a fox fur cape and hat. Their arrival and their purposeful pace toward Bow Hill showed beyond doubt that Bubeck had been successful there.

A hundred men. A tenth of all the Flint Lord's army.

Tagart brought down his hand: Fodich jumped.

The great hornbeam trunk creaked and cracked and was set free. Smashing aside the few branches still in its way, it charged downward and swept into the body of soldiers. At the far end of the trap the second hornbeam trunk was released.

They had been penned in.

Their commander, the man in the fur cape, was already dead. He had been hit by the second tree trunk and crushed against the ground, but one of the three surviving unit leaders, a plume of ocher feathers on his helmet, took command, yelling orders. Each man unslung his ax.

Before they could group properly the first volley of arrows whirred from the trees on the north side of the road. Many soldiers fell: another volley thinned those still standing. In the wake of the arrows a double rank of women and warriors stepped from the forest, spears held ready. For every soldier there were at least five nomads.

"Give ground! Give ground and regroup!"

They ran in terror across the verge, away from the oncoming spears, straight on to the spikes concealed in the undergrowth.

When it was over not a soldier remained alive. Two nomads had been killed and eighteen wounded. While they were being cared for and taken away, a group of men removed the hornbeam trunks. The rest, working in pairs, quickly cleared the road of bodies.

The commander had not yet been moved. Tagart put his toe under the commander's chin and turned his face to the light.

"He's young," Fodich said.

"He's also dead." Tagart let the blond-bearded face fall. "You can send the runner to Bubeck now."

The distress signal from Bow Hill had been received simultaneously by Harting and the Trundle. From Harting no reinforcements could be spared, but from the Trundle four units, Gehan's own men, were dispatched within a few minutes and their young commander, Chanvard, was given orders to investigate and render assistance.

The departure of troops for the savages' camp, already under way when the signal came, had been stopped. The eighteen units of Vuchten had left the Trundle long before dawn. Six had gone too far to be readily called back, and runners were sent to catch up with them. The other twelve returned to the Trundle.

Gehan slammed his fist on the window ledge. This signal had thrown the campaign into turmoil. While the trouble at Bow Hill was probably purely local, it was essential to halt everything until the matter had been dealt with. Any rebellion by slaves had to be quickly and firmly suppressed: to have them at large, in a position to reach Valdoe, would be very dangerous. The ratio of guards to slaves, not only here but at all the mines and works, had been carefully calculated. If the balance were upset by an onrush of insurgents the whole force of slaves might be set free, with formidable results.

But the signal had also mentioned brigands. This was the first time they had dared to attack a fort. That such an attack had occurred in winter, and only three miles from the Trundle, was deeply worrying. And then—were they brigands, or were they more primitive savages? Were they perhaps the nomads whose clans Valdoe had begun to destroy the previous summer? Gehan recalled the spies who had been found at Apuldram.

Larr was doubtful. "We must not overestimate the savages, my lord. More pressing is the news from Bow Hill. Chanvard should have reported by now."

"I agree," Gehan said. "I'm going up."

They climbed the staircase and threw open the door to the roof. The signalmaster and his boy were at the smoke station; the fires were burning.

The signalmaster did not salute them. He was staring continuously westward to Bow Hill. Gehan looked and could discern little but the black shape of the fort: his eyesight could not match that of the signalmaster.

"Was that a double white, boy?"

"Single, master."

The smoke station consisted of three shallow stone hearths, each about two yards square, and a wooden shelter for fuel: wood chips, dried dung, leather scraps, wet leaves, and the like. Plank covers, operated by pulleys, could be raised or lowered over the hearths. For complex messages three fires were lit, generating pure white, blue-gray, and dark smoke. Over the years, using combinations of color and interval, a large and subtle vocabulary had been amassed.

"What are they saying?" Gehan demanded.

"They want to know if we have sent the reinforcements yet, my lord."

He looked at Larr. This should have been a matter for Hewzane: it involved one of his forts. But Hewzane was at Eartham and there had not yet been time to summon him.

"What do you suggest?" Gehan said.

"We sent a hundred men," Larr said. "There are already twenty-five in the fort, not counting the slave-guards. That should have been enough to deal with thirty brigands and a rabble of slaves."

"But if Chanvard has not yet arrived, he must have been waylaid."

"My conclusion."

"Then we must send more units. Five more. And this time we'll send Vuchten."

"That is the best plan, my lord. But before committing more men and upsetting the departure further, we should have confirmation of Bow Hill's message."

"Get it," Gehan told the signalmaster.

The reply came, slowly and painstakingly pieced together.

"Repeat . . . No . . . units . . . arrived . . . Enemy . . . laying . . . siege . . . We . . . are . . . alone . . . and . . . urgently . . . repeat . . . urgently . . . request . . . aid."

8 From the site of the ambush to the Trundle, by road, was a little over a mile and a half. The two routes that Tagart had chosen to convey his forces to Valdoe were longer, curving through the forest. One turned northeast, skirting the rise of the hill to emerge at the base of Levin Down, at Valdoe Village. This was to be the destination of two hundred and thirty-four of the nomads, who, together with the slaves from Bow Hill, were to be led by Bubeck in a raid on the village.

The other route, the one that Tagart and the rest of the nomads were now following, struck out southeastward and approached Valdoe from the seaward side, by means of the flint workings.

They were nearly there. Behind him, coming through the woods, were people from twenty or thirty different tribes, from every winter camp. Compared with the Flint Lord's soldiers they were ragged and undisciplined. The men and most of the women were armed with spears, axes, and bows. Some were carrying coils of rope and grappling hooks. All were laden with backpacks of food, clothing, bedding, and spare weapons.

Tagart felt physically sick with dread. He was trying to walk confidently, Fodich beside him, Segle just behind, but with each step the illusion became harder to maintain. The slaughter of the soldiers had left them all subdued; Tagart sensed that he was not the only one who was afraid. He knew he should try to break the mood; but he was too gravely occupied in thought, for now, too late, he feared that he had placed too much reliance on exact timing, exact coordination, and that it would all fail. And if it failed, he alone would be responsible for the destruction and death of the largest and best part of his own nation. If it failed, the nomad tribes might never recover.

The final plan had been settled the previous night, when his scouts had brought word that there were still a thousand men in the Trundle and that they were showing no signs of leaving.

The essence of the plan was the diversion of soldiers from the Trundle. While Bubeck's force attacked the village and drew most of the soldiers down from the fort, Tagart would advance on the flint workings and set the miners free. By that time the beacon on Levin Down would—if Klay had done his work—have signaled the start of the rebellion inside the fort itself. If all went to plan, the gates would be opened from within, Tagart's force would find and kill the Flint Lord, set fire to the Trundle, and escape before the soldiers could get back from the village.

A thousand men in the Trundle. A hundred had already been killed. When Bow Hill reported to the Trundle that these reinforcements had not yet arrived, more would presumably be sent, perhaps as many as two hundred, which would leave seven hundred or so in the fort. The second group of reinforcements would be well along the road to Bow Hill when Bubeck's force, almost three hundred strong, attacked the village. It seemed likely that the Flint Lord would send most or all of the remaining seven hundred to its defense.

Valdoe Village was over a mile from the Trundle, reached by a track which zigzagged at least half that distance again. In altitude the village was four hundred and fifty feet below the fort—a long and steep return climb for men who had not only already run down the hill in full armor, but who had chased an exasperating crowd of attackers from the village compound and into the trees: for Bubeck had orders to offer no resistance to the soldiers, but to retreat into the forest and try to lure them on, wasting as much time as possible before they realized the Trundle itself was under threat.

The timing of the raid would be controlled by the beacon on Levin Down. Its smoke would signal both the start of the slaves' revolt and Tagart's advance on the mines and Trundle. The man in charge of the beacon, who was already in position, had instructions to light it only when the soldiers from the fort had descended two thirds of the way to the village. This would give Tagart a margin of some minutes to allow for unexpected difficulties—but now, as he led the way out of the forest and into the aspen break at the bottom of Valdoe Hill, the nature and number of those difficulties had swollen and multiplied in his mind with terrifying speed.

They prepared to wait. Nobody spoke. The Trundle could not be seen from here, but through the branches the terraced diggings and heaps of the mines, half a mile up the hill, were easily visible.

The shelters and spoil heaps were being patrolled in a bored manner by ten or twelve soldiers, who occasionally paused to chat with each other, stamping their feet, before resuming their walk. The soldiers could be told by their helmets and fur capes. The other figures on the hill, scurrying back and forth, could not be so readily identified. Tagart knew that most of them would be slaves, hauling stone up from the shafts, moving timber about, running errands for the overseers.

The sight of the mines brought a quick and repulsive vividness to his memory. The ground had been green then, it had been summer, but the rest of it was the same, the servitude, the grinding labor and hopelessness of the slaves, and, worst of all, the confinement in dark holes and galleries of men who worked drenched in sweat, breathing foul air and chalk dust. Sometimes he had coughed until he had seen bursts of light under his lids, and always he had felt trapped by the closeness of the rock and the weight of earth above him. At this very moment there were men down there, laboring by the light of smoldering wicks, digging with deerhorn picks, with scraps of wood, with their fingers, to extract from the depths of the hill the flint that gave strength to their master, their owner, the man who lived in the Trundle, the man who was planning to exterminate all of Tagart's race.

"There!" cried Fodich, pointing through the trees.

On the eastern edge of the hill, among the thorn scrub, there was the movement of a leather flag being waved. Orick had been waiting there, watching for the smoke on Levin Down.

The smoke had come. Bubeck had attacked the village and lured the soldiers down from the fort.

Tagart's mouth was dry. He unfastened his ax from its sling, summoned a shout, and at a run led his people from the trees and onto the hill.

Coming down the track from the northeast gate, Gehan was appalled and fascinated to see that the brigands had now set fire to the Meeting House. Black billows were rolling from the roof and pouring into the compound, giving a hellish, other-worldly tinge to the scenes of murder and pillage that were being enacted from house to house. Dozens of other buildings were burning too. Both granaries, many of the workshops, the leather stores, four large barns, and at least a score of the best and most luxurious houses, among them those of the quartermaster, the roads Trundleman, and even the fine and stately residence of General Larr: all were ablaze. Flame had engulfed the three great ricks of firewood, sending intense heat downwind to melt the snow from long, oddly shaped tongues of gray mud. Steam was rising from the mud to add to the smoke and ash, slowly climbing into and sullying the sky. The village had been turned into something unreal, fiercely set apart from the rest of the landscape. As he descended toward it, Gehan heard its noise growing louder: the combined shrieks and yells of the brigands, the screams of the wounded, of the scorched and impaled, of those with their hair and clothes alight, the frantic squealing of pigs and goats and cattle trapped and burning in their stalls.

There were at least three hundred brigands. Such a large and audacious force had never been envisaged by those who had built the village, those who had decided that no palisade was necessary; and the delay between the alarm being given and the dispatch of help from the Trundle had allowed the fires to take firm hold. Where the brigands had come from, why they were attacking the village, why they had attacked Bow Hill: these were mysteries that Gehan and Larr had been given no time to discuss. A message had been sent immediately to Bow Hill, recalling all reinforcements. Larr had been left with fifty soldiers, the civilians, and command of the Trundle, for Gehan had decided, on an impulse compounded of anger and a need for action, to take personal charge of the defense of the village. Of the twenty-one units remaining in the Trundle he had chosen nineteen—four hundred and seventy-five men—and brought them at battle pace out of the northeast gate.

Gehan was in the center of the column, surrounded by his customary bodyguard of ten men. Behind him was one of the commanders, whom he had appointed as his lieutenant, a blond, spare-limbed man of thirty-five named Irdon.

At the bottom of the hill, three hundred yards from the Meeting House, Irdon shouted an order and the soldiers spread out across the rough, snow-crusted ground. In a few moments they had formed a huge half circle. All movement stopped.

"Spears!"

In exact unison they presented their spears, a long, curving rank of aligned and identical shafts, pointing inward to the center of the half circle—the village.

Some of the brigands had already run away. Others were following. The compound was littered with their abandoned spoils and with bodies, sprawled in grotesque attitudes or lying more or less normally, on the open snow, in burning doorways, on the steps of the Meeting House.

Irdon gave his instructions. The maneuver to be performed was a standard part of the soldiers' training. They were to pursue the brigands from the village and on to Levin Down, which, having a diameter at the base of only half a mile, was small enough to be encircled, the gap between each man being seven yards at most, reducing continuously as they climbed and drove the enemy to their deaths at the top.

"Vuchten Red Unit: take six prisoners! Hunt the others to the death!"

Gehan and his bodyguard were left behind. He watched the chase, his view partly obscured by burning buildings and drifting smoke. The brigands, women as well as men, were fleeing in a mob, being herded by the soldiers toward the trees. On the far side of the compound was an arable field, its clods and withered stalks unevenly covered by snow. Beyond this, across a frozen brook, many of the brigands had already reached the edge of the woods, which rose almost without a break up the steep scarp of Levin Down.

"My lord," said the leader of the bodyguards. "They've got a fire up there."

It was so. White smoke was rising from the top of the hill. A camp? Some sort of signal? Gehan could not tell. This was another mystery that the six prisoners would explain.

The uneven surface of the field had delayed a few of the brigands; one had twisted his ankle and fallen. The soldiers killed him where he lay and ran on. At the brook three Vuchten had caught up with and speared a pair of women. Yet more soldiers were spreading along the base of the hill and disappearing into the woods.

Keeping well clear of the worst fires, Gehan walked into the village to look at the damage. Larr's house had been reduced to a stark framework of charcoal spars bathed in racing flame. The

wood had burned away in cracked, reticulate patterns, leaving
rows of squares and oblongs, like runes which were continually
visited and abandoned by the caresses of the fire; even as Gehan
paused to watch, the key beam gave way and the structure collapsed into the blackened rubble of stone and ash which had been
rooms, bedding, clothes, the furniture of Larr's domestic life.
There were no bodies to be seen here, but in the next house, also
burning, he saw two dark shapes with spindled limbs and heads,
shrunken as if by tremendous age. It seemed that most of the
younger and more agile villagers had managed to escape, for the
infirm and old accounted for a disproportionate number of those
lying dead or pleading for help.

"Do something for that man," he told one of the guards, and
walked on, brushing soot from his shoulder, until he reached the
eastern edge of the compound, farthest from the cries of the
wounded and of the trapped beasts. Smoke was pouring overhead
in great surges, as if generated behind him by the sound of the
fire. He looked out across the fields. The chase had by now passed
entirely into the woods, and from the slope above him and to his
left could be heard, faintly but regularly, the shouts of the soldiers
keeping contact. It would not be much longer before the brigands
were brought to the top.

Hazy smoke under the morning sun spread thin, moving shadows over the flat fields in the valley ahead of him, fields bisected
by a winding track which eventually joined the road to the north—
along which his troops had that morning passed and repassed.
Gehan wondered whether the six units of Vuchten, recalled by
runners, had yet returned to the Trundle.

On his right, on the south side of the valley, rose the fields
that had been made of the face of Valdoe Hill, and above them,
where the ground was impoverished or the gradient too great,
was the scrub of tussock grass and thorn that reached all the way
up to the fort.

Casually his eye took in the distant form of the Trundle, black
against the whiteness of the hill: the timbers of the palisade and
guard towers, the jutting framework of the northeast gatehouse;
he even looked away again before realizing that something was
amiss. At a mile's range it was not immediately obvious that the
pennons had been struck and replaced with strips of sheepskin,

nor was it easy to see the continuous, white plume of distress that was rising from the signal station.

It was being carried strongly eastward by the wind at the summit, quickly evanescing, becoming one with the sky, and though it left no trace of haze it was being blown by the same impulses as the smoke from the ruined village down here in the valley, keeping company with it as it moved toward the forest and disappeared.

The Trundle was being attacked.

Klay saw the blond woman run into the hawk mews. He broke away from the fighting and followed her.

He reached the door and barred it behind him. The uproar in the enclosure outside had upset the birds: the owls, falcons, hawks and eagles. With piercing screams they were treading their perches; the more highly strung had already bated and were hanging head downward with wings and tails in a broken tangle.

Klay looked round. The far wall was divided into alcoves by wooden partitions from floor to ceiling. Each alcove held three padded perches at chest height, above which were shelves laden with boxes, bags, tackle, bundles of twine and cloth and leather. Below the perches were lockers. They were too small for her to hide in.

His heart was thumping. He had lost all sense of time. He felt elated, drunk on the blur of events. At the mines he remembered spearing two men at least, seeing their faces, and in the fighting by the southwest gate he had taken three more.

Tagart's plan had succeeded. The nomads had stormed the hill and cut down all the soldiers and overseers at the mines; the miners had come above ground as Klay had arranged, already armed with shovels and picks and lengths of wood. The slaves' quarters had been broken open and everyone there set free. Klay had been in the middle of the throng of slaves and nomads heaving against the ranks of oak logs that made up the gates. Almost at once the gates had opened inward, released from inside by the slaves in the Trundle, and the crowd had surged forward and into the enclosure.

At the start of the rebellion, when the signal from Levin Down had been seen, there had been about fifty soldiers and thirty civilians in the Trundle. The civilians were craftsmen and freemen and overseers in the various workshops and buildings in the enclosure; working with them had been about forty slaves. When the smoke had come these slaves had attacked their overseers. Many of the other civilians had tried to run and hide, and the soldiers had been divided between fighting the slaves and making the fort secure—for they had already seen Tagart's force advancing up the hill and toward the mine workings.

Once the gates had been opened, the few soldiers remaining in the guard towers and on the battlements had been pulled down and put to death; Klay had been among the fighting there. Other slaves and many nomads had already spread out across the enclosure, rampaging through the sheds and buildings in their search for overseers or soldiers left alive. Tagart and a group of more disciplined warriors had broken into the inner enclosure with ropes and grapnels, looking for the Flint Lord; it had been then that Klay had seen the woman, running toward the hawk mews. Somehow she had been flushed out of the inner enclosure. She was barefoot, wearing a thin white dress. And now she was somewhere in this building.

Klay noticed for the first time that he had been gashed in his right forearm. Spots of blood fell to the flagged stone floor as he passed from the hawk mews and came to the next room, a seven-sided chamber with a high, rafted ceiling. In the middle of the room, surrounded by a tier of seats, was what he took to be a cooking pot or caldron, a stone bowl on three legs, covered by a circular lid upon which was arranged a curious tripod of three bone needles.

He listened. Behind him was the screaming of the hawks, and outside, fainter now, deadened by the walls, he could hear human screams above the shouting of the slaves.

Klay's eyes jerked to the left. The wall there was covered by a curtain of dense woven stuff, yellow and white and black, hanging by a line of horn rings from a carved wooden pole. He had heard something: a moan, a low and involuntary whimper of fear.

He ripped the curtain aside. She was there, crouching in a niche, making herself as small as she could, tightly clasping her shins, her blond head bent low to show the nape of her neck.

He had not been mistaken. This was the same woman, the one in the village, the one who had encouraged the green-eyed youth . . .

Klay's hand trembled as he reached out his middle finger and allowed a drop of blood to splash on her neck. Her shoulders squirmed and she whimpered again, unable to deny to herself any longer that he was there.

Klay grasped her wrist and dragged her from the niche. She made no resistance and allowed herself to be pulled across the floor to the stone caldron.

"I have jewels," she said, barely able to speak.

Still holding her wrist, made slippery by his own blood, Klay reached out and took one of the bone needles from the tripod. With a dry rattle the other two fell to the stone surface of the lid.

"Look at me," he said.

"I'll give you anything—"

"Look at me!"

Slowly she turned her head and raised her eyes. They were blue: foreign eyes, cold eyes, the eyes of the farmers and the land across the channel.

"I am going to keep you in this room and lock the door," Klay said. "I will visit you every day until you die. Until then, I want you to remember my face." He gripped the bone needle and began to raise it. "Remember me well. Mine is the last face you will ever see."

9 He had gone.

Ika felt the coldness of the stone floor against her shoulders and knew that at last she had become still. She had taken her hands from her face and she was silent, even though it had seemed impossible, in the worst moments when she had confirmed with her fingers what had been done to her eyes, that her screaming could ever stop. And yet it seemed not to have stopped. It was continuing somewhere, somewhere else, somewhere beyond . . .

She was blind. She had been blinded. With a brutal hand clenched in her hair he had wrenched back her head and put out her eyes. She knew what had happened, and yet she refused to accept it. Nothing was permanent. Her eyes would heal. She could see something even now: the blackness that surrounded her was not complete. It was tinged with color. Red, it was tinged with red, almost as if that were the color of pain itself.

And as if to ward off the weight that was threatening to crush her into the floor she sat bolt upright, her hands came to her face and she was screaming again.

He had said that he would be coming back. The slaves had taken possession of the fort and he would come back day after day with new tortures until she was dead. But worse than that, she was already robbed forever of her sight and her face and fingers were sticky with blood and everyone had been murdered and even Gehan could not help her because she was alone in this excruciating darkness where there was only Rald's voice and someone shaking her shoulders, shaking and shaking, hurting her, slapping her face, and to make it stop she cried out and was no longer screaming.

"Get up! Get up!"

"Who is it? Rald?"

"We must get out before they seal the gates!"

"Rald?"

He had helped her to her feet and they were leaving the divination chamber and coming into the hawk mews, into the banshee screeching of the birds, the screaming that she had thought might be her own.

"Rald! Where are you?"

"Here, my lady." He touched her arm. "We must cover your robe or they'll see you. At first they went mad. General Larr is dead, and all the soldiers and overseers. But now they're taking hostages."

"Are they in the residence yet?"

"Yes. Quickly, my lady."

He had found some coarse, musty cloth among the falconers' lockers. Calmly she allowed him to drape it over her shoulders. He led her toward the door.

"I was nearly killed myself," he said. "The others hate me. I was searching for you, my lady. Then I saw him coming out of the hawk mews." He guided her to the left. Cold air and a change in sound told her that they had left the doorway. "Now we must be careful. Say nothing. Walk slowly as though your legs are hurt and I am helping you toward the barracks. That's where they're taking their injured."

Rald was keeping close to the line of workshops, making for the northeast gates. The slaves had opened these too, though it had been on the far side of the enclosure, at the southwest gates, that the worst of the fighting had taken place. Ika could hear voices, both nearby and far away, but the frenzy of the initial onslaught was over, and where there had been horrible cries of suffering there were now coarse shouts and even laughter. On her right, from the middle of the enclosure, came sounds of destruction. They were ransacking the Trundlemen's quarters and the Flint Lord's residence.

"The gates are still open," Rald whispered. "Not much farther."

The pain in Ika's eyes had started growing.

"I can't go on . . ."

"You must."

To be challenged now, as she was certain they would, to be taken and killed before they reached the gates, would be a kind of release: for she had thought that the first pain, soon after he had stabbed her, was the worst that could be imagined; but it had been a mere prelude to the remorseless, solid growth that

was spreading into her skull from the unendurable points that
had been her eyes.

"I can't, Rald. I can't."

His hold on her arm tightened. "We're coming to the gates
now."

She could scarcely understand him. Her feet slipped on the ice
and she staggered, but Rald was supporting her and would not
let her fall.

"We're through! Keep walking! We're through!"

Distantly she heard him speaking again. She was nearly unconscious and could recognize meaning only in the eager tone of
his voice. Groping to comprehend, she retrieved the word *Vuchten*, sensed that it meant safety, salvation, vengeance; and then
the rest of his words pierced her mind and before she collapsed
she knew that he had said:

"Lord Brennis is coming."

It had gone wrong. The rebellion had worked, and Klay had done
his part, but the rest of the plan was in ruins. Once inside the
Trundle, the slaves and nomads had been impossible to control.
Even people from Tagart's own tribe had ignored his orders and
joined in the massacre of soldiers and civilians. The whole structure of his carefully thought scheme to find and destroy the Flint
Lord was on the verge of being swept away. He had arranged for
a systematic search of the fort to be carried out: it had not been
done. He had arranged for the northeast gates to be kept sealed:
they had been opened and left unguarded, as had the southwest
gates. And now, unless the Flint Lord was up here, hiding on
the roof of his own residence, Tagart would have to face the fact
that his quarry had escaped and that he had thrown away scores
of lives for nothing.

The door to the roof had been locked from the outside. It was
at the top of a steep staircase which, dark and cramped, rose
from the landing connecting the bedchambers. Fodich had ripped
a length of rail from the wall downstairs, but there was not enough
room to use it to lever off the hinges, nor could two men stand
side by side to break the door down. The angle of the stairs
prevented the use of some heavy article of furniture as a battering-
ram. They had tried to split the panels with stone hammers and
failed. Now Fodich was hacking at the hinges with a felling ax.

The upper hinge and its cover had been reduced to a fibrous pulp. Chips and splinters of flying flint rebounded from the paneled staircase walls with each new blow and Tagart covered his eyes with his forearm.

Suddenly Fodich's ax hit the exact spot and the lower hinge parted from the frame. He kicked at the door: it twisted sideways and the upper hinge yielded.

Freezing wind and daylight filled the staircase. Fodich was first on to the roof, followed by Tagart, Berge, and a man from the Martens named Porth.

They found themselves on a gravel-lined platform, thirty feet square, edged by a low wooden parapet. The main part of the platform was taken up by three stone hearths and a sort of shed. Tagart saw at once that this was the signal station: from each of the hearths there issued a column of white smoke.

The fires had been fed with wet leaves by a small boy and a man of middle age with a bushy black beard, his hair plaited into a pigtail which hung to his shoulders. To judge by his horn and leather jerkin and fur leggings, he was not an ordinary soldier but held some official post. Tagart took him to be a signalman. He had armed himself with a pole and, the boy taking refuge behind him, was standing his ground on the snow-covered gravel near the edge of the platform.

No one else was here. The Flint Lord had eluded them.

"Put it down!" Porth growled. "Put it down or we'll throw you into the enclosure!"

The signalman laid down his pole. The boy clung more tightly to his jerkin.

From below rose the sound of the slaves running wild, wantonly breaking down doors, wrecking furniture, pulling down and fouling shelves and stores in the workshops, the barracks, the armory. And the Flint Lord had gone: it had all been for nothing. With his army and his network of outer forts, he could afford to vacate the Trundle if he wished and retake it at his leisure. But even that would not happen. The Trundle had not been abandoned; the soldiers had simply gone to defend the village, and nothing remained for Tagart but to make an ignominious retreat before they had a chance to get back.

He went to the parapet. This roof was the highest point on the Trundle, which itself occupied the highest part of Valdoe Hill.

On his left, to the south, spread a descending panorama of white and gray, running out four miles and more to meet the broad stripe of gray-green ocean. To the west he could see Bow Hill, to the north the wooded slopes of Levin Down and, in the valley at its foot, over a mile away and hundreds of feet below the Trundle, the eloquent smoke that described Bubeck's work in the village.

In a tingling premonition of horror Tagart's gaze flashed from the village, farther to the right, and there, flowing up the road that zigzagged to the summit, already two thirds of the way to the Trundle, he saw a dark column of men: five abreast, extending like a vast snake hundreds of yards long, sinuously winding up the zigzags, and as he listened he could hear their chanting and the crash of their boots on the hard-packed ice of the road.

"Shut the gates!" he yelled down into the enclosure, and cupping his hands he yelled again. "Shut the gates! Shut the gates!"

Fodich and the others rushed to the parapet.

"Porth! Berge! Keep shouting! Tell them to shut the gates! Fodich, come with me!"

Tagart paused before jumping through the doorway and down the stairs. "Keep that signalman! We may need him!"

Gehan was at the head of the column, separated from the empty road and the unguarded fort only by a line of bodyguards. He was carrying no pack or weapons, but otherwise was keeping up exactly with the relentless pace set by the Vuchten at the rear. Behind him, powering him forward, he sensed the outrage of his men and heard it take form in the exhilarating battle chant that was made of the two syllables of his name: *Ge-han Ge-han Ge-han*, and he forgot that this was also the name of the Home Lord; it was his name alone, shouted by these men with their life's breath, shouted in the rhythm of their feet as they surged up the hill and toward the fort, toward total and devastating revenge on the vermin of slaves and brigands who had breached the Trundle and profaned the sacred territory of Brennis Gehan Fifth.

On seeing the white smoke from the Trundle, Gehan had sent Irdon, his lieutenant, on to Levin Down to recall the soldiers. The slaughter at the summit had already taken place. A few brigands had escaped the closing circle; the rest, numbering about two hundred and seventy, had been caught and killed. A hundred and three soldiers had been lost. Irdon regrouped the remaining men and, together with six captive brigands, started back down the hill.

During Irdon's absence five units of Vuchten appeared from the west, drawn to the village by the smoke. These were the second set of reinforcements that had been sent to Bow Hill; their commander reported that the first, four units under Commander Chanvard, had been ambushed and exterminated on the road. The Vuchten had continued to Bow Hill, found that the brigands had departed, and at a forced march had returned to Valdoe.

Under Gehan's personal supervision the men were marshaled and the race up the hill began. Their goal was the northeast gatehouse; the gates yet remained open. Once inside they could sweep through the enclosure and if necessary pursue the enemy out through the southwest gates to carry on a running fight on the southern face of the hill.

During the marshaling of the men, the captive brigands had been made to talk. In the brief time before the column set off, Gehan was apprised of the nature and size of the enemy: he could not bring himself to think of them as other than brigands, yet it appeared that his advisers last summer had been correct. The fort had been attacked by savages.

The gatehouse was drawing nearer. Gehan was by now feeling the strain of the run from the village. His legs were aching; his brow was hot and wet. He grasped at each breath; the air scraped his lungs as he pushed himself on. He could not stop. The Vuchten were behind him. He hurriedly wiped sweat from his eyes and saw that he had not been mistaken—beside the road, blurred by his own movement, he had seen two figures, one a woman lying in the snow among the tussocks, the other a man kneeling by her, now rising and running forward to meet him.

Gehan broke free from the column and allowed it to continue rushing past him, a stream of men still chanting his name. They were less than three hundred yards from the gatehouse, from the high black walls of the palisade; beyond the bobbing river of heads and weapons and armored shoulders he was aware that the space between the gates was starting to narrow; and he was aware of Rald's outstretched arm, but brushed it aside and went to the woman. To Ika. Somehow the final safeguard of the inner enclosure had betrayed him: the sanctuary of his residence had been broken open and defiled, and from the filth and chaos of the fort everything he loved and valued had been vomited forth. As he came to her he saw for himself what had been done. Stunned, disbelieving, he fell to his knees beside her.

And looking up, wide-eyed, his knuckles in his mouth, he saw the slit of daylight vanish as the giant gates slammed shut.

PART THREE

1

Both gatehouses had been made to the same plan. With slit windows and raised roofs thickly guarded with spikes, flanked by shielded walkways which gave access to the rest of the battlements, each gatehouse overhung a pair of massive doors composed of ranked oak logs set in ponderous frames. These swung inward and were secured with a grid of locking-beams, which rested in sockets in the jambs as well as in rabbets cut from the timber of the frames. The grid could be hoisted clear with pulleys operated inside the gatehouse. And as a final precaution, oak buttresses could be slotted into special pits and jammed against the gates in times of siege.

By now it was well past noon. The locking-grids had been in place for over an hour, ever since the Flint Lord had returned from the village. Finding both sets of gates shut, the army had withdrawn to the southwestern side of the fort, a bowshot from the palisade. Fifty soldiers had been detached and sent down the hill; they had disappeared into the aspen break, the nearest group of standing trees of any size.

Tagart could guess what they had gone to fetch. He was keeping watch from the signal station, not only on the soldiers but on the ominously quiet woods and fields round the village. The houses down there were still burning. He could just make out figures against the snow, approaching the compound in small groups, and from their behavior it was obvious that they were villagers. Of Bubeck and his whole force of slaves and nomads there had been no trace.

Tagart was desperately trying to suppress his fears. Without Bubeck there would be no chance of leaving the Trundle alive. Sixty of Tagart's force had died during the assault, and a hundred more were too badly wounded to fight.

He looked down into the enclosure. The arrival of the Flint Lord had quickly sobered the slaves and those nomads who had disregarded orders during the assault. All the soldiers in the fort, including an important one called Larr, had been senselessly killed. So had many of the overseers and other civilians. The survivors had been spared only by the intervention of the chief of the Crows, who had locked them all in one of the barracks.

Even with the Flint Lord at the gates it had taken time to establish some semblance of order, and it was not before an hour had been wasted that a slave was found who knew something of the Flint Lord's army.

His name was Correy. In his early twenties, with wide-set brown eyes and a fleshy, slab-cheeked face, Correy was even dirtier than most of his fellows, who were washed and deloused only in summer. His beard was dark brown, somewhat lighter than his hair, which hung in ill-smelling locks about his neck. There was a boil beside one lobe of his nose, and another was visible through his beard, distending the line of his jaw. His remaining teeth were black stumps, and when he spoke Tagart tried to avoid his breath. But he was articulate and voluble and had worked both in the weapons shop and on a maintenance team.

Within a few minutes he had expounded the functions of the fort and the distinction between ordinary soldiers and Vuchten, whose darker uniforms could clearly be seen from the signal station. Tagart had estimated the total number on the hillside at five hundred and twenty, of which two hundred and ninety were Vuchten. It had been from the Vuchten that the tree-cutting detail had been taken: shortly after Correy had arrived, the men had reappeared, trotting up the hill, bearing something long and heavy which proved to be the trunk of a large aspen, newly felled and shorn of its branches.

Tagart and Correy went down to the enclosure. Slaves had lined the battlements, striving for a view of the Flint Lord. On Correy's advice the slaves were cleared and replaced with the best archers among the nomads, for whom extra arrows and bows were brought from the armory.

Tagart climbed the ladder into the southwest gatehouse, Correy behind him. The trapdoor opened into a plank-lined room three yards by five. The room was in semidarkness. In the rear wall, overlooking the enclosure, was a narrow window beside which stood the stocks for the pulleys and tackle of the locking-grids: ropes passed down through neat ovals cut in the floor. On the outward wall were four slit windows and a larger, central, aperture, two feet square, provided with a hinged shutter. Hanging on brackets above it, running the length of the room, was a trough-shaped board; below this was a curious device, a pair of wooden handles five feet long, attached to the wall with pivots and supporting a shallow basket fashioned from heavy osiers.

"That's the hoist. Those hooks in the ceiling are for the chute ropes."

At floor level was a horizontal slit a few inches wide and about four feet long. "What's this for?" Tagart said.

"The hose." Correy indicated the shutter. "You work it from there."

Tagart opened the shutter and looked out. The soldiers were so close that he could hear their voices. They had spread out on the hillside, with an order and regularity which were themselves intimidating, just beyond the furthest bowshot. In the middle of their ranks a tent, taken from the mine-workings, had been pitched, and next to it a fire, the largest of the several fires they had lit, was being fueled with pitprops by half a dozen men.

The tree-cutting detail had not yet reached the main body of troops. Tagart turned to Correy. "You don't think they'll try it in daylight, do you?"

"I do."

"They'll be shot. We'll hit them as they come."

"They have good armor."

Hanging just by the shutter, on a loop of cord, was a broadmouthed cone about a foot in length, made from reed leaves pressed together and laminated with glue.

"What's this?"

"A shouting-cone."

Tagart took it down and examined it. "By what name should I call the Flint Lord? Lord Brennis?"

"Yes. But he won't answer."

Tagart put the smaller end to his lips and leaned forward. "Lord Brennis!" The sound was amplified by the reed-paper trumpet and it seemed no longer to be Tagart's own voice. He shouted again. "Lord Brennis! Lord Brennis! I am the chief of the Shoden! I wish to talk!"

The soldiers were behaving as if nothing had happened. No one made a move toward the tent, and no one appeared at its flap.

"To speak to us would be to admit that we have taken the Trundle," Correy said.

Tagart tried again. "Lord Brennis! We must talk! Lord Brennis!"

For reply came a few terse commands and responses; the aspen trunk had been made ready, with twenty-five equally spaced slings of rope. Fifty Vuchten went and stood by it. Two hundred of the other soldiers strung their longbows and formed into four rectangular squads, each five men wide and ten deep. These four squads now set off toward the gatehouse, flanking and keeping slightly ahead of the men with the tree trunk. The first assault had started.

Behind Tagart, four nomads climbed through the trapdoor and took their places by the slits. Tagart looked impotently from side to side, at the approaching soldiers, at Correy: and suddenly Correy seemed seized with fright. He rushed to the ladder and scarcely touched the rungs as he slid to the ground. Tagart heard him shouting "The buttresses! The buttresses!" and, with the soldiers less than two hundred yards away, saw him directing a group of slaves as they manhandled across the ice, two for each gate, sloping frames made of oak beams.

Although the gates had been correctly closed, the locking-grids alone were not meant to withstand a battering-ram. Most of the slaves had known what was being prepared; all those on the battlements had seen the aspen trunk being brought up past the mines, seen it being brought ever closer to the Flint Lord's position, seen it being rigged with rope; but it was a measure of the confusion and indiscipline inside the fort that not one, not even Correy, had thought to mention to Tagart, or to Fodich or Crow or any of the other established leaders, the existence and purpose of the siege buttresses. Only now had Correy remembered them, and without reference to anybody he had taken men from their posts and was shouting orders at them as they tried to drag the unwieldy frameworks into place.

Fifty yards from the palisade the two hundred longbowmen, still in formation, had stopped to take aim and shoot, protecting the men with the battering-ram, who were keeping on, increasing their speed.

Tagart dodged aside as the soldiers let fly a howling volley of arrows, fanning outward on spinning vanes to cover the whole defended width of battlement, ending in shrieks and screams and a sudden loud crepitation against the logs of the gatehouse wall. Beside him one of the arrows had found a slit, found it and gone through, and the man standing there had been punched backward, his throat pierced, his hands clutching the arrow and already bloodied as he fell against the pulley stocks and crumpled to the floor.

The Vuchten with the battering-ram had kept on, and when Tagart glimpsed them in foreshortened view, fifteen feet below, it was as if he was seeing one creature, with one brain, blind, insane, a tree trunk for its body, horn and leather legs propelling it forward in a writhe of glinting gray and black, but each leg was a man, a human being, faceless behind an ugly visor, each one different, deformed, carved in the guise of nameless beasts and Tagart saw them no more and was thrown as the head of the creature struck its first tremendous blow. The whole gatehouse lurched. He grasped the shutter and pulled himself up. As one, with inhuman precision, the Vuchten had dropped the trunk and turned, ready to retreat for a second strike; but, ignoring the dense covering fire of the longbow squads, the men on the battlements had bent their bows and leaned into view. They let fly: a hailstorm of shafts and feathers converged on the Vuchten. Half fell dead or mortally wounded. Those who had not been hit tried to lift the battering-ram; others, with arrows sticking from their limbs, bodies, necks, added their ebbing strength and the tree trunk actually moved a few inches. But the trunk was too heavy, they could not manage it, and with each moment more devastation was threatened from the battlements. The order came for retreat. Leaving their dead, they dragged the wounded to the cover of the four squads, whose men, shields held high to deflect the nomads' arrows, were slowly backing away.

They reached the main position and were absorbed into the general body of soldiers.

Tagart could see the casualties being attended to by their comrades, and from the tent appeared the figure of a man in a fur cape of the palest gray. As he passed among the men he was shown the greatest deference; he cursorily inspected the wounded and from his impatient gestures seemed annoyed by what he saw.

This surely was the Flint Lord himself. Under his cape he was wearing a high-necked tunic of what looked like ermine, leggings and knee-boots of sand-colored hide, and gull gray gauntlets; on his head was a black or dark gray stormcap with ear muffs and neck flap. Beside most of his soldiers he was not tall, but even at this distance his bearing and carriage could be seen to mark him out from all the rest. Tagart found himself staring at the man, despite the need to leave the gatehouse to discover what losses had been inflicted on his own people. And at the back of his mind Tagart was trying to assess the chances of making a run for safety. The northeast gates, perhaps deliberately, had been left unguarded by the Flint Lord. It was as though he were inviting Tagart to try. Tagart's fighters were women as well as men, slaves as well as nomads, undisciplined, uncoordinated, lacking all training in warfare. Pitched against them were five hundred soldiers, awesomely well prepared and equipped. The odds were hopeless. But staying in the Trundle would be death. Before long, even more soldiers would arrive, from the outer forts. They would help the others to erect a temporary village and keep warm by burning timbers from the mines, and in a week, a month, supplies of food and water in the fort would run out. For a while those inside would eat snow and go hungry, but, when the last dog had been eaten, they would start eating each other. The dead first, then the nearly dead, then the weakest of those left alive.

The Flint Lord knew this. He had come to the forefront of the ranks and stopped, alone. Behind him was the movement of his men, the bright fluctuation of the fires; but he was motionless. To Tagart his stillness seemed uncanny, the product of an anger so deep and unforgiving that it wore the appearance of patience and calm, and at its center was his gaze, fixed on the fort, on the gatehouse, on the open window, on the face and eyes and soul of his adversary. Tagart took an unconscious step backward and his heel touched the paper cone, which had fallen to the floor. It rolled aside with a resonant scrape, and Tagart, who minutes before had been eager to use it, to bargain his way out of the trap into which he had sucked all the nomad tribes, now felt himself unable even to bend and pick it up, still less put it to his mouth and attempt to communicate with such a man.

Tagart made himself break the spell and look away. He had resolved to act, whatever the cost. He could no longer afford to wait for Bubeck: it was beginning to look as if Bubeck would never come.

Pushing back the conclusion of this thought, he glanced out again for a last glimpse of the man in gray.

He had disappeared. Something had drawn him back into the assembly. Tagart saw what it was.

Over to the right, climbing nearer through the thorn scrub on the western face of the hill, giving the Flint Lord complete superiority of numbers, was a column of a hundred and fifty men wearing the dark armor of the Vuchten.

There would be no escape.

Tagart left the gatehouse and in a daze went down into the enclosure.

There was a quality about the woman that preserved a part of her dignity even now. Like the Flint Lord's spotless and luxurious personal clothing, like the lavishness of his chambers and the costly contents of the chests and cupboards that had been emptied and looted by the slaves, she was of the best and most expensive breed: precisely the consort that a man like Brennis Gehan would take. Her face was grimed and bruised, and she was holding the torn flap of her robe to her neck, both to keep herself distanced from Tagart and to cover the flesh that had been exposed when the slaves had tried to rape her. She was exhibiting this rare pride, yet the manner in which she had been found, crouching in the bottom of an empty cistern, spoiled it all, and in her brown eyes it was easy to discern the terror that paralyzes someone facing imminent death.

"Take her upstairs. Give her new clothes and a private room. Her own room."

"The slaves want to kill her," Fodich said.

"Keep them away. Keep them away from this building at least."

Lookouts had been posted in the guard towers and on the signal station, but still there had been no trace of Bubeck or any of his force. Half an hour had passed since the attack on the gates. The aspen trunk was still lying outside, surrounded by the bodies of twenty-eight Vuchten. They had been sacrificed, perhaps merely to establish whether or not the buttresses had been erected, and any further attempt to breach the fort before nightfall seemed now to have been abandoned.

Three nomads, including the man in the gatehouse, had died in the attack; several had sustained serious wounds. They had been taken, with the rest of the wounded, to the barracks by the northeast gates, where women had been appointed to look after them.

The nomad chiefs were beginning to impose basic order. A handful of the most violent and uncontrollable slaves, most of whom had found jars of beer and liquor, had been bound hand and foot and locked in the prison.

Klay was alive; so was Segle. Tagart had been with her in the enclosure when word had come that the Flint Lord's woman had been found hiding in the residence.

He watched her being escorted to the stairway. She, perhaps, was the reason for the reckless savagery of the attack on the gates. And perhaps her presence in the fort explained the terrible gaze that had held Tagart helpless at the gatehouse window. For the nomads she represented hope: she was the key to deliverance.

Then there were the other hostages. They would add to Tagart's bargaining strength.

He left the dayroom, Fodich at his side. It was already getting dark. Cloud had spread across the sky: more snow was on its way.

In the gatehouse, Tagart picked up the paper cone and went to the window. The scene on the hillside had changed little. Other tents had gone up, and men were bringing more timbers from the mines.

The fire by the Flint Lord's tent was still blazing.

"Brennis Gehan! Brennis Gehan!"

At first, as before, there was no reaction. Then a man came out of the tent. It was the Flint Lord.

"Lord Brennis! We have your wife! We have her! She's alive!"

The Flint Lord seemed to be deaf. He turned and spoke to one of his soldiers.

"Lord Brennis! Lord Brennis! We have your lady! We have other hostages! Let us go and they will be spared! Lord Brennis! Give some sign that you hear! I am Shode, chief of the Waterfall tribe! We must talk!"

The Flint Lord had by now turned his back and was in earnest discussion with the soldier. The soldier pointed toward the mines and the Flint Lord nodded agreement. With that, he went back into his tent.

Tagart shouted until it was dark.

The tentflap did not move again.

2 Hewzane, as General of the Coast, divided his time between the seven outer forts. In winter he traveled from one to another by dogsleigh, which, although considered slightly indecorous, was quicker, safer, and capable of covering greater distances between rests than the usual slave-drawn sleigh. There were ten dogs in the team: sturdy, rough-haired animals bred for stamina and docility in harness. They pulled in a single long file, all but the leading dog wearing a withy muzzle, while Hewzane, seated in comfort under warm furs, flicked his whip and guided the light, elegant framework of the sleigh in a path that left two endless lines in the snow. On each side ran a pair of bodyguards; a fifth man went ahead of the dogs.

For the period of the campaign against the savages, Hewzane had opted to remain at Eartham, the first fort to the east of Valdoe. The demands of the campaign would weaken the Trundle; Lord Brennis had agreed that Hewzane should be on hand.

Soon after observing Valdoe's signals for Bow Hill, Hewzane had indeed been summoned to attend Lord Brennis and give advice, for Bow Hill was one of the outer forts and its defense the proper province of the General of the Coast.

On his way, Hewzane had seen with his own eyes the distress smoke coming from the Trundle. It had both alarmed and puzzled him, and, arriving among the soldiers on the hillside, he had been astounded to learn what had happened and to find Gehan in charge of a rash attempt to get back into the fort.

Gehan's mood had been such that Hewzane had felt it better not to criticize, and the attempt, predictably enough, had failed, whereupon Hewzane, after hasty consultation with the senior officer of the Vuchten, had offered his assistance. Using timbers from the mines, work had begun on a toster, or protective roof, which would cover the men when next they used the battering-ram.

Among the survivors of the uprising had been the mines Trundleman, Blene, who had managed to hide in one of the galleries. Blene was an expert, if not a genius, in the craft of joinery, and his flair for improvisation made him ideal for the work in hand. Hewzane had left him in charge, and gone to sit with Lord Brennis in his tent.

Gehan was distracted with grief and rage. He sat holding his sister's hand. She had been given a camp bed; her face, which Hewzane had formerly conceded to himself as pretty, even lovely, had been wiped clean of blood, leaving her complexion pale, blotched, and ugly. Her hair hung in damp strings. She fretted at her bandages, fidgeted continually, and was overcome by frequent fits of sobbing. As the day faded she grew quieter and more resigned and expressed a desire to sleep: Hewzane left the tent, to be followed shortly by his lord.

The Trundle, viewed for the first time from the outside by one denied access to it, seemed to Hewzane both magnificent and frightening. Set against the gray-blue of the snow at dusk, behind it the sweep of a lowering sky, the dead weight of its walls and towers soaked up the last vestige of daylight and gave back nothing. Here and there, glimpsed through cracks in the palisade, were twinkles of firelight, but they served only to emphasize the oppressive bulk of the fort, this structure that had been built to dominate an entire foreign land and bring it under control. That was the meaning of the word *Gehan*: control, continuing manipulation, exploitation; the Trundle, straddling Valdoe Hill, looking north to the vanquished land and south to the sea and the homelands, was the symbol and the embodiment of the Gehan name.

The soldiers had begun to settle the details of their comfort in this unexpected bivouac. What tents there were had been brought up from the mine-workings, from the wreckage of the slaves' quarters and from the smoking ruins of the village. There were only enough tents for the officers, though, and no timber could be spared. As a result the men were even keener than their leaders to breach the gates. The alternative was a freezing night in the open, hard enough when on the march, but intolerable when warm barracks were only a bowshot away. Meat, some of it already grimly roasted, had been brought from the village, and caldrons and cooking utensils had been salvaged from the slaves' kitchen and put to use, but there was not enough food to share among six hundred men, and Hewzane saw that many had already broken open their pack rations.

He removed, finger by finger, his kidskin gloves, and stood warming his hands at the fire. Beyond the flames, in the middle of the assembly, a space had been cleared for Blene and his carpenters, recruited from those soldiers who knew a little woodwork. With adzes and other tools rescued from the mines, they had prepared the members of the toster and now tenons and mortises and halving joints were being cut and tested before fitting the framework together. When finished, the toster would be twenty yards long and three across, a long, slightly pitched roof. Under it would be four files of men, to carry the battering-ram and the toster itself.

Hewzane pulled on his gloves: Gehan had emerged from the tent.

"How much longer, Hewzane?"

"An hour or two. Perhaps more."

Gehan looked exhausted. He had been chewing his lips; his cheeks were hollow, his eyes sunken, but Hewzane sensed that these personal and outward signs of distress had been occasioned solely by the harm done to Ika. As her brother, he was grieving and his anger was open. As Lord Brennis, the merciless extent of his rage had, by strength of will, been contained and kept ready for controlled use on those who had taken the fort. He had, it seemed, regained himself since the heated madness of the first attack on the gates.

"Come along," he said, and a way opened before them as they went to inspect the carpenters' work.

"Tell me about him."

"He is my husband."

"And you are carrying his child?"

Her eyes dropped.

"Why doesn't he care whether you live or die?"

She made no answer. Tagart studied her face; she was softly spoken and he had to strain to catch her replies. Her body slave, a motherly woman named Rian, seemed divided in loyalty between her mistress and the success of the rebellion. She had disclosed that Lady Brennis was pregnant, which made the Flint Lord's behavior even more difficult to understand.

Tagart had taken over the largest of the ground-floor rooms in the residence. Food had been brought and the lamps lit.

With the coming of night, he had shed the defeatism that had made his despair insufferable. The change had come suddenly. He had been talking to Correy, giving instructions for fires to be kindled and certain stores broached, when he realized that he had allowed himself to become diverted from his first aim. His experience in the gatehouse had unnerved him and made him less than himself, but now he was glad there had been no response to his shouts. He had been willing then to bargain with the Flint Lord, to exchange hostages for mere freedom, when what he truly sought was nothing less than the man's death.

Once this had been secured—though Tagart as yet had devised no way of bringing it about—there would be time enough to worry about Bubeck and about getting the rest of the slaves and nomads safely away from the fort. Perhaps, with their leader dead, the soldiers would lose both their direction and their taste for fighting. He did not know. Nor did he know anything of the habits and temperament of the man he had decided to kill, and that was why he had sent for Lady Brennis.

She was sitting on a cushion, her hands in her lap, her legs tucked inside the voluminous folds of a finely woven robe, pink and gray, the narrow edging down one breast embroidered white on black in an abstract pattern of birds and grasses. A ribbon of the same design held back her hair. She was wearing no jewelry; it had all been taken by the slaves.

"I am sorry if they hurt you," Tagart said, and she looked up defensively. "You must understand what this means to them."

Altheme said nothing. The bruises on her face were not serious. Only her composure seemed to have suffered, and she was doing her best to repair that. She had not deigned to ask Tagart who he was: she was trying, not very expertly, to give the impression that she regarded him, his questions, the rebellion, the whole upheaval of the Trundle, as impertinent vulgarities unworthy of her attention. Tagart felt himself losing patience with her. He had never encountered such a woman before. She bewildered him; he was unable to guess at, still less pursue, the line of interrogation that would tell him what he wanted to know.

"If you do not talk we will have to torture you."

She gave him a reproachful glance.

"In your place I would be worried," he said.

"In your place I would die of self-disgust."

He stood up, exasperated, and went to the window. If she were his woman, in the woods, at the camp, he would soon get the information out of her. These foreigners evidently allowed their women abnormal license: he could no more understand it than he could fully take in all the marvels of the Trundle and the Flint Lord's residence. The paintings, the furniture, the simple fact that this was a shelter that went up in the air, the casual, easy mastery that was manifested in every incomprehensible joist and panel: it was all beyond him; he had no words for it. Compared with this one room, the whole of his culture was clumsy and pathetic. And this woman was unlike any he had ever met. He tried to imagine her in the company of the Flint Lord, serene, languorous, amusing. And yet she was not a foreigner in appearance, for she was dark, like a nomad.

He put his hand on the window frame. The shutters were open, and he could see past the gate of the inner enclosure to the battlements, where two big clay caldrons were being heated on beds of glowing charcoal.

"Has he always lived here?" Tagart said, without turning round. "Or did he come from across the sea?"

"He was born in this house."

An answer at last. "Has the Trundle ever been taken before?"

"Perhaps."

"In his lifetime?"

"I have never heard of it."

"Does he have another woman he likes better than you?"

"You are impudent as well as stupid."

"Then tell me why he does not care if you are killed."

"I see how little you know about the Gehans," she said, with every appearance of pride, but Tagart knew his question had touched a raw place. "If Lord Brennis himself were your prisoner his men would ignore your demands. If they did otherwise he would kill them himself at the first opportunity, just as he is going to kill you tonight when he breaks down the gates, you and—"

Tagart did not wait to hear any more. Correy had called his name from the gatehouse: the second attack was about to start. Tagart snatched up his stormcoat and, pushing his arms into the sleeves, ran outside into the newly falling snow.

★ ★ ★

Soon after dusk one of Irdon's unit leaders, protected by a specially large shield, had tied the end of a long cable into a noose and dragged it to the aspen trunk. The savages had shot many arrows, at him and the cable, but he had retreated unharmed and the trunk had been safely and easily retrieved.

Gehan took a meal with Hewzane, Irdon, and a Vuchten commander, the senior man, named Speich. Now in his late forties, Speich kept his ash-blond beard and hair closely shorn. In the presence of superiors he was studiously correct, and allowed no expression of disapproval or disagreement to escape his lackluster, pale blue eyes. He had achieved renown among his men for his surgical, mechanical fairness: they feared and loved him in equal parts. He belonged to the "Garland," the inner circle of high-ranking officers whose loyalty to the Home Lord was beyond question. For the duration of the Brennis campaign he had been given charge of the whole Vuchten force.

"It will be as my lord desires," he said.

Persuaded by Hewzane, Gehan had decided to keep the Vuchten in reserve from now on and use ordinary soldiers to breach the fort. There was no possibility of failure: the toster would be effective, but there would perhaps be further casualties and the Vuchten would be better employed in rounding up and dealing with the enemy once the gates were down.

Irdon glanced at Speich and for an unguarded moment compressed his lips in annoyance.

"Yes, Irdon?" Gehan said. "Is there something you wish to say?"

"No, my lord."

"Then let us go and see how quickly we can be back in our beds tonight."

Gehan stood up and the meal was over. He led the way out of the tent—Ika had been moved to a warmer, more commodious shelter improvised from mine spars and skins—and saw the toster standing ready, sixty feet long, roofed with bark-clad planks, supported by twenty-five pairs of poles like the columns of a miniature but elongated pavilion. Blene had worked with impressive accuracy and speed. From conception to completion the toster had taken less than eight hours.

Snow was falling in small, busy flakes across the firelit clearing.

Behind him Gehan was aware of, but did not turn to see, Ika's shelter. He clenched his fists and felt a shiver ripple through him as Irdon shouted orders and the harsh responses came. Gehan had found his love too late and she had been snatched away. What they had left him only mocked her former self; golden Ika had been smashed and trodden into the ground. For her and for what he had missed his grief was a gulf that fifty lifetimes could not fill. All his work had been undone. The campaign, the months and years of planning, his enormous debts to the Home Lord and Bohod Zein, the memory of Gehan First, of his father, the hopes and aspirations, the sense of destiny that had burned in him with a clear flame, everything, everything had been turned to dross. Even the fort had been entered and violated, and with his own men he was going to do it further damage. And yet, far down in the abyss of his suffering, he felt the glow of an illicit twinge of excitement. It was as if, by losing everything, he had moved closer to the brink, the edge of the sea that had tempted him all his life.

The men had taken their places.

Irdon shouted "Forward!" and the unit leader at the head of the trunk repeated the order, using it to initiate the accelerating rhythm that would coordinate the men.

"For-*ward*! Ge-*han*! Ge-*han*! Ge-*han*!"

Gehan felt his blood stir as they all took up the chant and moved forward, away from the glare of the fires. He could still see the white-sprinkled roof of the toster and the men running beneath it, dark against the ground, heading for the greater darkness of the palisade. Beside him Hewzane said something he did not hear, for he felt himself being carried forward with the motion of his men. They were nearly at the gatehouse. Their chant had built into a run of irresistible speed: the end of the battering-ram would strike at the center of the gates with a momentum that nothing could withstand.

Above them an illuminated rectangle, window-size, suddenly appeared. A wooden chute was thrust forth, and behind it some wide-mouthed object was steadily being raised.

"The caldrons!" Hewzane said, but his words were buried by the crash of the impact and Gehan saw for himself the torrent of boiling lamp fat as it spewed from the chute and onto the men below. With the first screams of the scalded, a blazing brand was tossed from the window and the fat erupted in a writhing sheet of yellow flame that lit up the whole façade of the fort and residence: the palisade, the guard towers, the battlements crowded with white faces. The front of the toster had collapsed. It had been let down with buckled knees by burning men, men in flames, and he saw them trying to crawl out, trapped underneath by the weight of timber and the trunk itself, drenched with fire. So many had fallen that those behind could no longer maneuver the toster. They were unable to move, unwilling to come out and show themselves, for arrows were already thudding into the planks above their heads. Some of the soldiers at the front, their clothes in flames, had pulled themselves free and were rolling in the snow, away from the inferno of burning fat. As they came into view of the battlements they were shot, each man, with one, two, or at most three, powerful and accurate arrows.

Gehan stared at the debacle. Lurid flame illuminated the gates and he could see now that the battering-ram had made scarcely any impression on them. The fort was intact, invincible, unassailable, as conceived and constructed by Gehan Brennis First. The savages had discovered its secrets, found out how to work it, even down to the siege weapons, to the chute that carried boiling fat safely beyond the caldron-window and prevented the gatehouse from catching fire. They had, in the prescribed and regulation manner, delayed a few seconds before igniting the fat, thus giving it time to soak into the timbers of the toster and to liberally splash the soldiers' armor and clothing. They had turned the human and wooden debris under the gates into a hideous sort of wick. And they were still shooting his men.

"Withdraw," he said to Irdon. "Withdraw," and there came to his breath and almost found utterance a foul curse on Gehan First, on his father, even on himself, on all the Lords of Valdoe and all the Gehans of the Brennis line.

They had built the fort too well.

"Lord Brennis! Lord Brennis!"

"He won't answer," Correy said.

"Lord Brennis!" Even in the open, here on the battlements, the stench of the fat-smoke was overpowering and Tagart had to pause to wipe his eyes before shouting again. "Lord Brennis! You are the man we want! No one else! Come to the gates and surrender by dawn or we kill the hostages one by one! Starting with your wife!"

Below them the last of the soldiers had fled from the wreckage. The ground, dimly white, was strewn with bodies, the newly dead and the Vuchten who had perished in the first attempt, and among them were men who were still half alive, abandoned by their comrades.

"Lord Brennis! Listen to me!"

"He'll no more answer than he'll come at dawn," Correy said.

"What then?" Tagart said. "What will he do?"

"Let the hostages die. They expect to die anyway."

"And then?"

Correy shrugged. "He might try to make us waste our water with fire-arrows, that is if he doesn't care about burning down the gatehouse. Or he might decide on a tunnel. Or he might just do nothing. He can get all the supplies he wants from the villages."

Tagart looked out across the spiked tops of the palisade logs to the Flint Lord's position. The fires were still burning; the army was still waiting. In the clearing where they had built the shield, Tagart could see new activity. More timbers were being brought. He saw a soldier kneeling on a trestle, his arm rising and falling with the blows of a carpenter's hatchet, and, lagging behind each stroke, the sound of chopping reached the battlements.

"What are they doing now?"

Correy could not say.

3 The rasping and hammering continued into the night. As far as could be seen from the battlements, the Flint Lord's carpenters were assembling some sort of framework. It seemed to be about fifteen feet long, built of rectangular-sectioned timbers from the mines. No one knew what it was for, though a few of the slaves said it was an earth-moving machine for digging a tunnel. Others thought it was a winch to pull down a section of the palisade. Others still said it would be mounted on rollers and moved up to the gates, and in its shelter—the roof, if there was to be one, had yet to be fitted—soldiers with axes would cut through the hinge posts, fix cables, and back away, dragging the gates with them.

Tagart was by now entering a high, giddy state of exhaustion. It was as if he had been awake forever; he could not remember when last he had slept.

But he could not hope for rest just yet. First, an exact inventory of the food supply had to be taken. Closely rationed, there was enough to last for a month at most. Tagart ordered all the food and live animals to be brought to the residence and its grounds and placed under guard. Next he inspected the reservoirs. There were six, wooden-sided pits lined with clay and covered with boards. Each held seven or eight tons when full, but in the last few days, the slaves had told him, the supply had been allowed to run down and now perhaps ten tons remained in all. In addition there were two dewponds, now frozen, and butts fed by pipes from the roofs of the larger buildings. Several of these butts had been smashed by the slaves. Those still intact were emptied and their contents added to the reservoirs, which, like the food, were put under guard.

Next, with Fodich's help, he arranged a rotation dividing his force into three equal shifts which would take it in turn to sleep. That done, he made sure that at all times, and at both gates, caldrons of lamp fat would be kept heated in readiness for further attacks. Finally he organized lookouts for the guard towers, and, as a last act before going to the residence for a meager meal and sleep, he put a man on the signal station to watch for Bubeck.

Bubeck had been separated from the other five prisoners and left in the snow, his ankles tied to his wrists. It was night; he was behind some tents or shelters and could not see the Trundle from here.

The other five were all slaves. At the village they had told the soldiers everything they knew. He himself had kept silent.

The massacre on Levin Down had been so rapid, so controlled, that nobody had known what to do. He and the rest of the force had counted on hiding in the woods. They had thought they would be safe.

He could not rid his mind of the pictures of irresistibly advancing armor and the beast-faces of the soldiers' masks. They had seized him and dragged him to the bottom of the hill where the Flint Lord had been waiting.

Since then he had been tortured twice. He had refused to agree to their demands. They had beaten him and he could no longer feel anything below his waist. His right wrist was broken. His breath was sliced into narrow gasps and he knew a splinter of rib was making him bleed inside. And now the soldiers were untying his bonds again and he was being helped along, his bare toes scraping the ice, through a corridor of tents and men and casually inquisitive glances.

They brought him to a warm fire by a tent where, seated on an upended log, was the General, Hewzane, the thin, fastidious man who had questioned him before. Snow was hissing into the flames; in the background were sounds of scrapers and sandstones.

Bubeck fell when the soldiers let him go and lay with his face near Hewzane's boots. One of the boots slowly came toward him and touched him on the collarbone. His shoulder was grasped and he was turned so that he could see Hewzane's patient, mockbenevolent smile.

"Have you reconsidered?"

At once Bubeck remembered his disdainful voice, associated it with the pain he had received.

"Will you speak to Shode and tell him to surrender?"

Bubeck shook his head doggedly.

"He must open the gates eventually. The longer he refuses, the harder it will go with him. You will be doing your people a service." He smiled. "I have heard they are counting on you to save them."

He stood up and passed out of sight, walking round Bubeck in a circle. "Do you hear the carpenters? At daybreak we shall take the fort back whether you cooperate or not. If you do as we ask, you will save the lives of your friends. If not, they will die. Which is it to be?"

Hewzane resumed his seat on the log and waited, the fingers of his left glove beating a slow tattoo on his knee. Behind him, beyond the tent, the carpenters were still at work. Bubeck did not know what they were making. He could hear a voice issuing instructions, a voice like Hewzane's, foreign, effete. None of the words could be made out.

"Are you sure you have nothing to say?"

Bubeck remained silent. For the first time, he knew that he was dying. General Hewzane, the fire, the sound of the sandstones, were receding; his thoughts were already far away, in another year, in a summer under the trees when he had been young and had known nothing about the world. When the soldiers had dropped him he had felt a great pain in his chest and now his life was leaking away. Nothing Hewzane said was important. He heard him speaking again, and the anger in his voice was no longer concealed.

"As you prefer. You have two hours to change your mind."

And then, addressing his men, he said: "Take him away."

Tagart was asleep at last. He dreamed he was walking by the stream with Bubeck, but this was a Bubeck whose face was whole and unscarred. Tagart advised him to cross. Bubeck stepped onto the bridge and suddenly the water reared up. The water was fire and Bubeck was trapped and drowning in its center, his features melting. Tagart shrank back toward the alder copse, unwilling to help him, afraid for his own safety, and he saw Bubeck's head and body become a blinding glow of light, brighter than the sun, unbearably brilliant.

Tagart woke up, shivering, feeling empty and sick. He remembered where he was—on the floor of the Flint Lord's own chamber, lying on rush matting, Segle beside him. They had tried the strange, elevated bed, but found it uncomfortably soft, so had removed its covers and made their bed on the floor.

A lamp was still alight. The shutters behind it were of pale wood which cast a yellowness into the room, softening Segle's face. She was sleeping soundly, her mouth open a little, an arm thrown across his neck. Her lashes were long and thick, her nose small, her ears neatly formed and partly hidden by her hair. Tagart caught himself studying her critically, comparing her with the Flint Lord's woman. In coloring they were alike, but Lady Brennis was older by a few years, more sensuous, and, about the eyes, she gave evidence of an understanding that Segle would never attain.

Gently he took Segle's arm from his neck and covered it with the furs. He shut his eyes. He had to rest, to refresh himself. Dawn was an hour away, perhaps less. With daylight there could be some fresh and more terrible onslaught. He would need to be alert.

Despite everything that was crowding his mind, despite his dream of Bubeck, he made himself relax, made himself shut down his thoughts and allow sleep to come. He was conscious of his woman's breathing, sharing her body warmth. Except for the gentle and random creaking of timbers, the fort was quiet. From time to time there was a sound from the enclosure, a goat's bleat or the lowing of cattle. Occasionally voices could be heard. Tagart began to grow drowsy. He had left a guard by the door, and from the landing came a few words spoken in low tones: the guard had changed.

Tagart drifted toward sleep. He did not hear the door slowly opening, nor did he hear the careful footfalls on the rush matting. But he sensed the pressure of a man's weight on the floorboards and felt air currents moving, and it came to him that there was no cause for the guard to change, and with the thought he was rolling aside. Klay's ax, a full-sized felling ax swung from the shoulders, flashing downward in a powered arc, missed his temple by a finger's width and slammed into the crumple of bedding.

The force of the stroke caught Klay off balance. Tagart grabbed hold of his leggings at one ankle and pulled with all his strength, reaching out with the other hand for the ax. Klay fell backward and struck his head on the sharp corner of the dais.

Segle was awake and screaming as Tagart, still acting as by reflex, took firm hold on the ax handle and rose to stand above Klay.

Although dazed by his fall, Klay knew enough to hold up his hands to ward off the blow. Anger filmed Tagart's vision and surged into a contraction of his muscles. Impervious to Segle's screams, he went up on his toes to give the ax its swing. All the weight of the preceding weeks and days and hours, like the weight of an immense stone blade, were bearing down on the flint edge, a hairline of intolerable pressure that could only be released in one place: in the head of his betrayer.

But, with the ax at its height, Tagart tottered and arrested his swing. He had overcome himself, and slowly he let gravity bring the ax to earth.

Then he saw that Klay was no longer holding up his hands. The eyes were blank: the sight had gone from them. Tagart let the ax go, knelt and lifted his shoulders. A wet gleam in his hair showed where the corner of the dais had split his skull.

Segle's screaming had become hysterical. She scrambled free of the bedding and put her head to Klay's breast, listening for his heart. She kissed his face again and again, prostrated herself across his chest, embraced him, put her face next to his, sobbing and calling his name.

Segle and Klay. The stories had been true.

For the moment Tagart could not absorb what Segle had done to him. On top of everything else, this was a trifle, unimportant. In a world where only fears came true and hopes were never realized, it was almost to be expected, of a pattern with the rest of it. But even as he stood watching them, he knew that, like bodily pain, this pain would not start with the making of the wound. It would come later.

She did not look up as he gathered his boots and stormcoat and went to the door.

"Take his body away," he remembered saying to someone on the stairs.

As soon as he stepped outside, he realized that the hammering from the hillside had ceased.

Overnight snow had lined the enclosures and laid a fresh mantle along the roofs and palisades. Snowflakes were still floating down in the twilight before dawn. It had become very much colder; Tagart's mittens stuck to the rungs as he climbed the ladder to the battlements.

"They've moved it from the clearing," said Correy, who was among those watching.

"I see it," Tagart said.

"Are you ill?"

"No."

The east was already pale, the ground beginning to brighten. At the front of the Flint Lord's position, a high scaffold or gantry could just be distinguished, its spars emerging from the night.

"They built it on its side," Correy said. "Now it's standing up."

"What is it?"

No one knew. Gradually, under their eyes, the growing daylight showed them what had been made: a framework of timbers, somehow reminding Tagart of a huge stick-doll such as children played with in the camp. It was a puppet, a man, facing directly toward the southwest gatehouse. He was seated on the ground with his knees bent, his head and body leaning back at an angle. A concave seat or basket gave him what seemed to be a face. Connecting the flanks to the thighs were what appeared to be bundles of ropes. The knees were joined by a stout crossbar, and the base of the framework had, by the use of a roller, been made adjustable for rake. The whole construction was fixed to the ground with eight heavy piles.

Two soldiers went to the rear of the machine where, set on the frame, was a windlass with a four-spoked handle on either side of the drum. They set to work. One whole section of the machine, the part corresponding to the man's head and body, slowly tilted farther backward and, when they had finished turning, came to rest in a nearly horizontal position, the basket-seat almost touching the drum of the windlass, which the soldiers locked in place.

The bundles between flanks and knees were not ropes at all. They were tendons, now stretched almost to breaking point by this act of turning which had reminded Tagart of drawing back an immense bow.

"It's a weapon!" Correy shouted.

"To your stations!"

Four more soldiers were approaching, carrying a man's body slung between them. They lifted it onto the seat; a block of wood was inserted between the windlass and frame, held there by the tension on the rope.

The corpse was that of an unusually large and heavy man. It hung there limply, head lolling back, arms loose, legs splayed. The darkness at the pubis formed an odd pattern and, even at this distance, Tagart could see that the corpse had been emasculated. He felt a foreboding of recognition. The chin was raised; the face was at an angle and could not be clearly seen, but he knew then that it would be scarred and misshapen, the left ear missing, the hair and beard tufted and sparse.

The Flint Lord came out of his tent, his breath like smoke. He was wearing the same gray cape, the same immaculate gauntlets and boots. He strolled to the machine. A soldier in dark gray took up an ax and went to stand by the windlass, awaiting a final order.

Standing beside the Flint Lord was another man in a fur cape. Tagart saw him raise a shouting-cone to his lips, and, in crisply enunciated words that penetrated the walls of the Trundle and reached the ears of those within, he delivered the message that was the prelude to the end.

"Slaves! Savages! We send you your savior!"

Rising smoothly to his toes, the soldier with the ax paused at the height of his swing to confirm his aim, and swiftly and resolutely brought the blade down on the block.

The flint edge cut cleanly through the rope. The tendons, released from their torment, contracted so quickly that the uprights could not be seen in the moment before they slammed against the crossbar. The basket's load was ejected with a bang. It sailed upward and toward the fort, a man's mutilated body, slowly turning, arms and legs flung wide. Tagart watched it clear the spikes on the gatehouse roof and saw it crumple against the ground, thirty yards inside the enclosure.

This too was a dream. It could not be true.

But the visage of the corpse, twisted by chance toward him, wore a death-grin that was too real for any dream.

And now, as the corpse lay in the enclosure, there was no reassuring white light to consume the horror of Bubeck's death.

This flesh, propelled over the battlements as a grisly and symbolic warning, this was how the Flint Lord dealt with a man who had been revered, a chief, the choice of the Sun; and by this act he had announced the same summary fate for all those inside the fort.

4 The second projectile followed in a few minutes, when the cut end of the rope had been refastened and the drum rewound; but this time the load was the body of a living man, who survived just long enough after impact to gasp some unintelligible phrases. Four more living men followed one another at short intervals, thrown by the machine in paths of varying accuracy. One fell short; one struck the palisade and tumbled back into the ditch; two found their way over the battlements. Then, after a delay, corpses, both of men and women, the naked bodies of those slaves and nomads who had died on Levin Down, were hurled into the enclosure.

There was pandemonium. As each new body landed there were fresh cries from the slaves and many of the nomads, who had deserted their posts and wanted to risk their chances on the hill. However, as soon as Bubeck's body had been thrown over, a large contingent of soldiers had taken up a position on the northeast side of the fort, commanding the other gates. Despite their presence, a mob of slaves tried to open these gates anyway, and were only dissuaded by the rest with the use of force. And unknown to Tagart, a party of seven slaves on the eastern battlements found some rope and lowered themselves to the ground. They were seen, chased by three teams of soldiers, and clubbed down among the thorn scrub. Then their bodies were added to the pile waiting to be loaded onto the machine.

Besides the hostages and the hundred wounded in the barracks, there were just under three hundred people inside the fort. Over half were nomads; those from the Water Spirit were the most loyal to Tagart, who was doing everything possible to bring the slaves back under control.

They were going wild. Word had spread that spells had been cast on the bodies, that they were diseased, and, such was their fury to get out, a prolonged struggle took place at the southwest gates, directly opposite the Flint Lord's main position. The buttresses were thrown aside; the slaves clambered into the gatehouse and raised the locking-grid. They were fighting to open the gates themselves when it was realized that, for some time past, the bombardment had ceased.

Someone called out from a guard tower. The machine had broken down.

"How long will it take to repair?" Hewzane said with acerbity. The whole effect of the bombardment, which had been his idea, was threatened by the incompetence of Blene and his gang of bunglers.

Blene was working with his men. He did not trouble to answer.

"Answer me or Lord Brennis," Hewzane said. "How long will it take?"

"Not long."

Blene jumped down from the vurfer. One of the six great bundles of tendons had snapped near its point of insertion in the fixed part of the frame. As Hewzane watched, Blene's men continued to strip the broken bundle and prepare another.

"It's the cold," Blene said, pulling on his gloves. "We did our best to keep the tendons warm."

The design was Blene's: he had based it on those he had seen in the homelands, siege-engines for flinging rocks and fireballs. But here, Hewzane had no wish to do needless damage to the fort, and so he had hit upon a novel way of achieving his ends. Gehan had readily consented, leaving Blene and Hewzane to work out the details.

From the five prisoners who had talked, Hewzane had ascertained that the savages in the fort were relying on the chieftain, the sixth prisoner, to save them. This man had been apprehended, partly by shrewdness, mainly by luck, in the thick of the fighting on Levin Down. He had expired under interrogation. After his body had been suitably prepared and thrown over the palisade, he had been followed to the vurfer by the other prisoners whom, as punishment for their loquacity, Hewzane had left alive.

During the night, teams of soldiers had brought the corpses from Levin Down. Other teams had been sent to local villages to procure, among other things, a supply of long tendons. The vurfer's propulsive force, Hewzane admitted, had been estimated with commendable skill, but Blene's performance had otherwise left much to be desired. His shooting had been deplorable. To panic the slaves still more, Hewzane had wanted all the bodies landed in the same spot, on the roof of the little altar house where the Trundle slaves were allowed to hold their services. Nonetheless, the exercise had almost succeeded, as shown by the attempted escape of a few defenders from the eastern battlements, when, infuriatingly, this interruption had come.

"You'll pay for this, Blene," Hewzane said, and returned to the shelter, where he had left Gehan sitting at Ika's bedside.

They both turned toward him as he entered, Ika with the uncertain expression and raised face of the newly blind, Gehan with an almost furtive look that Hewzane had never seen before.

"Well, Hewzane?" Gehan said, naming him for Ika's benefit. He rose to his feet. "Well? What was it? What made them stop?"

Hewzane explained.

If not quite pleasing to Gehan, the news did not upset him greatly; it seemed instead to confirm him in some other course which he had already been considering eagerly. "Come with me," he said, taking Hewzane's elbow. Once outside, he began talking rapidly. He expressed the view that the bombardment could no longer succeed. Now that it had been interrupted, he felt, the savages would be able to recover their morale. The cumulative effect had been lost. Other tactics would be needed to get them out of the fort and avoid the deadlock of a siege. He suggested calling to their leader, Shode. The soldiers would offer to withdraw, and would indeed do so, allowing the defenders their freedom. Having left the Trundle, hindered by their wounded, they would of course be pursued and overtaken. Those who were able-bodied would be captured and returned to the slaves' quarters; the rest would be dispatched as worthless.

The idea, although dishonorable—in that it recognized the savages as equals who could be petitioned—was interesting, but behind Gehan's words Hewzane sensed something more. It was as though his concern for the fort had been subordinated to an ulterior purpose. And so it proved.

"I want the man who blinded my sister," Gehan went on. "A slave. She doesn't know his name, but he was a peddler, taken in the Village just after Goele. Rald knows his face. If they give up the man, we'll say the rest can go free."

Hewzane was nonplussed. The implacable will that Gehan had displayed only the previous evening, the ability to keep his emotions in check, had, it seemed, been dealt a decisive final blow by the incident of the toster. During the night, Hewzane had watched his grasp on reality weakening still further. Over the past months he had become increasingly irrational. He had been subject to violent fluctuations in mood. His attention to detail had at times become obsessive; at other times he had maintained a lofty indifference to particulars, leaving his officers to arrange everything, careless of the extravagant cost of importing mercenaries from the Home Lord's army. The signs had been there, long before the campaign, even long before Hewzane's commission, and they had been observed not only by Hewzane, but by those abroad who were students of the island country and the wealth it promised, students who viewed with disfavor the independent turn taken by Brennis Fourth. Then there was the question of Ika, the unhealthy rumors that had been circulating. Since her arrival, Gehan's sanity had been eroding ever more quickly, and now, perhaps, with the events of the preceding day, he had come to the very borders of madness.

"See to it, then, Hewzane."

"Very good, my lord." He signaled to a man nearby. "You! Fetch me the shouting-cone!"

Lady Brennis shuddered and tried to avert her face.

"Tell me!" Tagart said, and turned her chin so that her eyes were looking into his own. Her whole body was trembling; her composure had crumbled at last, unable to withstand this latest blow.

"Yes!" she cried. "They slept together. He's in love with her and he's insane!"

They were upstairs in the bedchamber where Lady Brennis and Rian, her body slave, had been confined. Tagart had run to the residence from the crowd in the outer enclosure. Although no one there knew anything about the Flint Lord's sister, Klay had been recognized from the General's description as the man the Flint Lord wanted. But Klay was dead and his body wrapped in furs, and no answer had yet been given.

Tagart went downstairs and started across the enclosure. Since the first hours of the siege, since fearing that Bubeck might not come, his mind had been almost permanently engaged in trying to solve the intractable problem which had its roots in a single fact: by shutting the gates, the nomads had cut themselves off from the outside world. The soldiers were free to draw on the resources of the countryside around them; they could change their position as they wished: they had no fixed or vulnerable point. In order to get at and kill the Flint Lord, these circumstances would have to change.

Tired and dispirited, he had tried again and again to arrive at a plan that might work, and every time he had failed. But he had never given up a glimmer of hope that Bubeck might come after all, and so the bleakness and finality of his failure had not confronted him in all its force. Only when he had seen Bubeck's body had he been compelled to accept the truth. It had shaken him and left him unable to think.

Tagart climbed into the gatehouse and took up the paper cone. The General was still standing by the machine, awaiting a reply.

This was the nomads' first and, perhaps, only chance. If Tagart wasted it, if the siege were allowed to develop to its inescapable conclusion, he knew that he and he alone would carry the blame: he alone would have committed the whole nomad nation to oblivion. It had given him its best warriors, the young men and women, and he had brought about their downfall. Half were already dead, heaped there in the enclosure or by the Flint Lord's machine. Those who had not joined the fight, those who had stayed behind in the winter camps, were the dependents, the children who could not look after themselves, and the old people who would be unable to breed a generation to replace the one he had destroyed. Unaided, they would linger for a time, like the prisoners in the fort, besieged by the forest, and one by one they would die. And although some of the children might survive, there would not be enough of them to maintain the old ways, and they too would eventually disappear.

Their future rested with him. If he ruined this chance, as he had ruined everything till now, it would be the end.

In all his life Tagart had never before recognized defeat. The elders had taught him their version of courage, a blend of tenacity and honor. He saw now that they knew nothing. They were innocents, like himself. The scale of their code was dwarfed by what was happening here; the Flint Lord was not an enemy that they would understand. He was a colossus, beyond evil, beyond humanity, beyond even the brain and body of one man. Somehow, among the villages and their fields, a monster had been spawned that might never be stopped.

His men served him, not for love, not for the respect that was all the reward the hunters ever craved, but for payment. If he was challenged by a man who could pay more, they would transfer their allegiance without a qualm; and, if that new master fell sick and died, they would go to whoever could pay them, and spit on his memory. These were the men who had built the machine, who were fitting new tendons, and one of them, their general, was standing there and waiting for an answer.

Tagart raised the cone. "General! General! It is Shode!"

"Do you have the culprit?"

"We do!"

"I fear treachery," Gehan said. "If I do as you suggest, there will be three of them, counting the prisoner, and two of us. I shall be in danger."

The savages' leader was insisting on several conditions before giving up the guilty man. He had asked for the soldiers by the northeast gates to be recalled to main company, and this had been done. He had then stipulated that the man was to be received by Gehan himself, alone and unarmed. He would be brought by the leader in person, also unarmed.

Gehan had refused this condition; it could have no object but to expose himself to attack. He had consulted Hewzane and Speich, the Vuchten commander. Hewzane had suggested a compromise: that each principal should be accompanied by a deputy. Gehan's would be Speich, an expert in close combat.

They were standing at the edge of the camp, the vurfer behind them; Blene had finished the repairs.

Impatient as Gehan was to apprehend the man who had blinded Ika, he had yet to lose either his caution or his common sense, and he found Hewzane's attitude quite inexplicable. They were very much in control: he saw no reason to yield to the savages' demands.

"But, my lord," Hewzane said. "If we refuse them this, they will not give up the man and your strategy will fail."

Gehan studied him, and Speich. It was almost as if they wanted him to put his life at risk.

"Your argument is absurd," he said. "Tell them to send the man at once or the offer is forfeit."

Gehan could see faces at the battlements, in the gatehouse, and someone was in the nearest guard tower, leaning on the parapet and looking down. They had all been watching. Two of the savages had lowered a rope ladder and brought the guilty man across the snow, leaving him at a point that was out of range of Gehan's and their own archers. Two soldiers had then gone to collect him.

Gehan would give them no mercy. Their insolent presence on the battlements, the proprietary way they had taken over the fort, affronted him beyond measure. The Trundle was his inner house, and they had besmirched it, smashing and wrecking and killing like the animals they were. These alone were crimes enough; but they shrank to nothing beside what had been done to Ika. And now this. A corpse.

"He is the man," Rald said.

Gehan tried to calm himself. "Hewzane," he said. "We have wasted enough time on these vermin. We must get back into the Trundle."

"I agree, my lord. We'll withdraw at once and allow them to escape."

"No!"

"They have kept their part of it, my lord. We can pretend to do the same."

"Their chief has shown himself a liar. He cannot be trusted. They will leave the fort on my terms, not his."

"But—"

"Blene. Can you make fireballs?"

"We have enough netting," Blene said. "And some straw."

"Lamp fat?"

"Pig fat. We got it from the villages last night."

"Send for boulders. We'll burn down the gates."

"Yes, my lord," Blene said, and made as if to leave.

"One moment." Gehan gestured at the body of the peddler. "This is to be our first fireball."

Gehan went to Ika's shelter and let the entrance flap fall behind him. She turned her face; he crossed to the bed and reassured her with a touch of his hand. She put her own hand on his and held it to her breast.

"Stay with me."

"Just for a little." He sat down.

"Have you got him?"

"He's dead."

"Dead?"

"Listen to me, Ika. We're going to take the fort back now. It may not be safe here. I want you to take Hewzane's dogsleigh and go with Rald to Eartham. Will you do that?"

She nodded.

"I'll send a man to bring you back."

She transferred his hand to her lap and made a chaplet of it, counting the fingers over and over again as if they were the prayer beads the villagers used in their supplications to the gods of earth and sky. Her head was wound with a new sheepskin bandage; her mouth, still the soft and voluptuous mouth he remembered, was moving in a silent petition. Was it only two nights ago? How different she looked now! And yet, the savages could not take away what had been. He had filled her; their union deserved to bring forth golden offspring. A son, a child to vie with Gehan First!

"What will you do with me?" she said.

"What a strange question!"

"Will we be together again?"

Gehan extricated his hand and began to rise. "We will be together always."

"As we were?" she said, anxiously lifting her face.

He kissed her lightly. "I must go now, Ika. Don't be frightened."

5 Ten tons of water: at two pints a day each, the supply would give out in less than a month. And each bucket being poured into the leather tank, bucket after bucket brought by human chain from the reservoirs, held one man's water for a week.

Everyone knew it. Very soon, the chain would break and the slaves would try to get out again. They had been quiet for a time, pacified by the hope that the Flint Lord would keep his promise to withdraw, until Klay's body had been set on fire and thrown from the machine. He had hit the gates and lain there, burning.

The slaves' panic had then been rekindled. Even before the first fireball landed there was yet another attempt to break out, restrained by violence. Then the slaves had been made to join the nomads in the work of preventing the gates from catching fire.

The ditch surrounding the palisade was nine feet deep: the two gatehouses were the prime targets for fire attack. This had been foreseen by those who had equipped the Trundle, and among the siege-goods stored under the battlements, Correy led Tagart to a contrivance which consisted of a collapsible frame supporting a large tank made of waterproof ox hides sewn together with seal-skin. A leather hose led from the front of the tank, near the ground, and to this fitted a pan-shaped box drilled on one face with many small holes.

When assembled, the tank occupied the best part of the floor-space in the gatehouse. The hose, fed out of the slit in the wall, could be maneuvered by means of a hinged rod. Where the hose joined the tank there was a tourniquet to shut off the flow of water.

Tagart had left Correy in charge of directing the spray onto each fireball as it arrived. Made of chalk boulders covered with netting and stuffed with straw and wood and fat-soaked leather, the fireballs were coming at regular intervals, loaded with smooth efficiency onto the machine. The ax fell; the throwing-arm slammed against the crossbar; the blazing ball was launched in a roaring trajectory and fell against the gates, or against the palisade, rolling back into the ditch where it burned uselessly, or fell among the wreckage of bodies and timber left by previous attacks.

It was inconceivable that the Flint Lord was unaware of the low state of the water supply inside his own fort. As Correy had said, one of the purposes of a fire attack was to make the defenders waste their water and shorten the period of the siege. In effect the Flint Lord was saying to them: "Either let the gates burn or yield to me when you are dying of thirst." The slaves understood this only too well. At the rate at which the precious water was being passed up to the gatehouse and poured into the tank, it would not be much longer before they abandoned their places in the chain and made a final effort to break out. Once the chain was broken, the fire would take hold, and the nomads would have no choice but to follow the slaves.

Tagart had not believed the General's offer to withdraw. He had known it for what it was, and had tried at all costs to keep the gates safely shut. But with the rejection of his conditions and the failure of his attempt to get within reach of the Flint Lord, he had, after considering whether to send an impostor or to go himself, decided he had little alternative but to give up Klay's body in case the offer was, after all, genuine.

If the soldiers had withdrawn then, he would have risked trying to run. But the whole army was still in its original position. What was more, none of the soldiers had returned to the northeast gates. In this Tagart saw not an oversight, but the shape of the Flint Lord's plan to recapture the fort. He was leaving the way clear for a breakout on the northeast side. Once it had started, he would move some of his men round the palisade and pursue those who had escaped, while other soldiers would enter the enclosure and chase those still within out through the gates and into the main position.

Tagart was in the dayroom, discussing this with the other chiefs: they were agreed that the slaves would eventually succeed in breaking out. Unencumbered, making a break and trying to outdistance the soldiers was now the best and only chance of survival; but there were more than a hundred wounded to consider. Of these almost half were nomads. Some of the chiefs were in favor of taking the wounded nomads and leaving the wounded slaves, since their able-bodied comrades would have deserted them. Crow

said that, if the breakout came as Tagart anticipated, there would
be no hope of taking any wounded. Every man would have to
escape the best he could: better that some should live than all
should die. Any who could not walk, or run, for themselves would
have to be left behind. With luck, they might be allowed to live
as slaves. No more could be hoped for them.

Tagart wanted to, but could not, refute this appalling and
ruthless reasoning. He had become numbed by the horror that
bludgeoned him on all sides. After the meeting had broken up
and the chiefs had gone back to the enclosure, he stood for a
moment at the window, staring through the gateway of the inner
palisade at the double line of people, one line passing full buckets
forward, the other line passing them back, empty, to the reservoirs.

There were footfalls on the stairway behind him. Lady Brennis
and her body slave were coming down. Tagart had removed the
guard from the door of her chamber: the man had been needed
in the line.

She raised her eyes and glanced at him as she stepped onto the
floor of the dayroom, turning slightly to allow a bag, which was
slung over her shoulder, to clear the staircase wall. She had changed
her clothing. Instead of houserobe and slippers, Altheme was
now wearing a thick fur jacket, hat and mittens, leggings and
snowboots. Rian was also dressed for travel, and, like her mistress, was carrying a bag.

"May she fill it with food?" Altheme said.

Tagart nodded: Rian left in the direction of the kitchen.

"Do you want our help with the water?" Altheme said.

"No. Thank you."

She looked anxiously outside.

"Where will you go?" he said.

At that instant there came shouts from the enclosure. Women
were screaming. Tagart saw slaves throwing their buckets aside,
running to catch and overtake the first few who had seized the
initiative and begun the rush to the northeast gates. And with
them, among the stampede, he saw nomads. He began to recognize some of those who had been defending the gatehouse; and,
as Rian returned from the kitchen, he saw Correy and then Crow
running past.

He grasped Altheme by the wrist and followed.

★ ★ ★

Speich, the Vuchten commander, stood at the fore of his personal
Gray Unit and felt his stomach fluttering with the old sensation
he knew so well. It never changed. From the day of his first battle
at the age of eight, through forty years of bloody campaigns and
slave raids in the glorious service of the Home Lord, this feeling
was the truth and constant in his life. His palms were sweating;
he tightened the bone-studded fingers and knuckles of his right
gauntlet on the haft of his ax and prepared to meet the exhilarating
moment when he and his men would be working as one.

The fire attack had succeeded in flushing the savages out of
the far gates. Four hundred and seventy-five men, in two con-
tingents of twelve and seven units each, had encompassed the
walls of the Trundle and converged on the open gates; the larger
contingent, led at his own insistence by Lord Brennis himself,
was at this moment running down and recapturing the escapees.
From here, where three Vuchten units had remained to guard
the southwest gates, little of this battle could be seen, but flag
signals were coming from the lookouts and keeping Speich in-
formed.

The second contingent had fought its way into the enclosure
and now, as Speich watched, the southwest gates opened and a
stream of slaves spilled forth. They were scrambling over the
smoking debris of the toster, the corpses, the battering-ram, the
heap of burned-out fireballs, being chased by the soldiers, driven
out of the fort and into the crescent-shaped formation which had
Speich at its center.

The slaves were coming closer.

"Units!" Speich shouted. "As ordered and detailed! Pre-pare!"

After the losses at the village and in the attacks on the gates,
Hewzane had given the commanders orders to regroup their teams
and units. Fifteen units of Vuchten and seven of other men remained. The heaviest casualties had been among the common
recruits from the homelands, then among the men of the Brennis
barracks. The Vuchten had escaped lightly. They now outnumbered the other soldiers by more than two to one.

Along the curve came the soft sound of visors shutting.

"Ad-vance!"

The slaves, with a few savages, comprised mainly the old,
women, and the walking wounded. They made little resistance.

In a short time, all had been captured and bound hand and foot, strung together ready for sorting. Some would go back into the slaves' quarters. The rest would be destroyed. Meanwhile, the fort had been made secure and the Flint Lord's pennons were again raised into the wind.

Irdon, the Brennis commander, his breastplate smeared with blood, took off his helmet and put his hand to the back of his neck, twisting his head from side to side. He had led the seven units, four of them Vuchten, which had cleared the slaves from the fort.

"What are our orders now?" he asked Speich. "Do we go back into the Trundle? Or do we support Lord Brennis on the hill?"

According to the flagmen, Lord Brennis had nearly finished and did not need support. Speich gave Irdon a long, calm look. His stomach had not stopped fluttering: this was the moment. It had been delayed, delayed again, by the sea, by the snow, by the superstition of Brennis Fifth and his soothsayer, and by the wholly unexpected invasion of the fort. Since yesterday the plan had been restructured, the details revised, Gehan's inclinations kept on course, guided by the sure, lucid logic of Hewzane's mind. The numbers had been carefully estimated, the casualties monitored and taken into account. On the hillside with Lord Brennis were eight units of Vuchten and four of his own men. The ratio here, at the main position, was the same: six to three. And it was a Vuchten unit that had stayed behind in the fort to secure the gates.

Irdon was waiting for an answer.

"You are my prisoner," Speich told him quietly.

"In there! In there!"

Half running, half kicking their way downhill through the snow, they were trying to reach a broad, piebald expanse of gorse. They had been seen by the soldiers and were too far from the bottom of the hill to do anything now but hide and wait for night.

Fodich had nearly reached the first bushes.

"Into the middle!" Tagart shouted.

Beside him, just keeping up, were Altheme and Rian. They were at the rear of the group of eight or ten who had managed so far to evade the organized, systematic pursuit which had already claimed at least half of those who had escaped from the fort. Tagart had seen Crow being run down and killed, and he had looked back to see Segle captured and led away.

The soldiers, three hundred of them, had divided into a dozen parties. Each party, alone or in conjunction with others, had concentrated on one part of the hill, for the escaping nomads and slaves, on leaving the gates, had fanned out. Most had gone directly northeast, making straight for the forest. Few of these had succeeded, for they had attracted the largest number of soldiers. Tagart himself had turned left at the gates and started westward.

The wind had strengthened and a near-horizontal blizzard was blowing from the northwest. Far below, in the safety of the valley, the fields of the settlement were blank, immaculate, their boundaries traced by white-drifted lines of spidery hawthorns. Between the fields and the fort, descending by steep scarps and slopes, the hill was patched with scrub.

Rian stumbled and as he helped her Tagart looked back once again. The soldiers were less than three hundred yards away now, a party of twenty-five in the brown armor of the Brennis barracks, carrying spears and axes. Behind him he thought he glimpsed ten or a dozen more, clad in black.

"Quickly! Into the middle!"

Heedless of the sharp green spines, they pushed branches aside and plunged after the others. The bushes were old and thick, in places towering above their heads, grudging, obstructive, barring their way with strong, springy arms densely dressed in painful prickles. Near the ground, where they had lost their needles, the branches were bare and peeling and snagged at their feet.

"Spread out!" Tagart cried. Ahead of him, the others had broken a passage through the gorse. They were making it easy for the soldiers to follow.

After struggling another fifty yards or so he judged that they had reached the middle of the thicket. In one hand he was holding an ax, which he had snatched up as he had left the fort. With the other hand he took hold of Rian's sleeve. "Get down on the ground. Down there. Don't move." He went on another few yards and called to her mistress, a little way to his right. "Now you! Get down!" He found a place for himself. "Everybody! Get down!"

As far as he could tell from their voices, the soldiers had stopped

at the edge of the thicket and were debating what to do. He
clenched his fists and shut his eyes, praying that they would be
called away to search some more profitable spot. It was after
midday. In two or three hours darkness would come and they
would be safe.

One of the voices was raised in a shout.

"Altheme! Altheme! Altheme!"

"It's him!" she said. "My husband!"

Tagart knew then that the soldiers would not be leaving. Others
would be called; they would surround the thicket and move inward. He had exchanged one trap for another, the Trundle for
the gorse.

But, in making the exchange, he saw that he had suddenly
earned the chance of one last, desperate attempt to achieve his
goal, to redress in some measure all that had been sacrificed. His
own life was now finished. It had finished with Bubeck, with
Klay, with Segle. He would die here on the hill. But the manner
of his death could redeem the futility of what he had done to his
people. If he remained strong, if he took his chance and got close
enough, he might yet kill the Flint Lord.

"Altheme! Altheme! Come out!"

Tagart crawled among the branches until he could see her face.
"You must go back to him," he said. "There is still time."

"Altheme!"

"Do you order me to?"

"I cannot," Tagart said. "You are free to choose."

"Then I choose to stay."

"You know what will happen to you?"

"Yes." She turned toward the place where Rian was hiding.
"Rian! There is no need for you to die."

"No, my lady. I am free now. I'll stay with you."

"Altheme!" the Flint Lord shouted. "Altheme! We are going
to burn the gorse! I have sent to the Trundle for fire! Come out
while you can!"

Despite the snow, the bushes and the ground beneath were
like tinder. With the wind blowing so strongly, everyone in the
thicket would be burned alive.

"Would he burn his heir?" Tagart said.

"He thinks it is not his."

Tagart met her eyes. "What do you mean?"

"It does not matter now."

"Tell me."

"If you wish." Quickly she explained about Bohod Zein, the agent from the homelands.

"Yet you were with child before then?"

"I was."

"Could he be convinced? Could Rian convince him?"

"It is possible."

"Then she must try."

6 "And he says she will be released after dark, my lord, and allowed to go back to the fort, if you withdraw now."

"Has he threatened to kill her?"

"No, my lord."

"But he might, if I make a move. Is that it?"

"I cannot say, my lord."

Gehan was torn between anger and concern for the child Altheme was carrying, a child which Rian had halfway persuaded him might be his own. A son! He remembered the moment in his chamber when he had struck Altheme. She had told him then, and he had not believed her.

He cared little for her anymore; but if it were true—if she were bringing him an heir—he could not risk her life.

"What made her go with the savage?" he said to Rian. "Why was she running away?"

"He took her hostage, my lord."

"And you? Why did you run?"

"I am my lady's body slave."

With a curt gesture at Rian, Gehan turned to the leader of his black-armored bodyguard. "Tie her up. When we've finished here, she can go back to the slaves' quarters."

"But my lord!" she protested. "He said I was to—"

She was silenced; Gehan stood glaring at the thicket. Anger had made him take personal charge of his men to pursue the savages on the hillside. It was his first reaction now. He wanted to fire the gorse; but he allowed to himself that Altheme might get caught by the flames. The savages had, by implication, threatened to harm her if he sent in soldiers to drive them out. But the alternative, conceding to their demands and leaving, could not be tolerated. Besides, the word of the savages' leader meant nothing. If Gehan withdrew, he would never get Altheme back. She would be killed and left here.

He had no choice.

"Flush them out," he said to the unit leader. "Kill any you find, but bring Lady Brennis to me."

The gorse thicket, sloping down in two directions across a crumbling scarp, was about a hundred and fifty paces across at its widest part, with an irregular outline like the coast of a dark, rocky island in a sea of white. At its edges were smaller islands, smaller clumps of gorse, but beyond them the ground was open, the surface of the snow humped with the suggestion of the tussocks below. The search had led Gehan and his men to the western part of the hill; the road to Apuldram and the southwest, its banks heaped with frozen slush, ran across the shoulder of land a little way above them.

"Look, my lord!" the unit leader said, before he had had time to act on Gehan's order. He pointed up toward the fort. Two units of Vuchten were descending. "Shall we wait for them, my lord?"

"Yes. We'll surround the gorse and close in."

Gehan watched the approaching Vuchten with satisfaction, his anger abating. Across the hillside, the exercise to catch the slaves and savages, which he himself had commanded, had been expertly and cleanly brought to its conclusion. Doubtless one or two slaves had managed to take refuge unseen; doubtless, in the zeal of the chase, one or two useful creatures had been inadvertently killed. On the whole, however, the invasion of Valdoe had been successfully dealt with, the rebellion quashed, the savages eliminated, the slaves restored to their proper quarters; and now the fort was again firmly in good hands.

Gehan smiled to himself. It seemed that the savages' force had consisted of the pick of the tribes from several, if not all, of the winter camps. The loss of these men would weaken forever the tribes of the whole country, and not just those in the south. There was every chance that here in Brennis, as in the homelands, the savages could be permanently stamped out.

Tomorrow, he decided, he would rally his men and march north as planned. Undefended, its warriors' bodies here on the hill, the waterfall camp could be completely annihilated. From there, if the weather and supplies allowed, the army would continue to the eastern camp and destroy that, and perhaps the western and northern camps also.

He reflected that, in some ways, the turn of events had proved more satisfactory than the original plan. Although the fort had been damaged and four whole units had been ambushed on the Bow Hill road, other casualties among the soldiers had been no worse than might have been anticipated in a straightforward campaign. Among the Vuchten, particularly, losses had been slight, which would reduce the burden of wound fees and death sums payable to the Home Lord.

From the military viewpoint, Gehan had turned the invasion to his advantage. The savages, the object of his campaign, could now be wholly exterminated; the work of forest clearance and expansion could begin unimpeded in the spring, and proceed without a check until the whole island was under cultivation and under his control.

These thoughts had occupied only a moment; but his mind darkened as he realized that not once had they dwelt on Ika. Compared with her loss this reckoning of wound fees was shameful and petty. Yet he saw now that this was the way he had been trained. Since boyhood he had been forced into the rigid military ideal, forced to dissociate himself from weakness, from his feelings, forced to prepare for the day when he became the Flint Lord. He had accepted the burden, embraced it, discharged his duty with diligence and skill, and in so doing had become a man split in two. His destiny, the heritage of Gehan First, called for single-mindedness; and he had striven continually and at great cost to himself to conform and to yield that which his duty demanded. He had left his feelings behind, drifting farther and farther from ordinary humanity. He had made himself deaf to the tiny whispering doubts which once had plagued him. Altheme was the personification of those doubts. In rejecting her and reaching for Ika, he had tried to close the chasm inside himself by denying its existence. But now Ika was destroyed and his need of her was over. He had transcended his dilemma: he was free. He was the master of himself, strong, enduring, like the hill, like the landscape and the climate of this land he had once imagined he could possess. He felt again the thrill he had known when watching the toster, and now realized that this was the most important part of him. It was the truth. It told him that the world, and all that was in it, were valueless compared with the reality and growth of his own spirit. To be free to cast away his heritage and all that was precious, to see it trampled and befouled, and not to care: this was a luxury sweeter than could be imagined.

His vision had suddenly cleared: he saw everything as it was. No longer would he be a slave of Valdoe. He would use Valdoe, as it deserved to be used, as an adjunct to himself. His duties would now be self-determined; no more would he chase the impossible phantoms conjured up by the memories of his father and Gehan First. Because it suited him, he would continue as Lord of Valdoe, and, if Altheme gave him a son, Valdoe would be bequeathed to Brennis Gehan Sixth.

She was in the gorse with the savages. He would get her out, with the help of the Vuchten units: they were now only a hundred yards away, approaching at battle pace.

Gehan stood his ground, waiting to speak to their commander.

Tagart had known from the first that the Flint Lord would not accept the terms he had set. He had wanted Rian's message only to delay the search and to stop the soldiers using fire, and to give himself more time to reach the edge of the thicket undetected.

His face was bleeding, jabbed and scratched again and again by the fierce spines. In his flight from the fort he had left his mittens behind, and his hands too were bleeding, making the ax handle sticky.

Close by, in the sound of the blizzard, he could hear voices. Each prick of the gorse, each moment spent negotiating a branch that had blocked his passage through the thicket, had spread fear into his body, and now he had to force himself inch by inch to crawl forward.

He moved aside another branch and saw that he had come to the last bush, exactly opposite the Flint Lord. For a few seconds Tagart watched him through the dark network of the gorse, his cape cloud-gray against the rising snowfield of the hill. He was not five strides away, and the way was open. The men in black armor, his bodyguards, were beside him, and Tagart was close enough to see their eyes and hear one of them hawk before spitting sideways into the snow. If Tagart moved now, if he burst through the last branches and ran, ax high, he would be able to fell him: with one blow he could kill the Flint Lord before his bodyguards had time to react. The Flint Lord's back was turned: he was looking up toward the fort.

Tagart edged forward to see what had attracted his attention. It cost him his chance; he had delayed and let the moment slip, for as he saw the Vuchten coming, the bodyguards moved stiffly into formation, a three-sided box surrounding their master and open at the front, and the back rank was between the Flint Lord and Tagart.

He watched the Vuchten drawing near. Again he saw the grotesque and sinister forms of their masks—their visors had been lowered and they were coming at speed, spears held ready. From the Flint Lord's men came a shout of recognition and welcome, and for that instant Tagart shared their belief that the Vuchten had come to help in the search for Lady Brennis. But before Tagart's dread had taken shape, his belief, like theirs, was twisting aside. The charcoal-gray breastplates and vambraces, the fur capes and leggings, the snow-caked combat boots kicking powder in the mechanical unison of their run: these were a preordained force, like an avalanche that could not be stopped by mere words and a shout of appeasing welcome. Their spears were not being lowered. They were coming on, ten yards from the Brennis soldiers, five, and from the expressionless beast-faces came a chant, a blood-chilling double chant of *Ge-han Ge-han Ge-han*, and then the Vuchten were colliding with the brown-armored men in a confusion of spears and screams. Gray and brown armor thudded together; spears were locked and raised to the sky, falling, drooping, as brute strength overpowered brute strength or from behind came an enemy's crippling thrust. Axes were being brought into use, and stone hammers with flailing heads on loose thongs. Tagart saw a man's helmet struck and stoved, his skull smashed. He saw a gray soldier run through, the flint spearhead puncturing his cape and backplate with a creaking report and bulging the leather at his breast before the point broke through, bringing with it a vivid gush as from a burst bladder. Where the browns were alone they were falling one after another to the grays, the Vuchten, who in numbers alone overwhelmed them; but where they were mingled with the blacks, the Flint Lord's bodyguards, wielding black-bladed axes and black spears, the fighting was so ferocious that even the Vuchten were intimidated, and gray after gray was going down.

Vainly Tagart searched among them for a glimpse of the man they were fighting over, but it seemed he had disappeared, swallowed up by the blizzard and the battle, the shouts and screams of pain and the clashing of wood and horn and stone. Then Tagart looked uphill and to the right. The Flint Lord, in his gray cape, holding a spear, had passed unnoticed between the fighting and the gorse and was now fleeing, staggering and struggling through the snow, putting yards behind him, making for the Apuldram road.

Before he knew what he was doing, Tagart had left the thicket and was running too, past the fighting men and on to the open hill. He felt the wind stinging his face. On his right was the darkness of the gorse; on his left the whiteness rising steeply to the fort. The battle was behind him. He fixed his eyes on the single figure ahead and with new resolve forced himself upward through the fresh furrow of the Flint Lord's tracks.

The snow here was deep and crusted and dragged at the legs, hampering progress, giving Tagart the advantage. He quickly began to gain, and as he gained he felt the shape of something evil inside him and the promise that it could be set free. His fear was forgotten. He let his ax swing wildly in compensation as he ran, keeping his balance, his boots finding the very pockets of snow and shade that had just been trodden by his prey: for this had become for Tagart a chase, the most important of his life, an ecstatic hunt to catch and in a frenzy of blood and elation to find release from the monster he had vowed to destroy.

The road was still a hundred yards away; the Flint Lord was laboring toward it as if toward an unattainable summit, every fourth or fifth step using the spear as a staff. In his movements he appeared to be stunned, uncoordinated, fleeing from the incomprehensible forces that had been unleashed below. He was veering away from the stench of betrayal that hung over the fort; he was toiling toward the road that Tagart knew would lead him to his ships. His army and power had been stripped from him, and now just his own flesh and sinews and a hundred yards of Valdoe Hill lay between him and the way to safety.

He paused to glance back at the battle and noticed Tagart for the first time, ten yards from him, following his tracks. He turned and halfheartedly made as if to climb again, seemed to change his mind and turned back, spear in hand, to face his pursuer.

Tagart sensed weakness. He was aware of the spear, but did not slow his pace. He prepared to swing the ax for the first disarming blow, to knock the spear aside, and in a rush, in a single impression before the collision, he saw the Flint Lord in close detail, his blood-blotched ermine tunic, his cape in the wind, his blond beard and disheveled hair, and his eyes: gray, remote, contemptuous, and in them alone Tagart saw that the weakness had been no more than a feint. And in a masterly, graceful movement, the exposition of years of weapons training and practice, the Flint Lord was floating backward and to the right. The ax missed its target and sliced into the snow, pulling Tagart forward. He tripped and went down, his face plowing into the crust of ice.

The spear hit him with the impact of a heavy, inconceivably thick bludgeon, in the back, below his left shoulder blade. It cut deep into his body before the blade twisted and was wrenched away.

His hands outstretched, his face rigid, Tagart rolled onto his side. He looked and through his agony saw the Flint Lord receding. He wanted to crawl after him, but everything tilted and ahead there was nothing but a gray sky streaked with snow. The streaks made the sound of the blizzard, piercing and cold, the remorseless breath of the Ice God, demanding Tagart's warmth, and slowly he felt his fingers taken by the snow and turned to crystal as a gift for the Moon. The winter was filling his body, pouring in through the breach in his back. He opened his eyes and was under water, under a white, limitless sea.

Then he raised himself above the snow and saw the cloud-clad figure of the Ice God, clambering over the wall of frozen slush at the roadside.

Tagart cried out and let his face fall forward.

7 During the retaking of the Trundle, Hewzane had followed Irdon's units to the northeast gates. There he had lingered, at a distance, until the fort had been cleared and made safe.

From the roof of the residence he had watched Speich capturing Irdon's men. He had also watched the progress of Gehan's exercise on the far side of the hill. Gehan himself had been lost to view when Hewzane had judged that most of the slaves and savages had been killed or returned in bonds to the Trundle, enabling the signal—green pennons hung from the guard towers—to be given for the Vuchten to attack the Brennis soldiers.

Two Vuchten units, led by the commander who was second in authority to Speich, had been briefed to shadow Gehan and wait for the green pennons. The other Vuchten were to take their lead from these two units. Their orders were to capture rather than wound, and wound rather than kill, all the Brennis men, except Gehan's bodyguard and those soldiers actually with him at the time of the attack. Gehan himself was to be unharmed: the Home Lord wanted him alive.

With the attack under way and the outcome assured, Hewzane went down to the main enclosure to inspect the captives. They had been tied together and herded into four groups in the shelter of the northwestern palisade. The snowstorm had worsened. Hewzane fastened the collar of his fur cape as he crossed the enclosure, Speich at his side.

Even this part of the operation had been meticulously planned by Hewzane and, in accordance with his orders, Speich's men were already processing the largest of the four groups, the slaves and miners. The healthy ones were being stripped, searched, and conducted to the slaves' quarters, which had been temporarily repaired. The injured were being assessed by the unit leaders and their fate decided. If they could walk and lift a small boulder they were deemed healthy. The rest were dragged or carried to the northeast gates, where, in full view of the other captives, they were being brutally dispatched by Vuchten with axes.

The second group, those savages who had either been left behind in the fort or brought from the hill, would be carefully examined and any potential slaves picked out. The third group, the Trundle freemen who had survived the rebellion, would be closely questioned. Any who showed a trace of loyalty to the Brennis Gehans would be put into the mines.

The last group, almost as numerous as the slaves, consisted of the vanquished and dejected Brennis soldiers. Those who could not be trusted would provide a useful source of further slaves; and the men of Hewzane's old command, in the outer forts, would be brought to the Trundle by false signals and given the choice between service in the barracks or at the chalk face.

Many slaves would be needed in the coming months. The Bow Hill workforce had been lost. The Trundle had suffered much damage. The mining schedule was behind: hundreds of essential timbers had been wasted and would have to be replaced. Tree-cutting in midwinter was a hazardous and time-consuming operation. Then, when the thaw came, there was a variety of other works to be put in hand, in accordance with the Home Lord's wishes. Concurrently with the program of forest clearance, new outer forts would be built, and these of course would need new roads, bridges, ferry stations. The villages could supply some of the labor, forced if need be, for the laxity with which the farmers had been treated hitherto was now a thing of the past.

So too with the savages. In a way, their unexpected appearance had not been entirely unwelcome to Hewzane. They had spared him the unpleasantness of executing Larr, his fellow general, who would doubtless have remained loyal to Gehan. They had also, albeit unwittingly, speeded the outcome of the Home Lord's design to win back the island country.

The original plot, known only to Hewzane and then to Speich, had planned to use the attack on the savages' camp to deplete the number of Brennis men. Then, on the return journey, well away from the Trundle and the outer forts, the Vuchten were to have turned on the other soldiers and killed them. In this way not only would Valdoe have been taken with the minimum disruption, but the lesser problem of the savages—rightly seen by Gehan as an obstacle to expansion—would have been solved at small cost, for Bohod Zein, who was not a party to the scheme, would be free to apply to Gehan as vigorously as he wished for the recovery of his debts. Bohod Zein's interests on the mainland were anyway too large for him to risk the displeasure of the Home Lord. The mortgages would be revoked, and Valdoe given a clean start.

The Home Lord's plan had been upset by the arrival of the savages, but his larger design had remained unhindered. Valdoe had been seized, the resident army crushed, and now, after the loss of so many warriors, the savages' camps were ideally vulnerable. In the next few days, Hewzane would launch a heavy force against them. The vermin, as Gehan had so aptly termed them, would be stamped out in their winter nests and never allowed to infest the island country again.

Of the sorry examples standing before him, in the second group of captives, Hewzane could see few who would make suitable slaves. Their leader, Shode, was not among them. Presumably he had been killed by Gehan's men. But Shode's woman, a girl of perhaps twenty, perhaps less, had been pointed out to the soldiers by some of the more garrulous and contritely toadying slaves.

"Bring her forward," Hewzane said.

Cleaned up, she might be amusing, and for a moment Hewzane toyed with the idea of sending her to the residence. But then, remembering what she was, a faint shiver of repugnance passed through him.

"Take her for your men," he said to Speich. "And pick out any others you think might be suitable."

The Vuchten continued with their work. Just outside the gates, the pile of bodies was growing. They would be taken down the hill later and left for the ravens.

The scene at the gates was having its expected effect on the other captives. Most of the freemen had renounced Brennis Gehan and were vowing undying devotion to the Home Lord who, through the heroic bravery of General Hewzane, had released them from lifelong and grinding tyranny. But some were silent, and among them Hewzane caught sight of Blene, one of the few Trundlemen to have survived. Blene's eyes were not drawn to the gates: they were instead following Hewzane and Speich as they moved along the line. Their expression bespoke hatred of Hewzane and loyalty to the old order. Hewzane sighed inwardly. Although, as a man, he disliked Blene, his talents were undeniable and would have proved useful in the months to come.

"That one," Hewzane said, pointing him out, "is to join the mine slaves." The thought of Blene toiling in the galleries tickled Hewzane's sense of irony and he smiled thinly. The smile vanished: Blene's technical knowledge would present a continuing risk of sabotage which could not be suffered to remain.

"No," Hewzane decided. "Take him out and kill him."

"Look there," said Speich, inclining his head toward the gates, where a Vuchten unit leader, one of the men detailed to capture Gehan, was making his way into the enclosure. He was alone. His weapons, his helmet, even his cape had gone; there was blood on his face.

Anxiety gripped Hewzane's heart. He and Speich went to meet the approaching man.

"I make no excuses," the unit leader said, when he had finished his story.

"Are you wounded?" Speich asked him.

"No, sir."

"Then go back and help your men."

Fifty Vuchten had been sent to capture Gehan, and they had failed. Forty-three, including their commander, had been killed or incapacitated in the battle with Gehan's bodyguards, who, together with a unit of Brennis soldiers, had allowed Gehan to make good his escape. All the bodyguards and soldiers had now been killed, but the damage had been done.

Gehan had been glimpsed running for the road to Apuldram, something which Hewzane should have foreseen and provided against: for there were loyal Brennis men at the worksheds and two ships in the creek, both seaworthy, and now, at midafternoon, the tide was high and on the turn.

Five of the Vuchten had already gone in pursuit. They would not be enough.

"Speich," Hewzane said. "Take your Gray Unit. Bring him back."

"I will," Speich said, and, scarcely pausing, he added: "My lord."

Plastered with snow on its windward side, the figurehead of the *Kormoran* nodded and rolled with the glossy black waves which, spumed and threaded with white, were being driven by the blizzard to break about the waterline and send spray over the deck and the icicle-hung rigging. The ship had turned into the wind: snow-blind, the jet and ivory head of the cormorant, fantastically styled with arched neck and hooked bill, had come to face the rough width of Apuldram Channel and the wintry salt marshes beyond. At the next mooring, riding its cable with the same measure but to a different time, a larger, less elegant vessel, the *Empire*, kept parallel company. Thirty yards of cold water separated them from the landing stages, where a big upturned coracle waited to be launched.

A wisp of smoke showed from the roof-hole in the main workshed. Everything seemed to be normal. Gehan hesitated no longer. He went to the door and threw it open.

Two men were inside, cross-legged on the floor, engrossed in some gambling game played with bone counters. They struggled to their feet and saluted him.

"Where is the harbor Trundleman?"

"Asleep, my lord. Our work is finished for today. We—"

"Get him at once."

The older man hurried outside. Gehan followed him to the door and yet again scanned the road from the fort. It emerged from the trees two or three hundred yards away and to the left, and in a gentle curve arrived at the precinct of the worksheds. The main shed was nearest the water, with removable panels along one wall to give access to the repair shop and storage loft. Next to it was a general storehouse, a seasoning shed, a boat-building shed, and, at the edge of the little group of buildings, stood the sail tannery, which smelled of rotting fish and urine and gave Apuldram its own peculiar odor.

The road was empty.

"You," Gehan said to the other man. "Come here. If you see anyone on the road, tell me immediately."

Gehan wiped his brow, took off his cape and, though he wanted nothing more than to sit down and rest, went to a trestle table where the two men's afternoon meal was half finished. He ate without knowing what he was pushing into his mouth, bread, salt fish, cheese, honeycake, indiscriminately mixed with beer drunk straight from a wooden jug. His heart was still hammering: he had run and slithered more than three miles without a break, not knowing how close pursuit might be, not even knowing if Apuldram would be safe. He was not used to heavy exertion. He found his hands refusing to respond properly; and he felt as if a broad strap were being tightened about his chest.

"Lord Brennis!"

As Gehan turned he clumsily knocked over the jug: beer flooded the table and dripped to the floor.

The harbor Trundleman, Tain, moved through the bluish rectangle of the doorway, a man of forty, bald and grizzled, wearing a fur and sealskin jacket with sheepskin lining and leggings. Like the men who worked under him, maintaining, repairing, building, and often sailing the Valdoe ships and boats, he was of a breed drawn from those coastal villages which fished as well as farmed. He had lived with the sea all his life; he knew every yard of coast for a hundred miles to east and west. At a glance he took in Gehan's appearance, the abandoned gambling game, the beer dripping to the floor.

"Is the *Kormoran* ready for sea?" Gehan said.

A look of alarm crossed Tain's face. "Not in this wind. It would not be safe."

"But is she ready?"

"She can be made so in a few minutes."

"Then do it. Quickly. And I want you to scuttle the *Empire*."

Now the Trundleman was openly astonished.

"Sink her Do it now."

The rest of the harbor men, half a dozen in all, had gathered meanwhile outside the door. Most were middle-aged or old like Tain, with sheepskin or doeskin jackets and capes. One had lost a hand, another walked with a bad limp, but all were skilled men. Tain sent them to their work.

"Do you keep snowshoes here?"

"Yes, my lord."

"I want a man to go to Harting fort with a message for Commander Awach." Again Gehan looked out of the doorway toward the empty road. "The message is this. There has been a mutiny at the Trundle. The Vuchten have attacked my men. Awach must signal all the western forts, including Bow Hill. On no account are any instructions from the Trundle to be heeded. The secondary forts are to be kept sealed until my orders come. These orders will be coded with the word . . . cormorant. Is that clear?"

The Trundleman repeated the message without fault. "I have just the man to send, my lord."

"The rest of you will come with me. We'll sail east and beach below Cissbury fort."

Outside, in the creek, axes were sounding in the hull of the *Empire*. The coracle's painter had been tied to the sternpost; the men had already freed the *Kormoran*, which was being drawn on a long cable toward the shore. Plaited rush fenders crushed and squeaked against the frozen timbers of the landing stage, and the hawsers were looped and knotted round two oak bollards.

The youngest and fittest of the harbor men, given a stormcoat, backpack, and snowshoes, set out for Harting and Commander Awach. For the first half mile he was to follow the edge of the creek, leaving no tracks.

The *Empire* started to list. Two men appeared on deck, clambering free of the fountains of dark water gushing in from below. They let themselves down into the coracle, cast off, and paddled back to help their comrades carry sails and essential gear from the sheds to the *Kormoran*.

In his haste to be gone, Gehan joined in the work, with numb fingers helping to rig the mainsail and raise the boom. He scarcely looked at the *Empire* as it upended and, in a boiling rush of bubbles, sank into the mud at the bottom of the creek. Briefly its prow reared into the air for the last time, high, defiant, hovering uncertainly between life and death. The figurehead, the emblem of the Gehans, a lavishly carved serpent picked out in scarlet and green, stared indifferently into the blizzard and began its slide to oblivion.

"My lord! Look! The road!"

Five men with spears, a team of soldiers, Vuchten, had appeared between the trees, and were running toward the worksheds. A team of Vuchten against five old men: Gehan would stand no chance.

"Get aboard!" he shouted to the three who were still by the sheds. They dropped their bundles and ran to the ship. With the Vuchten less than two hundred yards away, they freed the hawsers and scrambled up the gangplank, while the others, Gehan included, found poles and tried to push the *Kormoran* into the current, against the full force of the blizzard.

But the wind was in the northwest, blowing onshore. Like a sentient, malevolent being, it was keeping the ship pinned to the landing stage. A strip of water appeared below Gehan's pole, narrowed, widened, narrowed; he looked up and saw the Vuchten almost at the main shed.

As they reached its precinct, Gehan heard a violent commotion above and behind him: the sound of tearing ropes, a sudden cascade of opening leather. There was a bang, a squeal of sheets running in their blocks, and with a jolt that shook the whole fabric of the ship the boom swept the afterdeck and was checked. The mainsail had come undone. Instantaneously the wind surged against the expanse of russet leather; the *Kormoran* heeled over against the landing stage, water flooding over the gunwale and rising up the deck. Gehan clawed at the shrouds to stop himself from falling. There was screaming below him, to his left. The Trundleman had been hit by the boom and knocked overboard, trapped between the hull and a pile of the landing stage. And, despite its list, the *Kormoran* was slowly moving forward, timber grinding on timber. Gehan saw Tain being rolled and crushed into the weeds and barnacles before his body was released and floated into the water with the motion of the ship; and they were beyond the landing stage, out of control, veering with the wind and running diagonally across the few yards that separated them from the shoals at the creek's edge.

The *Kormoran* ran into the stones at speed. The port bow crunched and splintered. The shrouds sliced into Gehan's fingers: he lost his grip and was flung forward, his feet fouling something on the deck.

The water hit the side of his face like a slab of granite. Splinters of rock were thrust into his sinuses. Membranes burst with the green tons of water pressing down from above. He was upside-down, his face being driven into the stones, and the green was changing to black, the solid universe black of the hull rolling on top of him, and his legs were caught, tangled with the rigging. His back was breaking.

And then the *Kormoran* was free, moving into deep water. Beside him Tain was hauling on a rope, bringing the boom under control. The mainsail filled again and Gehan felt the whole ship grow taut. It leaped forward, running with the wind, plunging joyously into the storm. Pellets of freezing spray stung his face and drenched his clothes. He looked back and already the Vuchten and the Trundle and the scenery of his life were becoming small.

At the tiller stood the man with one hand, watching the vast skyward sweep of leather. On either shore the snow and scrub were sliding past. They passed Cobnor Point and turned southward, leaving it forever, carried by the eager tide into the open estuary. Over Pilsey Island which he knew so well, low and flat, he saw a congregation of tiny shorebirds, flying in a cloud that changed from dark to light as with one will they changed direction and turned to show their breasts. And here, at the prow, his own cormorant, the raven of the sea, was marking his course in jet and ivory and leading him to sanctuary.

From brown water they moved into gray, into the broad ocean, and now the waves were breaking over the bows and the wind was in his face. The ship was disintegrating, its passage done. He called to his men and felt the wind under his wings and he was being lifted clear. Below him the boards were breaking and the sails shredding with the spindrift and the storm. He saw his men in the sea. Their heads were bobbing, their hands and arms clutching at wreckage. He soared on wide wings and they were drowning below, but he was free. He was no longer a raven: he was an eagle, borne in majesty to the heights where sea and sky were one, out of the blizzard, out of the clouds and into the sun.

8 Tagart was not dead. He had been lying here alone for a long time, and he was not dead. Voices had come and gone away again, but now he was not certain that he had not imagined them. Twice he had raised his head and dimly seen the snow. The first time he remembered seeing the Flint Lord. The second time the Flint Lord had not been there, and it had stopped snowing, and the sky was darker, and to keep himself alive he was trying to discover whether the voices had been real and whether they had come before or after the second time. The thread of memory was fragile and difficult to follow, dissolved by pain.

He had known pain before, but never like this.

Never like this.

He seemed to be waking, and there was a voice again. He was confused. Was this one of the voices he had heard before? Or was this imaginary too? But it was a voice he knew, and it was speaking a familiar word, a word from his old life, before his back had been opened.

"Shode! Shode!"

It was Fodich's voice, and he remembered then that he was no longer lying alone on the hillside. Fodich and another man had come for him some time before dusk and carried him to the thicket. They had laid him face down on something soft, massaged his hands and feet and covered him with furs. He had listened to them talking. Rian had been taken by the soldiers and they were worried that she might tell them that Altheme was still in the gorse. After that the furs had been removed. Someone had touched Tagart's wound and started to clean it and he had lost consciousness.

There had been some daylight left then; now it was dark.

"Shode! Shode!"

Long ago, in his sleep, Tagart had known that Fodich and Altheme and all the others in the gorse were dead, surrounded by the soldiers, burned alive. He had even seen the orange flames, black smoke drifting down the hill; but it seemed the smoke had been in sunshine and in this he was mistaken too. He had thought Fodich and the others were dead. He had thought he would have to crawl away from here by himself.

But it was not true.

He was here with them, in safety and shelter. They would help him and heal his wound.

Tagart reached out his hand.

"We want to lift you now," Fodich said. "We're going back to the forest."

Tagart stretched his hand further, to confirm the sound of Fodich's voice, to confirm that Altheme was kneeling beside him and speaking too.

He felt his fingers move. He touched the hard spikes of gorse. He touched the spears and icicles, the palisade. The fort was under his fingers, black, a few lights twinkling. By his grip he could crush it, crush the Trundle, crush the Flint Lord.

But when he closed his hand they had already picked him up and were carrying him away.